HE COULD PLAY GAMES WHEN THEY MADE LOVE, HE COULD ATTEMPT A BRIEF DOMINATION, BUT ULTIMATELY SHE WAS IN CONTROL. CARL WAS HER CREATION.

She had made him ... and turned him into Manifold's prototype of the perfect man. She had instructed him, groomed him, educated him and chemically moulded him into every woman's ideal man ...

Watching him sleep she knew that what she and the rest of the team had done in creating Manifold was probably a greater advancement for women than gaining the vote, entering the workplace or the introduction of the Pill. Finally, she thought as she looked tenderly down on her peaceful lover, women could take control.

ABOUT THE AUTHOR

Jane Gordon was born in 1956. She worked for ITN until the birth of her first child in 1980, then returned to work in 1986 for the launch of the newspaper *Today*. She wrote a weekly opinion column subtitled 'The Heart of Today' until she left the paper in 1993 to write *Hard Pressed*, which is also published in Signet. *Stepford Husbands* is her second novel.

Jane Gordon now lives in Chiswick with her three children and pretends to be a 'Total Woman' – that is one who works in the few spaces left by family life. She writes regularly for *The Times*, the *Daily Telegraph*, the *Daily Mail* and the *Mail on Sunday*.

JANE GORDON

STEPFORD HUSBANDS

A SIGNET BOOK

PENGUIN BOOKS

Published by the Penguin Group
Penguin Books Ltd, 27 Wrights Lane, London w8 5tz, England
Penguin Books USA Inc., 375 Hudson Street, New York 10014, USA
Penguin Books Australia Ltd, Ringwood, Victoria, Australia
Penguin Books Canada Ltd, 10 Alcorn Avenue, Toronto, Ontario, Canada m4v 3b2
Penguin Books (NZ) Ltd, 182–190 Wairau Road, Auckland 10, New Zealand

Penguin Books Ltd, Registered Offices: Harmondsworth, Middlesex, England

Published in Signet Books 1996
1 3 5 7 9 10 8 6 4 2

Set in 10/12pt Monotype Plantin
Typeset by Datix International Limited, Bungay, Suffolk
Printed in England by Clays Ltd, St Ives plc

To Demi and Petie,
with love and gratitude.

PROLOGUE

Caroline was so tired she wondered if she would be able to make it through that evening. She had left home at 6 a.m. in order to be in the office in time for a meeting prior to a presentation to a new client. She had written three reports, negotiated a difficult contract on a dull but lucrative account and had managed, midway through the afternoon, to get the grocery shopping in between two post-production meetings on the new Mistral ad.

The moment she entered the flat she sensed that Nick was depressed. Despite the brightness and heat of the day he had pulled down the shades and shut the windows. He was slumped on the sofa watching *EastEnders*.

'Had a good day?' she asked tentatively as she headed straight to the kitchen to deposit the warm, wilting shopping.

'You can't switch on creativity like a fucking television,' he sneered from his position low down on the sofa where, most nights now, he slept. Ignoring his mood – well, nowadays it was an almost permanent ill-temper rather than a mere mood – she cleared up the mess in the kitchen, packed away the groceries and began to make him a salad.

'You haven't forgotten, darling,' she began in the placatory tones she adopted with her husband. 'I'm seeing Juliet and the girls tonight. Nicola's finally come home.'

He didn't bother to answer, merely grunted and wandered to the fridge to get a can of lager.

'You look dreadful,' he said as he passed her.

I

She blushed. She had felt sick for most of the day and the heat, which she had always hated, had made her look blotchy and bloated. So much so that now, as her husband crept contemptuously past her, she wondered if he might not have guessed her secret.

Probably not, she thought as she watched his return to the sofa. The occasion on which they had last made love – nearly five months ago she realized with horror – had been brutal and unsatisfactory, and fuelled by anger and alcohol. Not only would he not remember he would probably not believe it possible that new life could have come out of such a meaningless and obscene union.

'I've left you something in the fridge,' she said, moving away towards the calm and cool of the bathroom.

She locked the door and took off her clothes. There was a pungent smell about her body that she had never previously noticed. And, although there were no real discernible signs of the changes that were taking place, her slight, boyish figure was – at least to her own critical eyes – beginning to thicken. Before she entered the shower she paused and looked at her reflection in the mirror where, in the early days of their marriage, she and Nick had watched each other making love.

All that was visible was a slight paunch. A small bulge no bigger than that on any average woman of her age. She turned the shower to cold, to the blue indicator on the dial, and stood for a moment relishing the iciness of the water beating on her body and through her straight, short-cropped white-blonde hair.

She had told no one. Most of her friends knew that Nick didn't want children and that there had been a kind of pact, what he had called a 'creative contract', when they had married, that they would remain childless. Certainly at work no one had even hinted at a link between her current pallor and a pregnancy.

She was, she thought as she put on a bathrobe and moved to the bedroom to find something to wear, behaving like some lost teenage girl, the kind you read about in human-interest stories in women's magazines. Girls who maintained their silence over a pregnancy until the moment of birth. Girls who then drowned their babies in the bath or wrapped them in a towel and abandoned them in bus shelters. Except that she wasn't a girl, she was a sophisticated, successful woman in her early thirties hiding her child from her husband, her friends, her colleagues and even herself.

She had always favoured a masculine look. She knew that the contrast between her mannish clothes, her slender body and her delicate pale features was dramatic and appealing. In fact, in the early days of her relationship with Nick they had virtually shared their wardrobe. It had somehow contributed to the feeling that they had of being twin souls. Apart from the obvious difference in their colouring – his hair was as dark as hers was fair – they might indeed have shared the same genes, not just the 501s.

She put on a crisp white shirt, a pair of Lycra trousers and a long jacket. She was certain, when she checked her appearance in the mirror, that her friends would not notice any change in her. At thirty-three she still had the look of a fragile young girl on the verge of puberty. She was the child, she thought with relief as she examined her reflection, rather than the madonna.

Even tonight, with the women she loved and trusted most in the world, she wanted to hide away her baby. She would deal with it soon, she thought as she checked her make-up and made her way back into the sitting room, noting that the only sign of life from Nick had been the switch of the remote control that changed the channel from 1 to 3. From *EastEnders* to *The Bill*.

'I'm off,' she said as sweetly as she could manage. She wasn't sure that he had heard, was certain that he didn't care and was almost gratified to hear, as she slipped out of the door, the familiar grunt of recognition that usually greeted her arrival and departure.

The children were late coming out of school and Georgia was getting fretful. Not because she had any worry about the girls, but because in her head she was making an inventory of all she had to do before she could escape that evening to London.

Richard was always saying that she was incapable of delegation. And it was true. The staff his privileged position in life had pressed on her were as out of control as her children.

She spent the greater part of her life doing for others what they should be doing for her, or at least for themselves. Giving Sandy the nanny room service (well, taking her tea in bed each morning), colluding with Mrs Henderson over the hours she worked each week, doing the children's homework, feeding their hamsters, walking Tamsin's dog, picking up the children from school, as now, in place of nanny or Mr Henderson, Richard's driver.

It wasn't that Georgia was an especially kind person. Privately she screamed and fumed and berated herself for her weakness. But she was that most old-fashioned of notions, responsible. And she reasoned, to Richard's apparent distaste, that if she couldn't be a proper mother to her children or wife to him (when he wasn't in Westminster), what else was there in her life? The only job Georgia had ever held down – and then only for two months between stints as a chalet maid – had been as a shop assistant in YSL in Bond Street. *Vendeuse*, as it was fancifully called.

Whenever Richard talked glowingly of two-career couples like Ken and Barbara Follett, Tony and Cherie Blair or even Virginia and Peter Bottomley – a tandem team as one of his fellow politicians put it – she would remind him that he was the man who professed a belief in family values and that she, as the ultimate in traditional wives, was the embodiment of his political dream. Even if, right now, that embodiment, well, that body, was physically repulsive to him.

Emily emerged from school first, her face set in that familiar frightened frown. Sitting herself in the passenger seat of the Espace, she looked up at her mother with a brief, shallow smile.

'Good day, darling?'

'What do you think?' Emily replied, implying, as she nearly always did, that all that had gone wrong in her day was somehow her mother's fault.

Tamsin followed, looking more relaxed but no less accusatory of her mother. She was the only girl without a cheque for the deposit on the outward-bound holiday, the only girl without proper Nike trainers for games, the only girl who didn't have a packed lunch and was forced to eat the muck the school served (and so on).

Even Tom, of late, spent most of the time with his mother issuing a series of complaints, denials and demands. It sometimes seemed to Georgia that she was being eaten alive by her family. That gradually over the years they were consuming her, leaving her weak, uncertain and spineless.

By the time they got home and Georgia had explained to Sandy where her supper was, served the children theirs, fed the dogs and bathed Tom, she had precisely ten minutes in which to get ready. Not, she thought as

5

she escaped to her own room, that she was exactly spoilt for choice when it came to clothes. The Marina Rinaldi jackets she had bought last year were already a little tight, but she absolutely refused to go above a size 16. Still, when she held her head up to the mirror she was pretty. There was yet a glimmer of the Deb of the Year 1979. Beneath the folds of loose skin that threatened, with all the extra weight she was carrying, to turn into jowls, you could still see what Dempster had once described as her 'kittenish' beauty. Those slanting violet eyes, that tiny turned-up nose and the small but full-lipped mouth were still there, even if, she thought as she scrutinized herself, you had to search hard to find them.

On her dressing table, next to her three-sided mirror, sat a picture taken by Terry O'Neill when she was eighteen. The contrast between her younger self and the 35-year-old woman frantically patting powder into the creases of her facial flesh so frightened Georgia that she was tempted to put the picture in the bin. But there was more to life, she thought as she picked up the photograph and looked at it closely, than mere physical beauty. She might not enjoy the reflection that returned to her from the mirror this evening, but she had certainly enjoyed the years that had turned her from a luscious young girl into a plump middle-aged woman.

The greatest gift in life, she believed, was not looks, intelligence or talent but children. And it was the creation of her three children that had wrought the changes in her physical appearance. It was the love and the worry over her babies that had settled into little lines on her forehead and the physical burden of child-bearing that had settled into the pockets of flesh that now puffed out her body. She could not complain, she thought as she put down the picture and looked at her 35-year-old face, if she had gained more than just her children in the last ten years or so.

A feeling of contentment overcame her when she finally boarded the train for London. It was such a treat to see her friends, such a delight to escape – for a few hours – the tedium of her domestic life. She prayed that Juliet would be kind to her, that Nicola would not comment on how fat she had become in the last four years and that Richard had remembered that she was staying in town with him tonight. It would be just like him to forget.

Amanda was in two minds about cancelling out of this evening. She was feeling depressed. Work had been difficult, she felt guilty about leaving Anoushka and she looked terrible. She always felt that when she saw the girls she had to put on a brave and glamorous front. Sometimes she thought that they regarded her nowadays as a sort of charity case. At any rate she knew they pitied her, and if there was one thing that Amanda resented – apart from Steve – it was pity.

It was far too hot to be travelling on the Tube in the rush hour. And the heat on the streets, when she finally emerged from Kennington station, had swollen her feet so that her stilettos cut uncomfortably into her heels.

By the time she reached the childminder's flat – a block away from her own – she was scarcely able to walk for the pain. But the sight of Anoushka's pale and unhappy face lessened her own agony. Because while Amanda was strong enough, hard enough even, to withstand their reduced circumstances it was clear that her five-year-old daughter – 'Princess Anoushka' as her father had called her – was confused and upset by the dramatic changes in her life. She clasped her daughter to her and the two of them made their way home.

Once behind the closed and barred door of their two-bedroomed flat it was possible to shut out the rest of their mean new world. Amanda had managed to hold on to one or two of the good pieces of furniture she had bought in the heady days – incongruous though they looked in this characterless setting – and their beauty gave her some comfort against the ugliness of her surroundings. Anoushka's bedroom – barely big enough to accommodate her draped four-poster and her possessions from her other life – was her haven. Inside their over-furnished rooms mother and daughter could pretend they were somewhere else and not sandwiched between the flat of a teenage mother and her two noisy children and what Amanda thought might just be a crack house.

The doormat, as ever, was littered with brown envelopes. Two OHMS from Steve and two OHMS from the Inland Revenue.

There were several abusive messages on the answerphone from people to whom she owed money, followed by the bright, clipped tones of Juliet making sure that Amanda had remembered dinner that night. She would go. She needed to get out, even if it would be hard, this evening, to leave Anoushka with a babysitter and to suppress the envy she now felt for her friends.

Amanda still had a few reminders of her previous wealth. A few bits of jewellery, some outrageous clothes bought for her by Steve and a row of Manolo Blahnik shoes.

It would, of course, be difficult to explain to Nicola about the events of the last few years. When she had last seen her she had been affluent and, she decided now, happy.

She sat on the bed in her room for a few minutes,

trying to make up her mind what to wear. In the old days she had dressed to impress. She had liked nothing more than causing a stir of interest in a crowded room. Amanda had an odd, exotic kind of beauty that she had, over the years, very carefully cultivated. She was quite petite – no more than 5 foot 4 inches – but her large features (a classic Roman nose and a huge, sensual mouth), her disproportionately long legs and her penchant for very high heels gave a false stature.

She knew that her friends had always disapproved of her taste. They thought that her love of leather, leopard skin, rhinestones, studs and anything else that could add glitz and glamour to her clothes was terribly vulgar. But then glamour, even now, was more important to Amanda than good taste and respectability. Why, even her hair was what Juliet would sneeringly describe as 'eighties big' – worn brushed and backcombed so that it framed her face and added to the false impression of her height.

In the end she put on a Versace frock, not just because she looked good in it but also because it filled her with nostalgia for the way things had been. For the days when she and Steve had been on a roll, moving forward in a relentless and ultimately dangerous way.

She didn't stop to read his letters. She didn't want to break the spell. The man who wrote the sad, lost notes from Ford Open Prison was not the man she remembered when she wore this dress. Amanda and Anoushka's prince was now a pauper, serving a five-year sentence for fraud.

It was so hot that Juliet had decided they should eat outside in the little courtyard that she had carefully created with York stone, pots, statuettes and topiary.

Georgia always used to joke that Juliet's garden was

more sumptuously furnished than her house. But then Juliet absolutely hated clutter. She had spent much of her adult life distancing herself from her sister. This house, with its conventional Edwardian exterior and stripped minimalist interior (which had featured in the most recent Conran design book), was as dramatically different from Georgia's grand country pile as it was possible to get.

Everything was organized. Peng, the Filipino maid, had been in to hand polish the sandstone and wood, iron the table linen, polish the glasses and buff up every glittering clean-cut surface in the house. Juliet had picked up the food in a taxi on the way home from work. Cooking was beyond her and besides she was in a position now when things like catering and shopping were done for her, by fax from her office to the fifth-floor deli at Harvey Nics or to Harrods or even, on occasion, to one of the smarter London restaurants that discreetly offered top-drawer takeaway to special customers.

Indeed, she had come to wonder, in the last few years, why on earth anyone would equate shopping with sex. The sexiest people Juliet knew never went near a shop. Like her, they sent out for everything. In fact, there was very little that Juliet had to do of a domestic nature any more. Sam was stashed away at prep school and she didn't live with Harry, so she didn't have to worry about the usual clutter of everyday life.

Juliet was, as Georgia often pointed out, rather pleased with herself at this point in time. Everything in her life, with the exception of Harry, was absolutely under her control, absolutely as she had wanted and planned it.

She glanced with approval at the image that was thrown back at her by the gleaming mirror in her bedroom. She had worked as hard on her appearance, in the last few years, as she had on her career. She had transformed herself from Georgia's gawky and rather plain younger sister into a truly elegant woman. Her straight brown hair had been highlighted, lowlighted and cut so that it now lay sleekly shining in a burnished bob. And although she would never be as naturally pretty as her sister, she had cleverly contrived (with the help of a deal of cosmetics and some cunning piercingly green contact lenses) to turn her dull but regular features into something approaching beauty. Her body was as slender as Georgia's now was plump, and through a ruthless exercise regime she had managed to achieve a hint of curve (actually solid muscle) in the most important places. Checking her profile in her short, sharp Amanda Wakeley suit, she smiled warmly at her reflection before making her way downstairs to await the arrival of her friends.

She thought it appropriate, that night, to have some champagne in the fridge. Ordinarily when she and Georgia got together with Amanda and Caroline it was more casual, pasta and white wine. But tonight was special because Nicola, who, with a front cover on *Time* magazine, was now the most successful and established of the five friends, had come home after four years in America.

Juliet was especially keen to impress her. When she had last seen Nicola, before she had taken up that post in the States, Juliet had been in decline. Her marriage had just broken up, Sam had been diagnosed as educationally subnormal and, to add insult and envy to injury, Georgia's Richard had just been made Secretary of State for Social Services.

In four years she had turned her life round. Had, through rigorous application and encouragement, pushed Sam into a goodish school, had forged ahead in her career (thanks, largely, to the unexpected interest of Richard), and had become involved with the famous and devastatingly attractive Harry.

It had been Richard's money – and Richard's sense of timing – that had set Juliet up in her exclusive letting business. She now presided over twenty branches in London, Brussels, Paris and New York offering a fantastic clientele (many contacts of Richard) fantastic properties. Sometimes it worried her a little that Richard did not declare his interest – both in the House of Commons and at home in the country – in Juliet's flourishing business. The brief affair that had preceded the deal that had changed her life – and substantially increased his income – did vaguely disturb her. But she knew that Richard was never going to tell Georgia, and, besides, what did Georgia expect? Nowadays she looked like a freak, a grotesque distortion of the sister who, ever since they had been children, Juliet had envied. Georgia should have guessed that whatever she had, eventually, Juliet would get.

Nicola lay down on the bed in her hotel room and put a call through to Carl in New York. She still felt a tremor of excitement when she heard his voice. They had been together for two years now but their relationship was as intense, as passionate and as satisfying as it had been in the first weeks of their affair.

'How've you been,' he said.

'Missing you . . .'

'It won't be long now. I'll be with you in a matter of days.'

Their conversations, whenever they were apart, were long and tremulous and emotional. They talked, this time, for over half an hour until the moment when

Nicola realized that she would be late for dinner. She had told Carl about her friends – about the rivalry between ambitious Juliet and lovely Georgia, about sweet Caroline and the glamorous Amanda – although as yet she had not told her friends about Carl.

As she got up from the bed and smoothed down her dress she wondered if they had changed as much as she had. She was sure that they would be as astounded by the transformation in her as she was herself. For Carl had brought out the little girl in Nicola. A little girl that, particularly in childhood, no one else had ever noticed. He made her feel vulnerable, and feminine and sexy. Which was astonishing because Nicola had always been the one who had said she could happily live without a man. Nicola had been the one who would, everyone had predicted, put her career before her own emotional fulfilment.

But Carl had changed all that. He had even managed to change her physical appearance. At school Nicola had endured endless slights about her looks. She had that particular shade of red hair – accompanied by very pale skin and transparent eyebrows and eyelashes – that inevitably resulted in cruel nicknames. Falling in love with Carl – or rather Carl falling in love with her – had given her the confidence to escape from the self-image that she had carried, like some awful disability, since her schooldays. She had learnt how to apply cosmetics, how to make the most of her striking looks. Carl had even managed to persuade her, from time to time, out of her previous pleated Jaeger skirts and into something a little more contemporary.

She could never have imagined that a man could play as important a part in her life as Carl now did. She had thought that only work could truly excite and satisfy her.

But then, she thought as she made her way down to

reception and the cab that would take her to Juliet's house, Carl now was her career. Or at any rate the hidden agenda in her career.

Proof positive, she thought with a smile, that the perfect man did – or rather COULD – exist.

ONE

They talked that night with unusual honesty even if, it later transpired, they all had secrets they did not dare share. Their mood could have been attributed to the champagne or the heat or even their hunger (the food that Juliet had prepared, rather like the woman herself, was more attractive and fashionably dressed than substantial and satisfying), or it might have been linked to the fact that at last they were five again. Nicola was back.

They had been friends since their school days. Educated at a small but smart London day school – famous for the production of a couple of Royal mistresses, several television presenters and a Booker-prize-winning novelist – they had stuck together through adolescence, geographically divided university years, diverse professional callings and turbulent emotional relationships.

There was no doubt, though, that the five of them had changed more in the four years that Nicola had been in the US than they had in the previous fifteen.

At first there was a stream of silences, minutes when the five of them seemed lost together. Exposed in the stark interior of Juliet's house – you couldn't call it a home – it was as if they had misled the previous intimacy and affection they held for each other. But any initial awkward moments were soon dismissed, aided perhaps by the alcohol. Amanda had always said that the reason that the five of them had stuck together was that they knew each other so well they had no need to pretend. They understood each other so well that they could detect, beneath panstick make-up and a fantastic outfit, the merest hint of depression.

They were, indeed, astonished at the change in Nicola. She had always been so bookish, so untouched by vanity. But the years in the States had put a gloss on her, transformed her so that, while still not as glamorous as Juliet or Amanda, she nevertheless had a glow about her. Her red hair shone, her skin was radiant and her clothes, which had always previously been picked for practicality, were now close cut and flattering to her long, lean body.

'I saw the piece about you in *Time*, Nicola. Even Richard was impressed,' said Georgia. 'You have done so brilliantly well.'

'I just had this idea, well more of a conviction really, that not enough had been done scientifically to control man's inhumanity to man, if that doesn't sound too pompous,' Nicola said.

'And you've done something about it?'

'Well, not me exactly. Together with a group of similarly minded people I have helped to create a revolutionary new series of drugs. One or two of them that might even cure man's inhumanity to women,' she said with a dry laugh. 'We're mostly women, I admit, but there are a few brave men committed to the project. They had done a great deal of work before I even joined them. We've just completed three years of trials on the drug, which is why I'm here. I'm here to put out some feelers for a British launch of the drug.'

'You mean, it's a drug purely for men?' asked Caroline curiously.

'Well, yes. There wasn't much more that could be done, scientifically, to control the moods and behaviour of women. Fortunes have been spent on research, and fortunes made in the pharmaceutical industry through the control of women. Science, male-dominated science, has battled to understand, overwhelm and manipulate women. They have drugs to stop us ovulating, drugs to make us ovulate, drugs to make us feel, at an age when we no longer ovulate, as if we are ovulating. They have given us smart drugs to eradicate emotions that we might feel are, in a man's world, inappropriate. They have even created syndromes and disorders out of female hormonal and emotional imbalance, and yet, all the while, the real problems of the world have to do with male imbalance, male hormones . . . But don't start me off or I will drive you all crazy with my theories and my plans. I want to know about you.'

Then Nicola quizzed them in turn about their lives. Georgia talked sweetly of her children, her life and the astonishing success of her husband, a man whom, she readily admitted, she now scarcely knew.

'I think if he was in any other profession but politics he would have traded me in by now,' she said. 'You know how everyone is saying that there is no job security any more, no jobs for life. Well, in the same way there is no marital security any more, no marriages for life. Unless' – she paused and giggled – 'unless, that is, you're married to a politician. Whether Richard or I really want it or not, we have a marriage for life.'

'Georgia, you can be so silly. What woman wants a marriage for life nowadays?' said Juliet thinking guiltily of the flat she had just discreetly arranged for Richard's latest House of Commons researcher.

'Do you know that 73 per cent of divorces are insti-gated by women?' said Caroline earnestly. 'I've been working on an account for a big stationery company that has introduced a line of divorce greetings cards. Women are opting out of marriage and celebrating their free-dom. They perceive life without a man as a positive thing.'

'And married life with Nick, Caroline, how is that?'

Nicola enquired. 'Is he still writing the great British novel of the nineties?'

'He is developing this extraordinary theme. He is taking the most popular television soap series and weaving them into a kind of allegory of life today. He says it will be the contemporary *War and Peace*. He's called it *War in Peace*. It's quite brilliant but it totally absorbs him,' Caroline said, her face flushed by the sudden attention.

'You mean, *Armageddon in Albert Square*?' said Amanda with a hoot of laughter that was quickly echoed round the little candlelit garden.

'Or *Rambo in the Rover's*?' added Juliet.

'And are you happy?' Nicola asked, aware that the mockery of her husband's pretensions had embarrassed Caroline.

'Well, you know. It's difficult. Creative people like Nick aren't easy to live with. Until the book's finished there is no money, so he has to live off my earnings – and he absolutely despises what I do.'

'He gave up journalism?'

'It gave him up. Well, the money was lousy and it was taking up so much of his time there was no space left for the novel. People don't realize that writing proper literary fiction is not something you can pick up and put down. It's a constant. Even if he only writes fifty words in a day it can be emotionally and physically backbreaking . . .'

Juliet raised her eyebrows and cleared away their plates as Nicola's gentle interrogation continued.

'You haven't changed your mind about children?'

'How could I?' Caroline said. 'Nick can barely relate to me living alongside him, let alone a child. And anyway I couldn't afford a child. I can barely support us and the mortgage. I don't earn enough to cover childcare as well.'

'Nick could become a house-husband. Role reversal is perfectly acceptable now,' said Georgia, her voice slightly slurred from the alcohol.

Amanda knew that Nicola's dark brown eyes would fall on her next. Nicola must know about the court case. It had been a big thing in the tabloids over here and there was little doubt that one of the other girls – Juliet probably because she generally took the lead in keeping the five of them in contact – would have warned Nicola of Amanda's difficulties.

'I wonder if any of the men we are involved with could seriously cope with a role-reversal situation,' mused Georgia. 'The idea of Richard looking after the children and the house while I work is ludicrous. And I'm sure that Harry, if you lived with him, Juliet, would loathe to be your domestic drudge.'

'Darling Georgia, why would I need a role reversal? Sam is at boarding school. Harry and I maintain our independence in every area of our lives but in our sexuality. We have the perfect arrangement,' said Juliet smoothly.

'Role reversal is out for me too,' whispered Amanda. 'Steve would no more want to serve my current sentence than I would his.'

'I'm sorry about Steve, Amanda,' said Nicola.

'He was lucky in some ways. He could have gone down for much longer. He's hoping for parole in about six months' time.'

'Are you still together?' Nicola asked.

'For half an hour once a fortnight in an atmosphere of misery and hatred, surrounded by people that frighten me more than they do Steve. More for Anoushka's sake than mine. But it would be mean, wouldn't it, to desert a man at a time like this? Particularly when I enjoyed so many of the good times.' Amanda paused, looking down at the last vestiges of those times. A Cartier ring, the Versace frock and the Blahnik shoes. 'Besides I should share some of the guilt. I didn't stop him. I should have seen that it was all a mirage, that it couldn't last. And I didn't. I was as taken up with having more and pushing further as he was. But I haven't been the conventional little woman while he has been inside. That would not be my style,' she said with a grin that restored life and humour to her extraordinary face.

Amanda had always been the most sexually adventurous of the group. She had, the others thought, always been essentially a man's woman. And perhaps in order to deflect the conversation firmly away from her husband she began to relate the tale of the fabulous man she had picked up at a wine bar over the road from her office the previous week.

'He was as near the perfect physical specimen as you could get. Everyone in the office fancied him. I'd flirted with him, we all had, but I didn't really think about it until that evening. Anoushka was staying with my sister and I was free, and I suppose I was a bit drunk. But anyway I just asked him if he wanted to go somewhere when he finished and he said yes.'

They listened intently to her story, whooping loudly at crude details and sighing in exaggerated envy.

'But then, you know, immediately after we'd made love I felt curiously disgusted with myself. And him. I didn't know how to get rid of him. I remember this disgusting man once telling me this joke about how his ideal date would be a woman who would turn into a pizza and a six pack immediately after they had had sex. And suddenly I understood what he meant. I just wanted this man to evaporate. I said, 'Thank you, that was wonderful. But it's time for you to go.' But he wouldn't, he wanted to talk. Talk! He drove me insane for three hours talking about his insecurities, his fears for the future, his inability to make lasting relationships.'

'Isn't it strange,' interjected Juliet, 'that when you first meet a man, all they want to do is talk. Harry and I – we talked and we talked and we talked when we met. It was as if he was getting it all over in one swoop. We only ever talk nowadays when we are with other people or when we are arranging where we are going to meet or what we are going to do.'

'But darling, don't you and Harry have the perfect arrangement?' Georgia slurred.

'It should be, but it isn't. He's away a lot working and I worry about who he's with. I've never suffered from that kind of jealousy before, but then I've never been with anyone who spends all his time looking at beautiful women. And then I think that even if he isn't sleeping with any of the models, or even attracted to them, there is something wrong because if he really did love me, would he not want to live with me, marry me? It's like there is this tune playing in my head that I just can't escape from and do you know what it is, Nicola, it's "One day my prince will come".'

There was an embarrassed pause before Juliet, un-characteristically candid, continued, 'But then, here we are, independent, successful women in charge of our lives – well, perhaps not you, Georgia darling, or you, Amanda, but then you always were different – and what do we really want? We want the perfect man in the perfect relationship. And where is he? Can we find him? Have any of us ever encountered him? Haven't we all settled for something less than perfect? Or' – she glanced across at Caroline and Amanda – 'something downright imperfect?'

Nicola remained silent. She had sensed a despond-ency and disillusionment amongst her friends that had not been present four years previously. She longed to tell them that perfection was possible, attainable even, but it wasn't the moment to talk of her own happiness.

'But then, not many men would claim to have the perfect woman either,' Caroline said, thinking of the expression of distaste that had flooded her husband's face when he had looked at her earlier that evening.

'Men are far more easily satisfied,' said Juliet. 'Their perfect woman is Pamela Anderson. We wouldn't settle for the male equivalent. We want . . . oh not just Pamela Anderson with balls, but Pamela Anderson with a brain, with a sense of humour, with a sensitive soul and an enquiring mind, a massive bank balance and a winning way with children.'

'I did think once that Steve was my perfect man,' said Amanda cautiously. 'But it didn't last long, that feeling. And now I think that there is no such animal.'

'I still fantasize about meeting my prince, though,' went on Juliet. 'You cannot undo two thousand years of conditioning in two generations. I still have this expectation, this need, for my dream man.'

'Tell us what he's like,' Nicola asked.

'Dark – rather swarthy, actually. Masterful but still aware of the feminine side of his nature. Successful – he'd have to be – and yet able to cope with the boring minutiae of life: setting the timer on the video, putting the pasta in the microwave, you know the kind of thing. His only hobby would be me.'

They went round the table, then, each pointing out the characteristics that would make up their perfect man.

'Wouldn't it be wonderful if you could go and buy one in some sort of genetic supermarket?' said Amanda. 'If you could order one with a Cary Grant cleft chin, Mel

Gibson's eyes and the wit but not the weight of Clive James.'

'Or the bum of Sean Bean mixed with the charm of Hugh Grant and muddled with the acumen and charisma of Richard Branson.'

'Without the goatee.'

'He'd have the appeal of Brad Pitt, the intelligence and perception of Anthony Clare, the body of Stallone and the humour of Billy Connolly.'

'Without the goatee.'

'Mine would have the brain of Bill Gates, the eyes of Colin Firth, the lunchbox of Linford Christie, the wit of Robin Williams and the voice of Robbie Coltrane. I just love men with Celtic accents,' said Juliet.

'He'd have to like real women. To admire a woman for what she was and not what she looked like,' said Georgia with misty eyes. 'He wouldn't be aware of other women. He would put me on a pedestal and keep me there.'

'He'd be a bit like my father when he was young,' said Amanda. 'Enormously interested in me but protective and nurturing and kind . . . but hung like a stallion.'

Caroline took a pencil and a piece of paper from her handbag and drew a stick man with little arrows pointing to parts of his body which were represented by different, desirable, men.

'Here, ladies, is our composite man. Our perfect creation.'

'The prototype for the perfect male. The Stepford Husband,' said Juliet amidst peals of hysterical laughter. 'I'll pin him to my fridge door to remind us all what we are missing . . .'

TWO

Georgia held on to the strap in the back of the cab on her way to Lord North Street as if her life depended on it. And in a way it did. The man at the wheel was driving with such speed and aggression that Georgia, who had consumed more champagne than was sensible, was frightened of falling off the seat and into the glass partition that divided her from him.

She was so relieved when they arrived at the little London house where Richard spent the week that she thrust a ten-pound note into the hand of the driver and told him, in slurred tones, to keep the change. The house was dark. She had known Richard would have forgotten she was coming. It was stuffy inside, but then it was stuffy outside that night, and anyway, with all the security you needed in a London house these days, it wasn't possible to open a window.

The bed was unmade but Richard wasn't in it. The signs were that he had left in a great hurry that morning.

Perhaps he had one of those interminable dinners or a late-night sitting at the House. She unpacked her little overnight case, ran a bath (after first liberally dousing it with spray-on-wipe-off cleaner) and lay wallowing in the tepid water, relieved at last to be cool.

In many ways the regular suppers she shared with her sister and their old school friends were the highlight of her life. She had long since removed herself from what she regarded as the real world. The dreariness of her own existence was such that she could enjoy their lives – even Amanda's with all its current problems – vicariously. It was as if, when she listened to tales from

Amanda's life, suddenly, by proxy, she herself were slim and beautiful and desirable.

In reality Georgia had reached a stage in her life when she viewed her body as she did horrific pictures of starving children in Africa, with half-closed eyes. Only her own body, of course, didn't show signs of malnutrition. Her body, on her 5-foot 1-inch frame, displayed signs of First World indulgence rather than Third World neglect. It was too late, she had decided, to enjoy her body. She had let it go. Hadn't, she understood now, even enjoyed it when it was a splendid vision. She'd always thought herself too fat, to fulsome, for the fashion of the time. Even during that period of glory when Dempster named her Deb of the Year and she had been briefly linked with Prince Charles (she had, in fact, rejected him in favour of Richard), she had been ashamed of her body. Now, when she saw photographs of herself taken at the time – like the O'Neill picture that sat on her dressing table at home – she wondered why she had wasted that body, why she hadn't spent more of her younger life flaunting and enjoying it.

She giggled to herself when she remembered the conversation about the perfect man. How far from the fantasy Richard was! But then, how far from Richard's fantasy of perfection was she now? she thought with a bitter grin, never mind Prince Charles's?

Her husband had not made love to her in a long, long time. She didn't let herself think too much about what Richard did with his sexuality these days, just as long as it wasn't too sordid or shocking like that poor MP who had died with the black plastic bin-liner over his head and the orange in his mouth. She was fairly confident that Richard had no hidden perversions. He had always, at least in the days when he had wanted Georgia, been desperately – and predictably – conventional. He still occasionally made a stab at it with her. Perhaps just for the sake of form. As if to appease her in some way or allow her to imagine that she did still produce a faint stirring of lust in him. But it was never very successful. Partly because, she knew, he was not aroused by her present blubber and partly because, since she had never bothered to go back on the Pill after the third child, she would always be saying, when his flaccid penis did manage a minor erection and he was able to enter her, 'Don't come inside me, Richard.'

She fell asleep wondering just whom Richard did come inside these days, and if anyone – let alone the perfect man they had conjured up at dinner at Juliet's – would come inside her ever again.

When she woke up it was light, bright even, the sun that slipped through the curtains already bringing an intense heat to the bedroom. Putting on Richard's towelling robe, she wandered down to the kitchen to make herself a drink.

She was sitting at the tiny table, sipping her tea and reading the pile of papers that were delivered each morning, when Richard – looking tired, whiskery and dishevelled – burst in through the front door. Just for a moment, when he caught sight of the small tubby figure in his dressing gown, he was frightened. As if his wife, so rarely seen in London, were a burglar or assassin.

'Georgia, what are you doing here?' he said, as he might if addressing some remote acquaintance who had suddenly appeared in his home.

'I did tell you, Richard. And I left a message with that new secretary of yours,' Georgia said somewhat defensively.

'She's a researcher, Georgia, and has more on her mind than my domestic arrangements,' Richard replied irritably and not entirely truthfully.

In fact, he had left the new secretary/researcher just half an hour previously curled up in bed in the luxury apartment that Juliet had arranged for her. Thank heavens, he thought, that they hadn't stumbled back here last night. 'Bloody all-night sittings, I'm knackered,' he said, recovering quickly and saving himself from any further explanation with the oldest excuse in the politician's book. (Even though a quick glance through *Hansard* would find him out.)

'Do you want some tea?' Georgia asked calmly, despite the fact that some intuition or sense (smell perhaps) told her that her husband had been at an all-night, well, an all-night shagging rather than sitting.

'Yes, and something to eat. I'm starving and I've got to be back in for a Select Committee Meeting at eleven. Be a sweetie and get me something while I have a bath,' he said.

Richard had come to expect a certain level of servility from everyone he encountered. His considerable political power and influence had made his life such that he was always surrounded by flunkeys who would, at a second's notice, cater to his every whim. Whether it was a toasted bacon butty or a blow job.

Georgia, who realized that in the scheme of things she was about the lowliest of the lowly flunkeys (on bacon-butty rather than blow-job duty), began a desperate scramble through the fridge and cupboards in search of a hearty breakfast for her faithless husband.

She felt rather awkward, half an hour later, when Richard came down all smooth and smart and smelling of some preposterous aftershave. She felt odd and out of place sitting across the kitchen table talking to this slick, successful, sophisticated man. He had, she thought, weathered the years rather better than she had. But then slightly thinning hair, the odd wrinkle and a certain thickening of the body were considered signs of character and experience in a man. And his hazel eyes had that devastating glint that power lends a man. In fact, in many ways, at least on a physical level, the years had improved Richard. Age had lent gravitas and interest to a face that had once been, at best, plain and, at worst, weak and chinless.

'So,' he said, 'what brings you to London?'

'I had a girls' night at Juliet's. You know, supper and a few drinks to celebrate Nicola's return.'

'Do I know Nicola?' he said with the tone of disinterest he used when discussing anything with his wife.

'Nicola Appleton, you remember, she's been in America for the last four years, working on a new superdrug.'

'Oh now yes, I do remember her. Rather plain redhead. Done some interesting work. Part of the nineties' Brain Drain. Our best, I think the PM said, being used abroad. How on earth do you know Nicola Appleton?'

'I was at school with her,' Georgia said despondently.

'Surely not, Georgia. Nicola Appleton is one of the brightest women of her generation, how can she possibly have been at school with you?'

'She was in Juliet's year. Two years behind me in the A stream.'

'Ah, that explains it. Juliet. Well, that I can believe. Juliet and Nicola Appleton.'

Richard had always suspected that he had married the wrong one of the Hamilton girls. Juliet would, in almost every respect, have been a much more appropriate and effective wife for a politician of his standing. Might have been a bit more trouble, though, to fool Juliet, and anyway the electorate – God bless them – liked a politician with a homely wife.

'Nicola's been working on that drug that can make men nice to each other,' said Georgia, 'and nice to their women.'

28

'I think it's a little more complicated than that,' he said with a mocking laugh.

'I thought maybe I would invite her down for a week-end. If you don't mind.'

'Good idea. That could be rather useful. Get Juliet and Harry and some other suitable company,' Richard said in commanding tones.

'I'll organize it.' Georgia was certain that Richard would not regard Amanda as suitable company. He had been horrified by Georgia's close connection to the no-torious Steve Minter, despite the fact that, during the good times, he had enjoyed a great deal of Steve's hospit-ality (holidays on the Minter yacht, all-expenses-paid trips to the far reaches of the Minter empire and, some said, the odd backhander for an appropriate question in the House).

He had forbidden Georgia to attend the trial. Insisted that it was inappropriate, however fond she might be of Amanda, for her to be photographed by the tabloids at her friend's side. She'd given in, she usually did in the end. But she reckoned that with Steve still in prison he couldn't object too much to her inviting Amanda. Or Caroline and Nick, for that matter. That way she could turn a piece of Richard's politicking into something approaching a girls' weekend.

She was enormously relieved when her husband finally left for the House in his ministerial car. She couldn't wait to get home. To get back to a place where she belonged with people – well, the children – who loved and needed her and wanted her with them.

Caroline's sickness was getting worse. Some days, like today, she felt as if the thing that was swelling out her stomach was nothing more than a mass of nauseous bile.

Nick had lashed out at her when she had got home from Juliet's the previous night. Launched into one of his desperate tirades, accusing her of being shallow and bourgeois and of having sold her soul to commerce. She hadn't bothered to argue because she was simply too tired and too frightened to mention – when he was in such an agitated state – that their lives rather depended on her shallowness, her bourgeois nature and her ability to bring home enough money to support the mortgage on their negative-equity flat (not to mention his increasing need for alcohol). The night had ended when he had moved to strike her and she had locked herself in the bedroom and fallen into a deep but distressed sleep in which her dreams were visions of doom.

It was not as if, she thought as she searched her desk for some research data for the Mistral account, her work was exactly easy. She didn't even like it since she had been moved away from copy-writing to an executive role within the agency. She wasn't suited to it, or perhaps not physically up to it, because she found herself forgetting quite important things and making mistakes that, she feared, would soon be found out. Besides she didn't think that she had the stamina for this new life. Conferences, seminars, late-night meetings and early-morning starts were difficult to cope with on top of the demands of living with Nick.

She felt trapped between her need to appease her husband and her need to hold down her job. She knew that privately her colleagues regarded her as a rather distant person. She was always the first to leave the office, a meeting, a dinner or whatever. Always the first to be glancing anxiously at a phone if work had run over into the evening. She was not, she knew, what they would call a team player. In fact, over the years the intensity of her relationship with Nick had isolated her from everyone else in her life, apart, on the rare occasions that they managed to get together, from her old school friends. And while in the early days the strength of their love had somehow made up for the fact that Nick would not, could not, bear her to have anyone else in her life, she now felt terribly alone.

She couldn't confide in him, and, because she had never really established any personal relationships outside her marriage, there was no one at work whom she could trust. And in any case she was probably even more terrified about the office finding out about the baby than she was about Nick discovering the cause of her nausea. She needed the job more than she dared admit.

Of course, she knew this state of denial could not continue. That soon she would have to tell someone. Occasionally, when she had a sudden tightening pain in her stomach, she wondered if something was wrong, but she couldn't bring herself to go to the doctor. Couldn't bear the idea of acknowledging what was happening to her. Of becoming a hospital number, a statistic on the books of some ante-natal clinic and, she had no doubt, in the divorce courts. Instead she had found herself, that lunchtime, in Waterstone's reading quickly through a book on pregnancy. The pains, she then decided, were Braxton-Hicks, and nothing to worry about. Nevertheless, she bought the book and locked it away in a drawer of her desk.

Georgia rang her in the office during the afternoon – her friends knew better than to ring her at home – and invited both Nick and herself down for a weekend at Gallows Tree House. It was, Georgia said, a continuation of the celebration of Nicola's return. For a moment Caroline had been excited at the idea but then, after she had put down the phone, she realized that it was impossible. Should Nick come, he would, she had no doubt, spend the whole weekend being rude, patronizing and aggressive towards her friends. And should he not come, she would spend the whole weekend worrying, knowing that her return would be greeted by another frightening scene.

Quite unexpectedly, though, Nick was calm and serene when she got home from work. He had written over a thousand words that day and was clearly relieved. The writer's block – which had become like the Berlin Wall in their home – had apparently been demolished. He seemed almost pleased to see her. Sat her down and talked to her about the new idea he had about the novel. She was so relieved to see him in this mood of optimism that she sat next to him on the lumpy sofa and listened with interest.

She cooked dinner and he opened a bottle of wine and they sat and talked like an ordinary married couple. Warmed by his mood and the wine and the unusual intimacy of their evening, Caroline went over to him and kissed him.

He came to bed with her and they made love, gently and happily. She remembered then how much she had once loved the exclusivity of their relationship, how much she had liked his need to share everything with her. He had been jealous, something she had found enchanting at the time, of any moment they spent apart. He had resented her friends – even her old schoolfriends – and their life had been gloriously limited to each other. In those days they shared everything, each other's triumphs and thoughts and bodies as well as their clothes. These days the only things Nick had to share with her were his frustration and his anxiety. She prayed, as he moved in and out of her, that this change was real, that it would lead them back to the way things had been.

Afterwards she cried and Nick cradled her in his arms and, made brave by their love-making, she tried to talk to him, to share with him her secret. 'Nick, wouldn't it be wonderful if we could have a baby?' she said softly.

'I should be everything to you, Caroline. You are my muse, my lover, my wife, my mother, my child, my confidante. Why am I not everything to you, why do you need a baby?'

'It wouldn't be just my baby, it would be our baby. Your genes and mine merged. It would be a reason for all this . . .' She stopped, realizing that she had lost him again.

'If you were to have a child, it would be the end for us,' he said, releasing her from his arms, turning over and falling asleep.

It was ironic really that Amanda should be working as a temp at the head office of the building society that her husband had so massively defrauded. Not that anyone else working there realized – she had reverted to her maiden name – or would even have appreciated that irony. The office block in Vauxhall was filled with ghastly inadequate men – and a few token women in cheap business suits – whose main ambition had been to get to the lower reaches of middle management.

Still, none of them asked any questions – they didn't have the imagination – and she could work monotonously at her terminal with anonymity. She had created an office persona for herself vastly different from the real Amanda. During Steve's fantastic rise in the property business in the eighties she hadn't had to work, although, she supposed, she had contributed to his success. Done all the things that the wife of a major businessman should – entertained, advised, travelled with her husband. Which was why, at the age of thirty-three, she was still temping. There had been no need to develop any particular skills when she was with Steve. She had been a secretary when she met him and, ten years on, she was a secretary again. It depressed her that her friends – well, Juliet and Nicola and Caroline – had advanced so fabulously in their careers – but she accepted her present situation. Preferable, after all, to Steve's. Temping suited her. It meant that she could remain aloof and distant from her workmates. And it meant that she could move on when she wanted with no worry of anyone finding out who she was, or rather who she had been.

Nowadays she restricted her sexual activity to casual pick-ups whenever she could make arrangements for Anoushka. Men whom she could use and discard. Men she was sure she would never see again.

If Amanda had a weakness, it was her constant desire for the attention and admiration of men. She knew that she shouldn't need to seek the approval of strangers, but she did. She had lived for so long in Steve's world – a world where a woman was only as good as she looked – that she felt insecure and disturbed if she didn't (at least five times a day) receive an approving glance from an interested man.

In any case she had to have something else in her life apart from her mindless work and her daughter. The men she met were, she reasoned, a harmless but essential hobby without which her life would be totally empty. She justified her actions by telling herself that she couldn't have a meaningful relationship at this moment in time – it would be too disloyal to Steve – and that the only way she could satisfy her physical need for sex was to indulge in occasional meaningless encounters. But one-night stands could not alleviate her loneliness or her unhappiness. Her parents, who lived in Hong Kong, had disowned her at the time of the trial and the only family she had, apart from Anoushka, was her sister.

She visited Steve once a fortnight, but they didn't talk much. After visits he would write to her, telling her how pleased he had been to see her, but during them he looked sad, dejected and angry.

Georgia was the only person she could talk to, be honest with, although she didn't dwell too much on her own misery. She supposed she found Georgia a comfort because she sensed that her life, with that ghastly husband, was very nearly as difficult as her own. Most days, during her lunch break, she would ring Georgia and chat. She was rather astonished, that day, when Georgia asked her to stay for a weekend of celebration with Nicola.

She spent much of the afternoon planning what she would wear and how she would treat the awful Richard (who had once made an appalling and gross pass at her). The other good thing about being a temp, she thought as she noticed the clock shift to five-thirty, was that she could leave on time to pick up Anoushka at six.

The journey home, that evening, was made easier by the fact that the afternoon rain had lowered the temperature about ten degrees. She felt buoyant and excited, as she hadn't done for ages, when she picked up her daughter, aware that the forthcoming weekend would be as much of a break for Anoushka as it was for herself.

It was not until the moment that she came out of the steel graffiti-covered lift, hand in hand with her daughter, and approached her flat, that her precarious happiness evaporated. The door was ajar and the lock had been jemmied off: they had been burgled. She hesitated for a moment outside the door – afraid for Anoushka's emotional and physical safety – and then pushed it open to see if there was anyone inside. Once she was sure that whoever had ransacked their humble new home had long gone, she went in.

Her jewellery had been taken, of course, and the television and video. All the little electronic conveniences of life – like the microwave, the alarm clock and the radio she kept in the kitchen – had disappeared. Even the answerphone. Anoushka's room was a mess, but the real things of value – the furniture – were still in place.

She knew that it was a tragic fact of life that the less you had the more likely you were to be burgled. She wanted to cry, but she didn't because she had to be strong for Anoushka. She couldn't even ring the police or Georgia or anyone who would care because the phone had gone. Eventually she went next door, to the lesser of the two evils that were her neighbours, to the woman with the children that screamed. Threw herself and her daughter on the mercy of a startled stranger.

Juliet was, she freely admitted, something of a control freak. It explained her success, really. She was born to boss, her mother had always said (had once given her a T-shirt bearing this legend for Christmas), and in her business she could do just that.

She was also a brilliant delegator. Which explained how she could take two hours out of her day for a work-out and massage at the Harbour Club. Of course, she rationalized this chunk out of her day by assuring herself that it was good for business. After all, she had quite a lot of Chelsea Harbour apartments on her books and the people you bumped into in the juice bar or on the step machine were often jolly useful contacts. She was edgy today, though, despite the efforts of the woman who was giving her an aromatherapy massage. Juliet's mobile phone rang as the masseuse – the same one, actually, who pummelled the flesh of the Princess of Wales – reached a delicate area of her anatomy. She jumped as if the woman had hit her with an electric cattle prod. 'Damn,' she said, 'I'll have to answer. You'll have to stop for a moment.'

It was difficult to pick up the phone when her hands were covered in aromatherapy oil, but she was anxious to speak to Harry and she guessed it would be him. She'd left several messages at his office that morning urging him to call her and strict instructions at her own that no one else was to disturb her at the Club.

'Juliet, what is it?' Harry asked tersely.

'I just wondered what you wanted to do this evening. I thought we could stay in at my place and have some dinner,' she said, desperately trying to keep the lavender oil out of her hair as she hung on to the phone.

'Juliet, when are you going to get it into your head that I don't like routine. I'm not a "Wednesday is our night in" kind of man.'

'But I thought we'd agreed . . .'

'Something came up, Juliet. Don't set your clock by me. Don't let me rule your life. I've got a big commission from an American magazine. I'll be away for a few days. I'll call you at the weekend.'

'Richard and Georgia have asked us to stay the weekend of the 20th June in the country. You will come, won't you?'

'I can't promise. I'll try. Can you hear me . . .?'

'Yes, loud and clear,' said Juliet.

'Are you there? I can't hear you . . .'

At which point he faded from his mobile. She quickly dialled his number only to get that irritating message that 'The mobile phone you have called is not connected. Please try later.' The bastard must have switched it off on purpose. It enraged her when Harry did that. Her mood was made worse, when she finally got back to the office, by the discovery that Sam would be on exeat on the 20th. Harry would be even less likely to want to spend a weekend with her with Sam in tow. She was irritated and deflated, and so thoroughly frustrated that she couldn't get a grip on Harry that she spent the whole afternoon and much of the early evening making her staff respond to a series of pointless and petty demands.

Nicola was making a presentation of the Manifold concept to a group of important city investors. She was accomplished now at talking in layman's terms about the marketability and importance of the drug. Using powerful statistics on the growth of male depression, on violence amongst young men and on the increasing figures on family break-up, she had managed, at least in the States, to convert some of America's most important decision-makers to the cause and the commercial sense of her company's – The Malestrom Foundation – creation.

'Gentlemen,' she said, looking round the table, 'you have been shamefully neglected by the pharmaceutical industry. Your needs, your desires, your feelings have never been considered as important enough to warrant the expensive research and the exhaustive clinical trials that are necessary in the creation of new medication. Why? Because men, through the ages, have been expected to get on with it. To accept their lot. To hide any worries, any anxieties, behind a macho mask while their women' – she paused, threw back her glossy red hair and smiled sweetly at the men – 'have been given seemingly endless scientific help and aid to get them through the difficult moments in their lives.'

She paused again, for effect, before introducing the idea of a drug that could improve the quality, productivity and happiness of a man's life. 'It is impossible to deny that there is a link between the crisis of masculinity that is being experienced by young men today and the increase in urban violence. That was the starting point for the creation of Manifold. What if, we reasoned, it were possible to create a drug that could finely tune the emotional, intellectual and physical capabilities of young men. Not merely by balancing hormones but by using the radical new smart drugs that we know can dramatically improve the quality of a person's life. And gentlemen, there now *is* such a drug.'

She waited a moment, aware that the men around the table were interested, that they had begun to grasp the enormity of the scientific advance that the Malestrom Foundation had made.

'We have been testing such a drug on volunteers within the penal system in the States and the results are astonishing. We are confident of FDA approval – our drug is a revolutionary concept that can channel the aggression of youth without limiting their creativity or inventiveness or ambition. It is, quite simply, the most exciting thing that science has ever done for man. And indirectly, of course,' she added with a bashfully feminine look, 'for women.'

She paused, then went for the kill, leastways with this group of ageing, balding mid-life men. 'Not that Manifold has an age limit. For the older man frightened that he is past the most creative period of his life we have developed a type of Manifold that will increase his energy, his confidence, his output and, should he need it,' she added with another girlish giggle, 'his sexual performance. Manifold 2 has been rigorously tested on an élite group of volunteers with extraordinary results. In time we believe that we will have a Manifold for every man. It is a concept, gentlemen, that has no limits . . .'

She had them now, she knew. A drug that could cure depression, excess aggression and any sagging sexual power was irresistible.

'Is there a young man in the developed world who wouldn't, given the chance, want to improve his capabilities? A man over forty who wouldn't want to prolong his mental and physical prowess? Is there a man round this table who can afford to turn down the opportunity to invest in a drug that can give us all a better future?'

They applauded when she sat down. There was a buzz of questions, most of which she skilfully answered. If there had been any nagging doubts in the minds of the money-men, they were gone by the time they had shared lunch with Nicola and her statistics.

When she got back to her hotel at five there was a message for her to call Georgia. Riding high on her success, she called her friend – her favourite of the group – straight back. 'Darling Nicola, I can't tell you how happy I am you're back with us. And even Richard is pleased. In fact, that's why I rang. We were hoping that you could join us for the weekend of the 20th. Juliet and Harry are coming and Amanda and Caroline and Nick. You will come, won't you?'

'I'd love to, but I have a problem . . .'

'Business?'

'No, pleasure, really. You see, I am in love, Georgia. I met a man in America and he is joining me later this week . . .'

'I'm so pleased, darling, you deserve it. It explains that glow you have. How silly of me not to realize that there must be someone special in your life. You will bring him, won't you . . . ?'

'Can I? I know you'll like him.'

'What's his name and what does he do? I can't wait to tell Juliet.'

'He's called Carl. Carl Burton. He's everything I ever wanted in a man and never thought possible to have . . .'

'You can come down with Juliet on the Friday night. I think that Richard and Harry will be joining us on the Saturday. It will give us time to get to know Carl,' Georgia said.

THREE

Georgia had been fluttering around nervously all day. She wanted this weekend to be special. She had carefully planned every meal and activity. Making arrangements that would mean that she and her old schoolfriends would have moments on their own while the men – well, only Richard, Harry and this Carl were coming – did mannish sort of things (she did wonder, though, if Carl could shoot: Americans, she had a feeling, only went in for sports like golf).

She had precious little in her life to be proud of, she thought as she checked the menu for that evening's meal, but her home and her children. And she wanted to share them with her friends. She had even made an attempt, this weekend, to ensure that Emily, Tamsin and Tom would behave. Had offered all three of them fantastic inducements to be sweet and malleable with her guests, their poor little cousin Sam and Amanda's daughter Anoushka.

Gallows Tree House was made for weekend parties but rarely saw them. Richard was so busy through the week and so exhausted by the pressures of his ministerial entertainment programme (which rarely included Georgia) that when he was at home he was something of a recluse.

Nicola and Carl (Georgia kept repeating his name to herself to see if she liked it) had been put in the big green bedroom since they were the principal guests. Amanda was in the blue room – with her daughter in the dressing room beside it – and Caroline (who had decided to come without the difficult Nick) was down the corridor in the pink bedroom. Juliet and Harry, she reasoned, could make do with the red room, which shared a bathroom with the tiny single bedroom in which she had put poor little Sam.

She must, she thought as she put the final touches in her friends' rooms (small boxes of chocolates that they had all adored as girls and a framed photograph of the five of them on the front steps of Queen Anne's School), stop thinking of Juliet's son as 'poor little Sam'. She was sure that Juliet had only had him in order to offer some sort of competition to her and her growing, glowing happy family (as it was in those days). In fact, she was pretty sure that Juliet only got married to Mark Burrows – a youngish Tory MP hotly tipped for greater things – in the first place out of misplaced envy of Georgia's life. Sadly, though, Mark Burrows had lost his seat and his reputation (a nasty scandal over some unfortunate financial deal) and the marriage foundered. Well, Juliet was not the kind who hung around in times of trouble. Money and status were more important to her than love and affection were to Georgia (who had somehow acquired, to Juliet's constant irritation, money, status, love and affection).

Poor little Sam was the flotsam of the relationship. Georgia had tried with him, she genuinely loved children, but he was charmless and unattractive and exactly the sort of child other children loathed. Her own had groaned at the idea of having him for a whole weekend. It worried her, disturbed her conscience, that she couldn't get close to him and that she couldn't – at least on the odd exeat at Gallows Tree House – offer him a loving refuge from his cold world.

Gallows Tree House was not as old as it sounded. Built on the spot where the people of Henley – in the days before the Criminal Justice Bill, Richard always joked – had hanged their felons, it was a fitting place, Georgia privately thought, for their MP to live. If Richard had his way, they would bring back the gallows and he would be hangman. Constructed in the late thirties in a Tudor style, it was, she knew, of little historic or architectural interest. It was just an impressive pile. A vast place with twelve bedrooms, three staircases, five reception rooms and even a ballroom (nowadays limited to a snooker-and-games room). Big rather than beautiful (a bit like me really, Georgia thought), the house was nevertheless, thanks to Georgia's warmth and preference for chintzy clutter, a home.

She heard the first car pulling up on the gravel drive outside the house just before six. It was Juliet, who had driven Amanda, Anoushka, Caroline and poor little Sam down from London. Georgia opened a bottle of champagne, something she ordinarily only did when Richard had expressly given her permission, and the four women sat down in the small sitting room – Georgia's room – while Anoushka and poor little Sam went off with Emily, Tamsin and Tom.

They were mad with anticipation by the time that Nicola and Carl arrived at seven. They had spent much of the previous hour speculating about their old friend's American lover and the extraordinary confidence and glamour that he had cast on the previously rather bookish Nicola. From the very beginning Georgia liked him. There was something different about him. He was handsome, of course, if a little too hirsute for Georgia's tastes (he had that curious colouring, very black hair and very blue eyes – he was probably of Irish descent, she thought), and polite though not too much so.

She took the two of them upstairs to their room, leaving Caroline, Amanda and Juliet whispering and giggling behind them.

'I thought since it was just the six of us this evening that we could eat in the little family dining room. You'll probably want to unpack and settle in, but maybe you'll join us for champagne in half an hour?' Georgia said, backing out of their room.

By the time they went in to eat they were pretty well relaxed with Carl. He had an undeniable charm. Even Juliet, who was the kind of woman who would never ordinarily be interested in a man until she had seen, as it were, the colour of his bank statement, was apparently enchanted. It wasn't that he flirted, he clearly had eyes only for Nicola, but there was an attentiveness about him and a sensitivity that none of them had ever encountered in a man before. He was coaxing and comforting and sympathetic. Indeed, they were so utterly at ease with him that they talked, and he generally listened, as they would were there not a man present.

Amanda, lubricated by the champagne and happy to be in an environment of luxury and comfort, told them about her burglary. 'I thought that I had been through just about everything that was possible – I mean, with all the publicity and the court case and the humiliation of what happened with Steve – but I'd never been burgled before. And it was horrible. I'd never thought of myself as inviolate, not even in the days when we had all that high-security protection, but I'd somehow never thought it would happen to me. But then, I never thought I'd find myself living in a council flat on one of the most notorious estates in London. Albeit in a Tory borough,' she smiled at this last statement.

'Darling, it's only temporary. You'll see, you and Steve will fight your way back, honestly you will,' said Georgia softly.

'Curiously, though, some sort of good came out of it. I'd been so cut off, so divorced from real life. And since I didn't have anyone to turn to I turned to my neighbour. This girl who looked so hostile, so hard, so absolutely unyielding, and she was wonderful. I mean, she was shocked by us at first. She had been as suspicious of me as I had been of her. But she kind of looked after us – even though she's only nineteen now with two children – and insisted that Anoushka and I stay the night with her. And she was so interesting, the sort of girl – on income support, of course – I would have dismissed in the old days as a stupid drain on the resources of the country. A member of the underclass we all used to tut-tut about.'

'Sounds like the sort of girl Richard and his colleagues would still like to condemn as a state scrounger,' Georgia said.

'No, really, she's a good mother. She's got her head together. She chose to be where she is now. She has decided that her kids are better off without their father. More secure with just her. And, judging from her stories, it's easy to understand why she has chosen to live alone.'

'It would seem,' said Carl softly, 'that the world is full of women who believe that men are dispensable.'

'Perhaps it wouldn't be,' said Caroline with a sigh, 'if more men were like you.'

'Anyway,' Amanda continued, 'I'd really like you all to meet her, then maybe you would understand. I think she'll make something of her life one day, and the lives of her children. And she'll do it her way, not the way her own mother did, putting up with the violence and disruption of a drunken and abusive husband.'

'It's curious, isn't it,' said Nicola, 'the way that people now talk about the importance of male role models for young boys growing up. How living with any man in the role of father is preferable to life with just a loving

46

mother. Well, I'm not so sure. If a boy grows up in a hostile home ruled by a brutal man, what is he going to take on with him? Brutality and hostility. While if he grows up with a woman who is sympathetic and offers him a genuine haven – even if there is no adult male figure in his life – then surely he will take with him into the world a far healthier view of humanity?'

'Do you really think so?' asked Caroline eagerly.

'Of course if a boy grows up with a father who is released from the macho tradition of his forebears, it is a different matter,' said Carl. 'I've seen how violence perpetuates itself through the family unit. The underclass you referred to, Amanda, is much more of a threat to the middle classes in America than it is here.'

'But how do we release men from the macho traditions of their forebears?' said Georgia. 'I mean, look at my Tom – and maybe Juliet's Sam. There is in them something, I don't know – innate, I suppose – that leads them towards things like guns, knives, video-nasties, dangerous machinery and football. Tom is like mini Mr Macho. And I can't blame Richard because he is never here. I'm a bit like Amanda's neighbour. Generally a single mother bringing up her children – obviously in rather better circumstances – and I haven't managed to override those macho traditions.'

'Of course, you can't eradicate them,' said Carl gently. But you can temper those instincts, you can make them more manageable. You can make them positive for humankind rather than destructive.'

'Why is it,' said Nicola to Carl, 'that all conversations nowadays naturally lead to Manifold?'

'Tell us Carl,' said Juliet. 'How have you managed to conquer those macho traditions?'

There was a moment's silence before Carl replied, 'I've done it through education and through. . . through

Nicola's help.' They were all touched – and not a little envious – of this tender tribute.

Alone in her room later, Caroline decided that Nicola had won the ultimate prize in life. She had found a man who understood and genuinely liked women. A true feminist, she thought, which was a rare thing. Most of the men that Caroline knew who professed a sense of support and sympathy for women were, beneath the surface, closet sexists. She knew that Nick had never really been able to grasp the concept of sexual equality because he had always – whether through upbringing or natural instinct – regarded the male as dominant. Carl's wise words stayed with her until the moment before she slept, and she dreamt, in astonishing detail, of being married to a man who talked like Carl but was Nick. A man who would nurture and love the child growing within her.

The pace and atmosphere of the weekend changed on Saturday with the arrival, in the ministerial limousine, of Richard and Harry. Georgia disliked Harry. He was too handsome, too celebrated and too smooth for her taste. Even when he was greeting her, as now, he couldn't manage to look her in the eye, largely, she suspected, because he found women such as herself boring and physically unpalatable. He was a man, she believed, with no conscience and no thought for anyone but himself. Perfectly matched, she had long since decided, to her sister.

In many ways Harry was a slightly younger and less aggressive Richard. The two were definitely classic examples of the traditional upper-middle-class English male, although, of course, Harry had attempted to distance himself from his roots by affecting a pony-tail, tattered jeans, a weathered black leather jacket and a pseudo South London accent, as befitted a man of his profession. But for all Harry's artistic pretensions – his photographs were hung and sold like fine art at places like the Hamilton Gallery – he was not that different from Richard – a typical product of the English public-school system.

Not ten minutes after his arrival Richard set about attempting to take over Georgia's carefully organized weekend by suggesting lunch at a local restaurant and tennis in the afternoon. Worse, Georgia found herself slipping into the role she played when Richard was around. That of a doting drudge. No, no, she insisted, they must have a light lunch at home and then Richard should take Harry and Carl shooting. It was all arranged. Richard conceded, but he was clearly determined to be, well, territorial. To display to the other men – and the women – that he was master of his own domain (even if he only spent a fraction of his time here).

In fact, the conversation at lunch was as different from that the women had enjoyed the previous evening – in the presence of the gentle and seductive Carl – as it was possible to get. Richard talked loudly and indiscreetly about some frightful parliamentary scandal of the moment (involving, for a change, a Labour politician), Harry braying with laughter at a series of his own smutty asides.

After lunch Juliet drove Amanda and Nicola into town for some shopping and the men departed for a little manly diversion. Georgia felt rather sad when she watched Carl being driven away in the Espace with Richard and Harry. It was just as well, she thought, that the only thing the men would be shooting today would be clay pigeons. She didn't think that gentle Carl would have the stomach for the real thing.

Caroline had opted to stay behind to help Georgia and amuse the children. Georgia had been quite touched by the way in which Caroline had taken to Tom and was overjoyed to see him responding to her and leading her, hand in hand, round the garden.

Mid-afternoon, when she was upstairs checking that Mrs Henderson had made all the beds and cleared the rooms, she heard what she thought was a sobbing sound coming from Caroline's room. Pressing her head to the door she realized that Caroline was not crying but retching. She found her friend kneeling on the floor in front of the loo, trying to be sick. At first she thought maybe Caroline had become bulimic – it was terribly fashionable these days – but then something clicked in her head and she knew, immediately, that Caro was pregnant.

'Darling,' she said excitedly, 'you're pregnant, aren't you?'

Caroline nodded, tears streaming down her elfin face.

'Well, it's an emotional time of life. When I'm pregnant the most extraordinary things make me cry. Do you know when I was first pregnant with Tom I was at some dreadful state function with Richard and after dinner, in the middle of this serious dull speech by some frightfully important diplomat, I began to sob.'

But Caroline just kept on crying until Georgia took her frail body in her arms and hugged her, realizing that she was suffering from more than just a hormonal overload.

'Darling, it is Nick's baby, isn't it?' she asked.

'Of course,' said Caroline between sobs.

'Then what's the problem?'

'He says he'll leave me if I have a baby. We agreed, Georgia, when we married that we were everything to one another. That we wouldn't have children. But it just sort of happened. And I haven't told him. I haven't told anyone.'

'How pregnant are you?'

'About five months, I think.'

Georgia moved into mother mode. She gently washed Caroline's face, smoothed down her short blonde hair, led her to bed and tucked her up. Told her to sleep for a couple of hours, and that everything would be all right. 'I'll talk to my man on Monday. Strictly confidentially. I'll organize everything. Nick needn't know anything until you are ready to tell him. But you must make sure that the baby is progressing normally. You simply can't go on ignoring what is happening. Heavens, by now you should have had a scan and goodness knows what.'

Caroline, still hiccuping from the pressure of the tears and the vomiting, felt better. Relieved that at last she had managed to share her secret with someone. And confident that she had shared it with the one person who could really help her.

Dinner was rather formal that night. The food, a little heavy and stodgy for the time of year, seemed to weigh down the conversation. Or maybe it was just the dramatic contrast between the previous evening's happy and casual atmosphere and tonight's more masculine and domineering air. Georgia did her best to keep things light and happy. To ensure that Richard didn't upset Amanda or Caroline and that Juliet didn't argue with Harry.

Right from the start there was a tension, prompted, Georgia decided, by the strict sexual divide. The women (and, Georgia noted, the sensitive Carl) were inhibited by the presence of Richard and Harry, and unable, for much of the evening, to involve themselves in the conversation. Richard, who had drunk a little too much a little too early, was being particularly boorish – to the evident enjoyment of his sycophantic sidekick Harry.

'Tell me, Amanda,' he said with a practised leer, 'how do you manage to retain your luscious bloom with your husband, er, away?'

Amanda wanted to make one of her classic retorts, but she didn't quite dare. Instead she smiled up at her host and said that she was not the sort of woman who depended on the presence of a man in her life for fulfilment, although, of course, nothing could have been further from the truth.

'I don't believe it, Amanda,' Richard pursued. 'I think that you are the kind of woman who needs the attention of a man as – as a car needs gasoline.'

Richard was the type of man who tended to attribute any depression or dissention in a woman to her sexuality. It was either 'the wrong time of the month' or she 'needed a damn good rogering'. It wasn't his fault, really. His mother had been a distant figure in his life, he had never had a sister, had been brought up in an all-male environment and was still, at forty-three, as puzzled and confused by women as he had been at fourteen. Still perceived them only in sexual terms.

'Why is it, Richard,' interrupted Nicola, 'that men of your type still believe that a woman is somehow incomplete without a man?'

'Because most women, Nicola, are incomplete without a man. You are an exception. At least you were until just recently,' he said, turning his head towards Carl. 'Real women are incomplete without a man.'

'The inference being, Richard,' said Amanda stonily, 'that Nicola is not a real woman?'

'No, no, I don't mean that,' Richard blustered. 'It's just that biologically most women are driven towards nesting – not creating superdrugs and competing in what is, essentially, a man's world.' Pleased with this little speech, and totally unaware of the mockery in the eyes of the five women round the table, he went on, 'A happy woman is one who has responded to the biological demands her body makes of her. A woman with a husband and children. Women are not suited to the cut and thrust of the world. They might like to think they want it, but they don't, not really.' He finished with a chilling grin.

'I hadn't realized you were so well informed about a woman's biology, Richard,' said Nicola coldly. 'I suppose you believe that everything that the women's movement achieved was a temporary change in attitude, not a radical alteration in the way of the world?'

'Women are rejecting all that feminist nonsense. They are coming round to accepting that their place, ideally, is in the home. There are as many women as men who want to see a return to the old traditional sexual roles.'

'A world where a man is a man and women are glad of it,' said Georgia with a giggle.

'Yes, Georgia, if you want to put it like that. This new species of male' – he indicated across the table to Carl – 'well they might go down well in America where the strident new female originates. Like fancy new housepets. But they won't do here. No wonder all those poor American males are running into the woods to celebrate their manhood. But I dare say that Carl doesn't need to beat his breast with a bunch of blokes. He's more comfortable with women,' said Richard.

There was an appalled silence. For a moment Georgia thought that a row would erupt or that Carl and Nicola would simply leave the table. Carl, with his fine intelligent eyes and gentle manner, had scarcely uttered a word the whole evening.

'I think you will soon discover, Richard, that the future is female. That it is men who will find that they cannot live without women and not the other way round. Biologically, as it so happens, we don't need men any more. Leastways, except for their sperm frozen in banks,' said Nicola with a winsome smile.

'And we are never likely to need a men's movement in Britain,' added Caroline softly, 'when we have the public-school system.'

'And football culture,' chorused Amanda.

Georgia quite understood when Nicola and Carl told her that they had to leave early the next morning. She had planned a big Sunday lunch but she knew that the atmosphere of the weekend had changed, been destroyed, by her husband. She wasn't surprised, either, when both Caroline and Amanda accepted a lift back to London. She now bitterly regretted the inclusion of the men – well, Harry and Richard, rather than Carl – in the celebration weekend. Men, well, the men she and her friends were married to, ruined everything.

FOUR

The only good thing to come out of the weekend at Gallows Tree House, Caroline thought as she sat in the antique-filled waiting room in Harley Street, was her confession of her pregnancy to Georgia. Within days of her departure (after that frightful dinner) Georgia had arranged this appointment with the man who was still described, in certain tabloid newspapers, as 'Fergie's Gynaecologist'. It was, she thought as she looked round the sumptuous consulting rooms, a difficult label for a man in his profession to live down. But an indication, she decided with a smile, of his discretion and professional competence.

She was nervous, unhappy and sweaty. The hot weather had returned and the palms of her hands were damp and dirty as she waited, thumbing through a copy of the *Lady*, for her appointment.

There was, she thought when she was finally shown into the great man's office, something very comforting about him. He fitted all her childhood images of a paternalistic, authoritative doctor. Tall, grey-haired and exquisitely dressed, he smiled at her and she wanted to sign her life over to him. To complete the image of the kind but stern father figure there was, she noticed, a bowl of Smarties on the desk in front of him.

She loathed internal examinations. The most shocking story that Amanda had ever told her was of the sex session she had had on the examining table at her gynaecologist's rooms. Caroline could imagine nothing more terrible than being subjected to this intimate examination by a sexually aroused man, but then she had always secretly wondered at the motivation that might make a man pick this particular specialist subject.

Mr Charlton removed his fine rubber gloves, washed his hands at the basin and told her to put her clothes back on. When she was dressed and had reseated herself in front of him at his desk he wrote a letter which he sealed in an envelope and handed to her. It was addressed to the Portland Hospital.

'You've left all this very late, Miss Evans,' he said, looking at her fresh young face and assuming, as everyone usually did, that she was no more than twenty.

'Mrs Evans,' Caroline said, although she wasn't sure why she was so bothered about him knowing that she was, in fact, married.

'I think we should organize an ultrasound scan straight away. I'll ring the hospital in a moment and see if we can send you straight over in a taxi. Do you know what a scan is?'

'A way of seeing the baby in the womb.'

'Yes, it's important you do not urinate between now and the scan.'

Caroline had been so preoccupied by her husband's reaction to the prospect of a child that she had given very little thought to the development of the baby. She felt a vague stirring of alarm and concern.

'How much do I owe you?' she enquired.

He winced. Obviously he was the kind of consultant to whom money was never mentioned. Even more expensive than Caroline had imagined.

'Mrs James is taking care of everything. If you will wait outside, I'll call the Portland now and see if we can sort the whole thing out today.'

'The whole thing? Is there a problem?'

'Not a problem, more of a complication, perhaps,' he said in a more kindly tone.

Georgia had been instinctively aware that her mother had something to tell her. It was unusual for Stella to make a formal request for lunch. What is more, the inclusion of her sister Juliet in the arrangement made her feel, somehow, that all was not well in their mother's world.

They met at 12.30 in the fifth-floor café at Harvey Nichols. It was a brilliantly hot day and, even with the air conditioning, the glaringly bright interior of the fashionably cluttered restaurant was uncomfortable. Made worse, for Georgia, by the fact that it seemed as if she was the only woman carrying, along with the regulation Prada handbag, at least two stone in excess weight. And the only one without sunglasses, so that her already flushed face was forced into a scowl as she scanned the dazzling room for her mother.

'How's Daddy,' Georgia asked as soon as she had kissed and greeted Stella, who, to Georgia's further frustration, looked terribly at home in the elegant throng. Cool even, Georgia thought, as she watched her mother cross her still-wonderful legs and smooth down her linen skirt.

'Your father? I wouldn't know,' Stella replied. 'Are you hungry, darling?' Her mother always knew how best to deflect her daughter's interest away from a difficult issue. Food, from the moment that Georgia had first been able to make herself heard, had been her primary motivation.

'Let's order. Juliet is always late.'

Georgia eagerly seized the menu, noting, as she did so, that she was probably the only woman in the crowded café who really intended to eat.

Juliet arrived as the waiter brought their starters. There was something about the combination of her mother and her sister that made Georgia feel like an outsider. As if she were some giant, ungainly cuckoo that had been dropped into a nest of tiny, exquisite jenny wrens. Her sister, who had caused a few envious glances over the top of a dozen pairs of sunglasses as she had walked to their table, looked wonderful.

What niggled Georgia most about her sibling's flawless appearance was the way in which it was meant to look so understated. Juliet, Georgia recognized, had gone to enormous effort to look effortlessly elegant. Her hair – the subtle autumnal colour of which, Georgia knew, had been achieved with a great deal of artificial intervention – looked absolutely natural and toned perfectly with her slithery silk dress and her gently sunkissed skin. The features that had seemed so plain at fourteen were – with the help of a great deal of subtle make-up and those dramatic contact lenses – now quite beautiful.

Although she hated to admit it, it was always something of a comfort to Georgia to realize that, despite her fabulous looks and her phenomenal success, Juliet was rather empty, unhappy and unfulfilled. Pushing the pent-up feelings of sibling rivalry to the very back of her mind, she smiled warmly up at her sister as she listened to her predictable excuse for being late.

'Simply frightful crisis at the office. Do you know, I'm not sure I could eat anything,' she said, throwing the menu back at the suddenly over-attentive waiter and ordering, to Georgia's absolute horror a 'plain green salad, no dressing, and a glass of still mineral water'.

After a small burst of mutual back-scratching between Juliet and Stella (what Georgia later described as 'you look at the labels on the back of my dress and I'll look at yours') there was a brief silence.

'Look, darlings, there is something you ought to know,' Stella said. 'Daddy and I have decided to part. Well, to be more truthful, I've decided to part from Daddy.'

Georgia was astonished. The idea that her parents – at their age – should part had simply never occurred to her. There had been times when she was a child when she had feared their separation. But the very fact that they had managed to stay together through the rows and recriminations that she had sometimes overheard had made her feel that her parents' marriage was inviolate. Even Juliet, who had been professionally trained to prattle at awkward moments, fell silent.

'There is so much that I want to do. And so little that your father can bear to do that really I think it is the . . . only way forward for me.'

Georgia wanted to say that at her age, surely you didn't need a way forward, at her age you should be looking back. Memories should be sustaining her mother now, not some fantasy idea of a golden future.

'Is there someone else?' Juliet asked coolly.

'Don't be silly,' Stella said. 'The whole point of my leaving your father is to lead my own life, not burden myself with another man. I am so envious of your generation. When I look at you, Juliet, I think, my God, if only I could be in control of my life.'

Georgia was now convinced that her mother was in the midst of some dreadful late-life crisis. She was also rather miffed by the fact that it was Juliet who was being held up as the person with the model life and not herself. Juliet with the broken marriage, the lover who wouldn't commit and the son who, at just seven, had his own psychotherapist. Not Georgia with her successful –

if not entirely happy – marriage, her three clever children, not to mention her husband's political power and influence which, at least in the days when her mother had been more, well, motherly, had seemed a great achievement.

'How has Daddy taken it?' she enquired.

'Not very well. He is not, as you both know, particularly good at coping with all those little things that most of us hardly notice we're doing. Do you know, he has never even answered the phone for himself. At the office he had a string of harpies who made sure no one got through to him, and at home there was always me or Mary or someone.'

'Mary hasn't left him, too?'

'No, but she's getting older and she's cut her hours right back. It means he has to do things like make his own breakfast and run his own bath and make his bed. He is being rather pathetic about it all.'

'You talk about him, Mummy, as if he were some dreadful, disagreeable invalid.'

'Darling, forgive me for sounding a little harsh but when did you last spend more than a couple of hours with your father? I think that if you did, you might understand how I felt. I simply could not go on sacrificing my own happiness for his.'

'Isn't that a rather selfish attitude to take?'

'Selfish? Well, maybe I am. But maybe it's time I was a bit selfish. And maybe it's time that you were, too, Georgia.'

In the weeks following the weekend at Gallows Tree House – which had left her feeling depressed and angry – Amanda and her neighbour Debbie had formed a strange alliance. It was a friendship that both of them, despite strong initial reservations, came to value. Most evenings, after Amanda had picked up Anoushka from her childminder's, they would pop next door so that the children could play together and Debbie and Amanda could talk.

If having a friend helped Amanda, it had been of even greater value to Anoushka, who had grown close to Sean, the elder of Debbie's two sons. Social acceptability in the hard but close community in which they lived was vital for Anoushka's happiness. Sean was the key to acceptance within the children's primary school they both attended, and in the series of playgrounds that surrounded the estate. Anoushka, who had taken to calling herself 'Annie', seemed happier than she had been since before the trial.

The only conscious guilt Amanda held from the old days was in not protecting her daughter enough. Steve's real crime, in Amanda's eyes, was not against society but against their daughter. In hurting their child and disrupting her life, and in not having made provision for her future. There had, of course, been persistent rumours in the press of a Swiss bank account and offshore investments. One paper had even run a picture of Amanda and Anoushka snatched in the run-down street by their home above an editorial condemning the council for allocating them their squalid flat. Speculation as to where Steve had hidden his money further fuelled Amanda's resentment. Did people really think that this dreadful new life was some sort of elaborate sham?

As far as Amanda knew – and on this she thought she could believe Steve – there was no emergency fund, no missing millions stashed away somewhere safe for the future. Apart for her own paltry wage, and a few nostalgic possessions, she was destitute.

Despite her ambivalent feelings about the company

that her five-year-old daughter was keeping – particularly when she contrasted it with the smart little group of friends she had previously mixed with at Hill House in Knightsbridge – she was none the less relieved that Anoushka's pinched little face had regained some of its former expression. And as her daughter relaxed into her new life, so did Amanda. She began to confide in Debbie as she had in no one else, not even kind, good Georgia. She told her of the way things had been, of the glory days with Steve, of her initial love for her husband, of his infidelities and the way, of late, she had come to resent, blame and despise him.

If Amanda was totally honest with herself, she would have to admit that part of the attraction of her friendship with Debbie was in the fact that she knew, deep down, that she was not being judged or pitied. All the friends that Amanda carried with her from her old life now regarded her with cautious sympathy, but with Debbie it was the other way round. In the supplementary benefit world in which Amanda found herself, she was still rich, still privileged and still the object of envy. Not that it was an entirely one-sided friendship. Debbie, in turn, told Amanda of her curious relationship with the father of her children – currently living with his mother on the other side of the estate – whom she had known since she was thirteen. Stories of his drunken binges, his physical abuse, his laziness and lack of purpose formed part of Amanda's education into the customs of the people she was now living amongst.

There was, then, a new and quite welcome rhythm to Amanda's life. There was no way that she was going to spend the rest of her existence in this place but for now, with Debbie's help, she could manage. Some nights, when the children had finally gone to sleep, they would sit together with a baby alarm linking the two flats. On one such night, a month or so after they had befriended each other, they were disturbed in Amanda's flat by a shouting and pounding on Debbie's door.

At first sight, when Amanda opened her own door on to the shared walkway between the flats, the object of her friend's fear seemed impossibly young and harmless. Dean was tall and thin and naturally fair with a babyish complexion, wide-spaced blue eyes, blond eyelashes and eyebrows. The only outward signs of aggression were a series of amateur tattoos etched into the backs of his hands and fingers, a very short haircut and the Millwall strip shirt that he wore with his jeans.

Amanda could scarcely make out what he said. The combination of a strangulated South London accent and alcohol had turned his speech into – at least for Amanda, used to the clipped tones of a more affluent society – a foreign language.

He was rude, of course, and dismissive of her. He walked into the flat, put his hand proprietorially on Debbie's shoulder and tugged her towards the door. Debbie, her eyes meeting Amanda's briefly behind Dean's back, whispered a farewell and followed him back to her home.

It was not possible for Amanda to distinguish the words that Dean used as he set about her friend. The accompanying noises, heard through the baby alarm and echoed through the paper-thin partition walls of the flat, were enough. She sat, terrified for her friend, as the tirade raged on for what seemed like hours. She wondered if the children were silent because they had learnt, through their short lives, that it would be worse if they were to protest, or if they genuinely slept through their parents' awful conflict.

Torn between the need to protect her friend and her fear of intruding in what might, after all, be an

63

accepted part of their odd relationship, Amanda lay awake until the early hours of the morning. Later she concluded that what disturbed her most was the fact that, when she next encountered Debbie, nothing was said. Indeed, her friend, without any visible signs of the fight Amanda had overheard, seemed happier than she had been since they had met.

But the incident had left a sour taste in Amanda's own mouth, perhaps because it reminded her of the compromises that she herself had made in the past in her relationship with Steve. More and more she was coming to believe that she was happier living without a man. She might not be able to survive without sex, but she had learnt in the period in which she had been parted from her husband that it was quite possible – and often more satisfying – to have sex without having to endure the constraints of an emotional relationship.

Nicola moved over towards Carl's sleeping body, putting her arms tentatively around him, longing for him to wake, to turn to her and make love to her. She was astonished by the way in which Carl had changed her from a rather passive, cerebrally controlled woman into a, well, into an abandoned, aggressively sexual being.

All her life Nicola had felt ill at ease with her body, gauche where her friends were elegant, embarrassed and revulsed where they were curious and sensual. She had, of course, been brought up by repressive, cold, academically driven parents in a house where physical intimacy was generally outlawed. As a young adult she was lumpen and awkward, and appalled by the idea of any sort of close physical contact. She had lost her virginity in a do-or-die moment, at a party of Amanda's when she was twenty-one. It had been an awful experience, as had her other attempts at a sex life.

Indeed, she had decided, just before she first encountered Carl, that she was essentially asexual, that for her work was the ultimate goal, not love and marriage. It was something of a shock, then, when she met him. As in all the old romantic clichés that she had previously rejected but nevertheless absorbed, she was immediately aware of a chemistry, one that her science could not quite explain. But she had been frightened, not only of the feeling he aroused but also by the man and his reputation.

Sometimes she did wonder about her lover's past life. About the other women he had been involved with and the awful things he had done in the days before they had met. But they had made a kind of pact, when they had become seriously involved, that they would not talk of his old life. That they would look forward positively. That she would not dwell on what had happened all those years ago. And, for most of the time, it was easy to go along with that pact. After all, wasn't Carl now the most sensitive, caring, funny, gentle man in the entire world? Wasn't he, she thought as she glanced at his strong broad back, a triumph for her work and a joy for her emotional life?

Just for a second, caught unawares coming out of sleep, Carl seemed suddenly hostile. His face contorted in a defensive motion. But when he took in the sight of Nicola looking lovingly at him, he relaxed and moved towards her.

'Is baby hungry?' he said with a smile.

She slid down and took his taut penis in her mouth, moving her tongue round it in the practised manner in which he had coached her. After a few seconds, when

Carl signalled, she shifted her body so that she was astride him, the hard thing within her.

'Come on, baby, harder, baby,' he said as she worked on top of him.

Beneath her he lay rather languidly his hands behind his head as she abandoned herself to his wishes. Even when she had come and he had seemed to ejaculate he was unmoved. But Nicola was so enthralled with him, so overwhelmed by these new feelings and physical sensations, that she did not notice his detachment.

FIVE

It was seeing that odd shape emerge on the screen that made Caroline finally face her responsibility. They had lain her on an examination table, poured some horrid, cold, glutinous substance on to her naked stomach and then traced around her flesh until they found what they were looking for.

At first it looked like nothing at all or one of those faded old black-and-white photographs of something that might just be the Loch Ness Monster. But then, as the woman explained what each bit was – this is a head, this is a hand – she suddenly understood the enormity of what was happening to her. An enormity, the nurse warned with a warm smile, that within a very few weeks she would more fully comprehend. For Caroline was expecting twins.

She was acutely aware that such news imparted in such a place – the most exclusive, expensive private maternity hospital in the country – would ordinarily be greeted with joy. But for her it just made the problem doubly difficult. Because, however instinctively thrilled and proud she might be by this extraordinary turn of events, she was nevertheless conscious that it further compounded the hopelessness of her situation. Nick would have no more pride in the procreation of two babies than he would have in one. Rather, he would, she felt, be doubly disturbed and disgusted by this news.

'What a shame,' said the sweet-faced nurse, 'that your husband could not be here to see this.'

Caroline had muttered something about him working abroad.

'Well, at least you'll have the Polaroid to show him. I'm sure he'll be overwhelmed when he sees it,' the nurse said gently.

Caroline hid the picture in the side of her purse and, in the days that followed, took it out when she was alone to study and wonder over. But she didn't really need the black-and-white image of her babies to remind her of the scan. The moment that she had managed to distinguish the heads and tiny bodies of her babies on that screen returned to her again and again without the prompting of a Polaroid. In the office, in the middle of a work crisis, she would suddenly see those blurred images. In the night – alone again in their double bed – she was haunted by visions of her babies.

Nick's brief period of inspiration – that had prompted their last attempt at love-making and communication – had long since turned into an even deeper depression. Unable to write, unable to go out, unable to talk to Caroline, he had become an aggressive and abusive recluse.

At work Caroline would daily make the decision to tell him about the twins, only to change her mind when she walked in the flat each evening and was confronted by his hostility. But gradually something inside her – no doubt encouraged by her hormonal confusion – was beginning to rebel. Now and again she would begin to think of a future without Nick. It would be hard, she decided, to bring up two children alone, but no harder than existing like this alongside her husband.

Caroline was rather shocked by this new feeling. She had truly believed that she and Nick would be a partnership for life. Their love, she had always thought, was deeper and greater than that of most married couples. They had counted themselves special. Sneered a little at the more fluid unions of their friends. Not once during their ten years together had Caroline for a moment imagined that she might ever leave him.

But now the image of the man slumped and sullen in front of the television held little appeal when she compared it to that picture of her babies on the hospital screen. If she had to make a choice, she now knew that it would be the twins growing within her and not the husband who had grown away from her.

Georgia's world had been turned upside down by the Prime Minister's announcement of a General Election. The party was in such a poor state, at least if you believed the polls, that Richard had been sent into a spin at the thought of losing his constituency. Not that such a thing was likely. Henley was, as everyone knew, never going to return a Labour MP. But nevertheless, in the spirit of party politics Richard had become an almost permanent fixture at Gallows Tree House, flying the flag at every village fête, school fair and garden party.

Georgia had forgotten what it was like to be needed by Richard. Not in a sexual sense, of course – he hadn't come near her in months – but in a purely political sense. His sweet, homely wife was his most essential accessory as the campaign gathered pace. For once Richard wore Georgia proudly at his side. He had even persuaded the children into one or two local picture opportunities, several of which had been used by the national Tory press.

Worse, though, than the frightful constituency excursions were the national events. Tonight they were attending a rally for a few select Tory supporters at the House. As one of the few well-known Conservative politicians as yet untouched by scandal, Richard was expected to mingle with the celebrity crowd accompanied, of course, by his lovely wife. She supposed she should have bought something for the occasion, but she had been so busy that she had not managed to get up to Selfridge's designer outsize department. So she wore her old favourite: a navy blazer over a wrap-round calf-length skirt and a white shirt. She was, she thought as she looked in the bedroom mirror, every inch the Tory matron.

'How do I look?' she said to Richard as she joined him in the Daimler for their journey up to the House.

He didn't answer. But then, Richard was not a naturally cruel man. He would never dream of saying to his wife that she looked fat and middle-aged, however much he might have thought it. But he did look her up and down and wonder what had happened to that pretty, petite girl he had married. As if to cover up this thought he then took her hand and smiled at her.

'Are you very worried about losing?' said Georgia, rather overcome by this show of affection.

'It would be a terrible blow. I have got so used to being in power. Being in opposition would be dreadful, the more so the longer it might last. Frankly, Georgia, if we lose, I doubt I'll be a minister again.'

It was odd, but for all the contempt that Georgia generally felt for her husband she could yet feel pity for him. Even though theirs was essentially a sham marriage, there was still some part of her that felt emotionally bonded to the man.

She felt genuine pity for him as he talked so uncharacteristically of his fears of defeat – not because she in any way enjoyed being the wife of a powerful man and the toast of the local WI. She was quite unmoved by the idea of losing the ministerial car, salary and status. But he was the father of her children and she knew that if he was unhappy it would have a knock-on effect on her life.

And in any case the way they lived now – with him in London during the week – rather suited her. The idea of his being around more appalled her. She would, she decided as the car drew into St Stephen's Entrance, be extra-supportive this evening.

It was all rather presidential, Georgia thought as she observed the decorations – giant 3D versions of the burning-torch symbols – that dominated the room. There was no doubt that the party were scared. Why else would they have rolled out all the old A and B list Tory celebrities along with three ex-Tory Prime Ministers?

Georgia was so rarely a part of Richard's London circle that she felt rather shy, even though, through force of circumstances, she was on first-name terms with the Cabinet and their respective wives. It was, she thought as she noted Sir Andrew Lloyd Webber and Phil Collins, rather like a Royal Variety performance without the royalty. Top of the bill was a rousing speech by the PM in which he paid tribute, amongst others, to Richard.

Boosted by the champagne and the spirit of evangelism engendered by the PM, Georgia relaxed and enjoyed herself as the entertainers were wheeled out – Paul Daniels pulling off an amazing trick involving a real blazing Tory torch and Jim Davidson telling a series of savagely funny and politically incorrect gags. She might not have noticed Richard slip out of the reception had it not been for the fact that at that very moment she had been scanning the room in search of a loo. The sight of her retreating husband, accompanied by that new secretary of his, sent alarm bells through her head.

She realized then that this must be his new woman. It didn't surprise her. A mistress was, after all, almost party policy right now. But while she had, over the years, come to ignore if not quite accept Richard's infidelities, she was enormously irritated that he should attempt to humiliate her here, in what was, after all HIS hour of need. She guessed that they were heading for his rooms and, after a few moments, followed them. The Palace of Westminster was a vast and daunting place, but she had been to Richard's offices – and to events at the House – often enough to have a rough idea the route they would take. She knew, too, that they would probably have locked themselves into his inner sanctum if they wanted to be alone. So before she disturbed them she found the loo and stood for a few minutes examining her reflection in the harsh strip lighting.

She was far, far too complacent, she decided as her eyes ran down her body. She had been ignoring an important part of her own life – and her husband's – for too long. It was time that she got herself in order. She had put so much of herself into the creation of her family that somewhere she had lost sight of that old Georgia, the one that had been fêted by royalty and pictured in all the gossip columns.

Presently she put some lipstick on and brushed her hair, although she knew these vanities were pointless. Then she made her way up to the confrontation. To Richard and whatever that new woman was called. They hadn't locked the outer office and she crept in and stood, breathing deeply to calm herself and to give herself courage, before making her move. Then she walked over to the other door and very gently turned the brass knob.

They had left this door open too. She was so quiet that they didn't even notice her. She stood watching them for a few moments. Richard was sitting at his desk with his head in his hands while whatever-her-name-was was gently massaging his shoulders and back. She had not, thankfully, interrupted anything urgent or obscene, but there was an intimacy to their movements that nevertheless alarmed Georgia.

72

She coughed and they looked up, as startled as if she had found them *in flagrante*.

'I wonder, Richard,' she said to her husband in the loudest voice she could muster, 'if the ministerial mistress will go along with the car, the salary and all the other perks.'

He was only caught out for a second. Not a lot could phase Richard. His years in politics had hardened him to surprise attacks, and he simply turned on his wife as he might an adversary in the House.

'I can't think what you are talking about, Georgia darling. I was just going through some papers with Louise. It will save me having to come back up to town tomorrow.'

'Richard, I am an adult. I am quite sure that whatever you are doing with her has nothing at all to do with the administration of ministerial business.'

'Don't be tiresome, Georgia, there's a good girl,' he said as if he were addressing one of the children. 'I simply cannot handle a tantrum right now.'

What upset her most was not her husband's obvious involvement with that woman but his utter contempt for her own feelings. He didn't seem even faintly embarrassed by the scene, nor worried enough about his wife's reaction to ask his secretary to leave. Instead he stood his ground, looked at Georgia as if she was in the wrong.

'Is there anything else I can do for you, Georgia?' he said curtly.

She realized quite suddenly then that he didn't even like her. She could pretend, from the warmth and safety of Gallows Tree House, that he cared for her, that, deep down, he was a family man, but he was – in fact – nothing of the kind. Lord knows she had never been sentimental about him, but she had once thought that he was basically a decent man. Now she understood the contempt he felt for her and she knew that she could not go on as she had been. It was time to put Georgia first.

'I'll take the car home. I am sure Louise will put you up for the night,' she said with a hint of a sneer. Then she swept out of his office down the steep stone stairs to the safety of Henderson and the ministerial Daimler.

Juliet was aware that she had angered Harry, although she wasn't sure how, why or when. They had been dining in one of his favourite restaurants with two of his closest friends when she realized he was freezing her out, casting long cold looks at her across the table.

She shifted in her seat and looked plaintively at him. If only she knew what it was that had upset him, she could apologize or attempt to right her wrong. She had, she thought, been perfectly civil to his friends, charming even. She had done everything that she could to please him. Worn her hair in the way he liked, the Ralph Lauren suit he had chosen for her, the shoes he had picked out to match.

Yet he was ignoring her, continued to do so as he drove her home. If she didn't say something soon, she thought as the car neared her street, he would disappear and she probably wouldn't hear from him for a week. He braked hard outside her house, but didn't turn off the engine. Obviously he didn't intend to stay.

'Won't you come in?' she said tentatively.

'No, Juliet,' he said.

'What is it, Harry. What have I done?'

'If you don't know what you have done, I am certainly not going to tell you,' he said with such utter disdain that she was frightened.

'But everything was fine –'

'Don't try to provoke me, Juliet. I don't want an argument.'

'I thought you were going to stay over tonight.'

'I was, but I'd rather not now.'

She knew the tears were coming and she knew that they would only serve to further enrage him. But she couldn't help it. If she could just get him to come in for a few minutes, everything would be all right.

'Please, darling,' she said, putting her hand on his arm.

'Look, Juliet, I've got an early start. Are you going to get out of the car or do I have to throw you out?'

'Please, Harry, please come in for a few minutes.'

'Juliet,' he said, narrowing his eyes spitefully at her, 'will you please get out of the car.'

'Don't you love me any more?'

'What kind of question is that? What do you think?'

Nothing in her adult life had made Juliet cry. Not the birth of her baby, not the break-up of her marriage. No man, woman or child had the power to move her as Harry did. She knew, from previous scenes such as this, that in a couple of days, maybe a week, he would have forgiven her. But still she was fearful that if he drove away tonight she would never see him again. She tried to move closer, but he brushed her away and then leaned over her and opened her door.

Convulsed with tears and overcome with shame, she got out of the car. He didn't even say goodbye, just accelerated off into the night. It was then that she began to really panic. She let herself into the house and rang him on the mobile in his car, but he had switched it off. Then she rang his flat and left a long, rambling, tearful message. Would he ring her back? Would he speak to her again? Why did she always make such a scene? Why did she always spoil things?

The early days of their relationship had been so different, so wonderful. He had made her feel as if she were the most beautiful, amusing, special woman on earth. For the first six months they had been quite literally inseparable. He had said that meeting her was like finding perfection. She was his muse, his soul mate, the one he had been waiting for all his life.

It was the memory of the intensity of the first months of their relationship that made her go on. She would, she decided, do whatever was needed to get back to that state of bliss.

She rang him again. Left another message. If only he would speak to her, she thought, they could sort things out. But she couldn't wait. She had to do something now. Rushing upstairs, she washed her face, put on some fresh make-up and furiously brushed her hair. She would go to him. She would drive to his flat and confront him, plead with him, do whatever he wanted just so long as he stopped hating her.

She was vaguely worried, as she drove the mile or so to his apartment, that she might be over the limit. But nothing could stop her now she had her mind set on a course of action. She was certain she was doing the right thing. When he saw her on his doorstep he would take her in his arms, love her again.

But the flat was dark, his car was gone and she had to face the possibility that he had gone somewhere else, that he was seeing someone else, that his coldness had to do with a new affair, a new soul mate, a new image of perfection. Or worse, perhaps he had gone to the wife that he had so cleverly never divorced.

She waited, in the darkness, for him to come home. She must have sat there for an hour, maybe two before she finally dropped to sleep with her head crushed against the car window. At five in the morning, when she awoke with a jolt and realized that he had not returned, she finally gave up her mission.

She went home, ran a bath and tried to remember the yoga chant that she had been told would calm her. Just before she slipped into bed she rang him again, first on the mobile then at his flat. This time she left no message.

Amanda was feeling so positive on the day the letter arrived that she didn't bother to open it. Rather, she assumed it was another one of Steve's dull missives and put it in her handbag to read later. She had noticed, that morning, that Anoushka had regained her old bloom. That her daughter, in this awful place, was actually flourishing. It occurred to her that even though they were parted during the day, they nevertheless enjoyed a far more intense and satisfying relationship than ever they had in the glory days.

Their life had flowed at such a terrific pace back then that there had never been time for Anoushka. Day and night nannies – rather than Amanda – had witnessed Anoushka's childhood milestones. While her parents flew relentlessly round the world their little daughter learned to sit, crawl, walk and talk with the hired help. Of course, she had always been Steve's 'Princess', she had always been indulged and cherished, but she had received very little parental attention in the early years and had grown – by her third birthday – into a sulky, petulant manipulator.

Removed from that life of privilege, Amanda now thought, she had been transformed into a generous, loving and intelligent child. Her ability to adapt to her new circumstances was astonishing and gratifying, and as they walked hand in hand to the childminder's flat Amanda felt something like contentment.

It wasn't until mid-afternoon that she opened the letter. The contents sent a spasm of shock and fear through her, so that she actually physically shook. She should have realized that sooner or later he would be paroled. She should have expected this news. But in her struggle to adapt to her new life she had forgotten that Steve's life, too, must go on. She hadn't expected that he would come out so soon, even though his crime was merely fraud rather than murder or rape, and his behaviour – at least within the confines of the prison – exemplary.

Two weeks. She had just two weeks to prepare for his release. She didn't just fear about their future together in their tiny flat, or worry about those feelings of hatred and resentment she had been harbouring for her husband in the last year or so. She was also frightened by the thought of the press reaction to his release. Just when Anoushka seemed to have settled into a happy and anonymous new life, she – they – would be thrown back into the headlines. More speculation about the lost Minter millions, more interest in their drab new lives, more exposure of those old wounds.

Nor was she certain that she wanted a future with him. Amanda had been a kind of trophy wife for Steve. She had met him in the early eighties when he was already successful and, although she had believed herself to be in love with him when they married, she now realized that her attraction to him had probably been very shallow. He had conducted an almost Mills-and-Boon romance with her and she, young and impressionable and from a quite different social background, had been easily overwhelmed by his charm and charisma. But she had quickly understood, within months of their marriage, that their relationship could never be equal. Steve had all the power, all the wealth and a very low boredom threshold. Keeping him happy was an exacting task. A year after they married he had a very public affair and Amanda discovered the other price she had to pay for being married to such a dynamically attractive and successful man.

He had loved her, she knew that, but he expected her to play the compliant, forgiving and essentially subservient wife. At the time she had gone along with things for fear of losing him, but now she despised the way she had behaved. And she had no intention of becoming his little woman again after his release from prison. Her new life, however financially limited, had given her a taste for independence and a new kind of confidence.

She decided not to tell Anoushka for a while. To keep the news of her father's parole quiet until she herself had adjusted to the idea. She told Debbie that night, confided in her the worries she had about any future that involved Steve. But she didn't tell Georgia when she called or Nicola when they had lunch together.

She would have to say something soon. But for the next week she would enjoy the sweet freedom she had while her husband lived through his last days of incarceration.

Nicola lay stretched out on the four-poster bed while Carl massaged her. For a man of his size his touch was remarkably gentle. Part of her felt guilty about the pleasure he gave her and the little that she thought she did for him, at least on a physical level.

He was so generous with his time, his emotions, his love. In the few unsatisfactory relationships that Nicola had endured before she had met Carl she had always seemed to be the one that gave. Never, not even as a tiny child, had she felt so protected, so cherished, so absolutely adored.

His arms swept down the small of her back – sweet, warm oil trickling beneath his fingers. She was aroused now and pulled her head up so that she could see him, let him know that she wanted him.

'Not yet,' he said with that still dangerous smile. 'Patience will be rewarded.'

He turned her over and began to caress her breasts and shoulders. She didn't think that she could bear to wait any longer. If he didn't make love to her soon, she thought, she would expire.

'Pleease, Carl,' she said in the little-girl voice she had adopted with him of late.

But he didn't seem to hear her and went on moving his hands sensuously across her stomach and down towards her thighs carefully avoiding the part of her that most needed him.

'I want you so much,' she said, a little petulantly.

'I want doesn't get,' he replied as he continued moving his hands down her legs and towards her feet.

Then quite suddenly, and with an unexpected roughness, he pushed her legs apart and entered her. She was so excited she didn't notice the look in his eyes as he thrust in and out of her or the words he whispered beneath his breath. And afterwards, when she felt so totally, blissfully content, she didn't think to question the change of pace in his love-making. For Nicola never needed to doubt Carl's love and devotion. He could play games when they made love, he could attempt a brief domination, but ultimately she was in control. Carl was her creation.

She had made him. Plucked him from a group of hopeless lifers in one of the most feared and brutal prisons in America and turned him into Manifold's prototype of the perfect man. She had instructed him, groomed him, educated him and chemically moulded him into every woman's ideal man. In three years she had turned a hardened criminal – a man serving out a twenty-year sentence for murder – into a sensitive, caring, attentive and compassionate companion.

She smiled to herself when she thought of the night she had introduced him to her friends at Gallows Tree House. None of them had the slightest inkling of what Carl was, or rather had been. They were all absolutely beguiled by his charm and gentility. All the more so, she thought, because their own relationships with their men were so unsatisfactory. Indeed, Nicola had thought on the night of the awful dinner with Richard and Harry that she had never, not even in the American penitentiary system, come across a group of men who were in more need of a prescription of Manifold.

She had a hunch that even in his dark and dangerous phase Carl would have been a more considerate partner than Nick, Harry, Richard or Steve. It had never been her intention to become personally involved with Carl – or any of the other men on the research programme – but there had been something about him that had interested her from the outset. She had known, when she first saw him in that frightful place with no dignity and none of the refinements, that he had now acquired that he was special. But if she was now addicted to him – passionately in love with him – he was equally dependent on her and the drugs that had caused his change of fortune.

She leant across his sleeping body and gently stroked his face. In a few days they would part again for a while. He returning to the States as part of his parole agreement and she remaining here for the last stage of talks with the European money-men. In a month, when Manifold was formally launched in the US, they would be reunited. Carl and ten other men, who had not so much been rehabilitated as reborn since their introduction to Nicola's drug, would be part of a huge promotional campaign throughout the country.

Watching him sleep she knew that what she and the rest of the team had done in creating Manifold was probably a greater advancement for women than gaining the vote, entering the workplace or the introduction of the Pill. Finally, she thought as she looked tenderly down on her peaceful lover, women could take control.

SIX

That morning when Caroline got dressed she discovered that the zip of her ubiquitous black Lycra skirt would no longer do up. It had taken the strain so far but would obviously go no further. When she looked at herself in the mirror, in the privacy of the bathroom, she realized that the bump was now quite clearly visible. She had always looked young, the cropped blonde hair, her slight figure and the masculine clothes she wore conspired to make her look like a pretty teenage tomboy. And even now, with her swollen stomach, she still looked oddly childish. But there was no way, she thought as she searched through her wardrobe for something that would still fit her, that she could keep her secret any longer. Either at work or here at home.

Putting on a drab dress with a high waist – bought on impulse in Marks & Spencer's a year before and never worn – she made her way through to the living room and past the sleeping form of Nick.

She was always very careful not to wake him when she left for work. He needed his rest, she still believed, more than she did. The creative process, as he was always reminding her, must be sensitively nurtured. She didn't even risk making herself a cup of tea in case it disturbed him, deciding instead to grab a drink and a piece of toast from the café round the corner from the office. The only consolation for the final visibility of her baby, or rather babies, was that at last the nausea had subsided and physically, at any rate, she felt good.

Telling them at work, in the end, proved unnecessary. Everyone, she discovered on what she was later to call the Day of Reckoning, had already guessed. One of the secretaries had stumbled across her clandestine copy of Miriam Stoppard's *Pregnancy and Birth* and word had quickly travelled round the building.

She went in officially to tell the Creative Director and he was kind and sympathetic. Privately Caroline thought that he might even be pleased at the news. Her absence from the office for a few months would give him an opportunity to reorganize things. Her recent promotion, even accepting the fact that she had been feeling so ill these past months, had not been a great success. The babies, he probably hoped, would be an ideal get-out.

No one in the office knew of the complexity of her relationship with Nick. Most of the people she worked alongside assumed that he was happy with the news. And she was in no hurry to disillusion them. She had this private fantasy, that could almost be a reality at work, of living a different life with Nick. Of him being attentive and adoring, supportive and strong. Of his longing for children as much as she now did. Allowing her colleagues to believe that the twins were happily planned gave life to this fantasy. In fact, her time at work on the Day of Reckoning was far easier than her time at home. Spurred on by the fact that her secret – rather like her big ugly Marks & Spencer's dress – had finally emerged from the closet, she resolved to tell Nick that night.

On the way home she bought a bottle of his favourite wine – one they had discovered together on their honeymoon in Umbria – and, to add to the nostalgia she hoped the evening would summon up, she bought a selection of Italian salamis, cheeses and breads.

Think positive, she said to herself as she let herself into the musty interior of the flat. She didn't exactly say,

'Hi honey, I'm home,' but the next most relevant thing, at least with Nick: 'Were you able to get any work done today, darling?'

'A little,' he said.

This was, Caroline decided, a good omen. It had been weeks since Nick had managed to write. Why, for him, this surly reply was a positive statement.

'I bought a bottle of your favourite wine. I was thinking about Umbria in the office today and how nice it would be if we could go back there one day.'

He didn't respond, although he did take the bottle into the kitchen to open it.

'I always think of it as our wine, our place. We were there long before all the *Spectator* readers discovered it. Do you remember that evening we spent with the Italian family? That meal they cooked for us?'

There was still no response and Caroline, suddenly tired, gave up her attempt at animated conversation.

'Nick, there is something I have to tell you.'

'Not more fucking Umbrian memories,' he said contemptuously.

'No, something more important.'

'What?' he said as he poured himself another glass of wine.

'I'm pregnant.'

'You're what?'

'I'm pregnant,' she repeated.

'Don't be absurd, Caroline. We decided not to have children.'

'Well, it happened. And there is more. It's twins.'

There was silence for a moment while Nick ran his eyes down Caroline's form, doubtless noting the unflattering dress and the emergent shape of the babies.

'How could you betray me?' he said eventually.

'I didn't betray you. The babies are yours, ours,' she

said. 'Here is the proof. This is the Polaroid of the scan – here are our babies.'

'But you know how I feel. And you know what a difficult time this is for me. The pressure I am under with the book. Why did you do it?' he said, throwing her precious picture on the floor.

'We both did it, Nick.'

'No, Caroline, because I didn't know I was doing it. To me it was just another sterile fuck,' he shouted.

'It was a mistake.'

'Then unmake it.'

She couldn't believe that he could be hinting that she abort the babies. Surely he understood her better than that. After ten years together he must know that she could never do something like that, however inconvenient the pregnancy was. However unhappy it made him.

'It's too late, Nick. I'm over five months pregnant.'

He came towards her as if to hit her. His dark eyes, narrowed in what she could only take to be hatred, were dangerous. The realization that he wanted to hurt her and that he could consider getting rid of their children finally gave her the strength to tell him a few truths.

'Nick, I am not asking you to support me financially. In fact, I have supported you financially for the best part of the last five years. I won't give up work. How could I? You haven't earned anything since that review that appeared in *Time Out* in 1992, and I think the payment for that was a little less than £75. I have made allowances for your great talent. I have, as you are always telling me, prostituted my own skills in order that you should have the opportunity to create your great work of art. I don't expect you to give up that dream, however unrealistic it now might seem. All I am asking of you is that you be a father to our children. Love them, care for them, love me. If you can't do that, then perhaps it's better that you go.'

It was the longest – and strongest – speech that she had made to her husband in the five years during which he had struggled to write his novel. Indeed, she was as stunned by the harshness and directness of her words as he was.

They stood for a few moments, looking at each other. Then he finished his glass of wine, walked into the bedroom, packed a small bag with a few clothes and left.

She was astonished at how relieved she felt. She even had a glass of wine, something she knew she shouldn't do now that she was a concerned, expectant mother. She felt a tremendous surge of optimism. Everything would be all right. It would be hard, but she could handle it. She put her hand down to her hard, swollen stomach and felt, in that moment, a flutter of movement from her babies. She sat in front of the TV and ate the Italian salamis before taking a long luxuriant bath and going to bed.

In the morning, when she rose to go to work, her mood of elation faded. Nick was back. Not contrite or in any way seeking an emotional reunion. Just asleep on the sofa as he was most mornings. He was even incapable of leaving home. He was as dependent on her as the babies within her. Only far less appealing. Her husband was now more like the child from hell – a moody, morose teenager whom she was expected to support, encourage and nurture without any hope of return or reward.

Georgia's relationship with Richard had entered a significant new phase after the revelation in the House of Commons. Not that it was a revelation, exactly; it was more of a realization of what he was and where she was going.

If she had dared to look at their life together at any time in the last twelve years, she knew she would have found a secretary, a researcher, a woman like Louise hidden away somewhere. She had been deluding herself for so long that she had simply lost sight of reality.

So much so that even after the insulting scene in Richard's rooms she still somehow expected him to come up with some stunning excuse or denial of what she now knew was going on. Part of her still clung to the old romantic image she had of Richard when he was a young man. The whole of the following day she had wandered round Gallows Tree House waiting for the phone call, the apologetic card, the bouquet of please-forgive-me flowers.

But they hadn't come. And neither had he. A short message on the answerphone – saying that he was campaigning in the most at-risk Tory constituencies in the North-East – was his only response to their crisis.

She toyed with the idea of talking to Juliet about her problems, but pride and fear prevented her. Instead she rang her mother – now living in a little cottage in Richmond – and arranged to go and stay with her for a couple of days. Without the children.

She had decided, in the days following her own drama, that she had not been sympathetic enough to Stella. She had mentally written off her mother's need for personal happiness and fulfilment. Georgia had reasoned that in her late fifties her mother had no right to pursue a new life without her father. But now, as she remembered odd scenes from her childhood, she began to understand Stella's actions, late though they were. Perhaps her father had been as faithless and manipulative as Richard. Perhaps the only reason that Stella had stayed in the marriage was for the sake of Juliet and Georgia. Certainly it was her own children's happiness that made Georgia even consider a future with Richard now.

She was enchanted by her mother's new home. Although Stella and Juliet shared a similar style of dress – and matching slender bodies – her mother's taste in home furnishings was much closer to Georgia's. She had filled the tiny, pretty Georgian cottage with perfectly proportioned pieces and warm, comforting colours.

Stella was not the kind of woman that you would immediately describe as 'motherly'. She had loved her children, but she was not, as Georgia was, a slave to them. But today, realizing that her daughter needed her, she greeted her emotionally, holding her tightly in a hug for several minutes after her arrival.

Georgia was instantly overcome by her need to tell her mother everything.

'Darling, I'm sorry but not in the least surprised. I knew that Richard was too emotionally stunted and basically dishonest to make you happy,' Stella said after digesting her daughter's story.

'You didn't say anything at the time,' said Georgia accusingly.

'Do you really think you would have taken any notice? You had made up your mind to marry Richard. And in many ways your decision was probably right. You have three wonderful children, a lovely home and a life of great privilege. Richard never beats you, does he? Nor does he deny you anything you want – apart from his fidelity. Perhaps that is as much as a woman can really expect from a man. In a marriage. At least it was for my generation.'

'But I want more, Mummy. I want more than I have

got with Richard and less, too. The money, the house, all that status stuff, I really don't need that.'

Her mother led her through the little kitchen and out into the courtyard garden. They sat together in the sunshine and talked. Stella was rather shaken to notice that, for the first time in her life, Georgia wasn't interested in food. Stella had raised Georgia so that every wound she encountered in life would be compensated for with a chocolate bar or an ice cream. A calorific treat. On hearing the news that her elder daughter was coming to stay – and realizing that this time the injury was serious – she had rushed out to M & S to fill the fridge with delicacies. But it was clear that today food was not going to appease her daughter.

She wasn't sure whether Georgia's rejection of lunch was due to her distress at the situation with Richard or a new vanity, maybe even a diet.

'Georgia,' she said, 'what has happened to your appetite?'

'Mummy, in the middle of all that business with Richard I finally realized what had happened to my body, to me. God knows appearance could never be as important to me as it is to Juliet, but I think that I owe it to myself to get my body in order. Being a betrayed wife wouldn't be so bad if I were thin. As it is, I have a daily reminder, if I dare open my eyes when I get in the bath, of exactly why my husband is sleeping with his secretary. Or should I say researcher?'

'Do you imagine that if you are thinner, you will be more desirable to Richard, or some other man?' her mother enquired.

'No, but getting thinner might be a form of revenge. I wonder if your leaving Daddy after all these years isn't a kind of revenge.'

'Maybe it is. But it's also because I cannot think of

any earthly reason to stay with him. Like most women of my generation I muddled along with him all those years because it was the most practical thing to do. Had I left him, it would have hurt you and Juliet and things would have been difficult financially. I was never trained to do anything, darling, except run a house and raise children. Well, I've done that and when my aunt left me some money – and this is going to sound terrible – I suddenly realized that your father had become obsolete.' She paused for a moment.

'And, Georgia, darling, I can't tell you how wonderful it is, after all those years, to be in control of my own life. To make my own decisions, to be myself. To no longer have to bend and stretch to fit into his idea of the way things should be. I've come to think that a truly fulfilled woman is a woman who is happy with herself. I'm sorry that your father has taken it badly, but there is no way I could go back now.'

Georgia grasped her mother's hand and squeezed it. Her attitude to Stella was probably rather like her own children's attitude to her. They didn't see her as a person with an existence outside of their lives. Heavens, Georgia was now thirty-five and this was the first time that she had ever considered her mother as an individual.

'Your problem, darling,' Stella said softly, 'is that you are living a life too like the one that I endured. You are out of time with your contemporaries. Like me, you thought the ultimate goal in a woman's life was to find her Mr Right, even if she knew that he was only Mr All Right. But Mr Right – like Prince Charming – is a myth. We can't expect men to make us happy, to take the blame for everything that goes wrong in our lives. Richard can't be all things to you, and nor should he be. You need to assert yourself, to find something in your life other than Richard and the children that will give you a degree of independence and identity. Look at Juliet.'

Georgia resented her mother holding her sister up as some kind of role model, and instinctively let go of her grasp on Stella's hand.

'Juliet isn't happy, Mummy. In fact, I think she is even more unhappy and dissatisfied than I am. More than anything else, she wants Harry to commit to her. She'd give up everything, I know, to be his wife. She told us all at dinner that some part of her feels incomplete without a man. She still believes that one day her prince will come. Isn't it extraordinary that, for all we have achieved, we still feel something is missing in our lives if we don't have a man?'

'We think society sees us as incomplete without a man, but of course we aren't. But it's difficult for us to forget those fairy tales we were brought up on and, even at my great age, part of me does still yearn for a shadow of what my perfect man used to be. My own personal Mr Right – a cross between Paul Newman and Pavarotti. But another, much stronger, part of me knows that it's nonsense. Here and now I am happier than I have ever been before in my adult life. Finally living without a man.'

'So what do I do, follow your lead and leave Richard?'

'Not yet. Not until you are ready. You must put yourself first for a while, Georgia. You must come out of this marriage having established what you want in life. Not what Richard wants and not what the children want. Although obviously they deserve greater consideration than their father. Stay with me for a few days. Pop into town and have lunch with your friends. Let Richard notice that you have gone. And yes, get thin if you want. It won't be the answer to your problems, but it will be a help.'

Georgia smiled warmly at her mother. That morning before she had left Gallows Tree House she had discovered that she had, in just one week, lost a stone. A drop in the ocean, of course, and the Atlantic at that, but enough of an incentive to help her push away the plate of food her mother had carefully left in front of her.

It was a full week before Juliet heard from Harry. He rang her at eleven o'clock at night and asked if he could come over. She said, as she always did after such absences, 'Come now.' Calculating that it would take him half an hour to reach her, she then launched into a frightful personal tidy-up. Putting on a deal of subtle make-up, working on her hair, changing out of her towelling robe and into a tiny dress that she believed especially flattered her figure. She felt so agitated that she had to have a drink before he arrived to calm her and to ensure that she didn't go against her own resolve to be sweet, compliant and sexy with him rather than whiny and critical.

At one o'clock in the morning, when one drink had become six and she was on the point of going to bed, he finally arrived.

He didn't say anything about their row. He just came in and demanded something to eat. He had been working late on a shoot, he said, and hadn't had a thing all day. Panicked again, Juliet rushed to the fridge to retrieve the few bits and pieces the daily had left there. Some goat's cheese, a crust of *ciabatta* and some olives.

'Hardly a sumptuous reunion feast,' said Harry, looking at her offering.

'But I didn't know you were coming. If I'd known you were coming –'

'You'd have baked me a cake?' he said with a snide smile.

'Well, no, but I would have got something in.'

Already she felt she was in the wrong. She had failed him, not lived up to his expectations.

'A drink, darling?' she said.

'I think you've drunk enough for both of us,' he said curtly.

'I'm sorry,' she said.

The trouble with Juliet's exquisitely designed house was that it was all sharp edges and hard surfaces. The sandstone bench – the only piece of furniture that could seat two – was hardly the place for a cosy cuddle or any attempt, on Juliet's part, to seduce Harry.

'Have you been working very hard, darling?' she enquired softly.

He grunted. Confused, drunk and dreadfully unhappy she moved over to him, unbuttoned his flies and began to fellate him. It seemed to take ages before she got any response. Eventually he became aroused and pushed her head harder down on him. It was the first contact he had had with her since he had made her get out of the car a week before, and she was pathetically grateful for it.

Never before in her life had Juliet debased herself in such a way to another human being. No one who knew her, none of her friends, colleagues or family, would believe it possible. In every other area of her life Juliet was confident, dominant, in charge. Saleswomen in Harvey Nichols flinched at her approach, secretaries scurried from her stare, painters and decorators trembled in her presence. Yet here, alone with Harry, it was she who was nervous, she who would do anything for peace and for what she believed was love.

Nor was this particular act to Juliet's, well, taste. She was the kind of woman – a slave to hygiene – who liked, after any exchange of bodily fluids, to shower herself down with a strong pH-balance cleanser and wash her mouth out with a double dose of Listerine. But now, in the ultimate act of contrition she swallowed his semen and – rather than rushing to the bathroom – shifted herself so that she could massage Harry's neck and shoulders.

'Is everything all right again now?' she said in the tone of a small and anxious child after a family row.

He looked at her blankly for a moment and then rewarded her with a weak smile.

'If you behave yourself, Juliet, everything will be all right,' he said.

'I won't do it again,' she said, although she still had no idea what it was she had done the previous week.

'Let's go up to bed,' he said.

He stayed all night, something he had rarely done, and Juliet felt so happy that she forwent her usual rigid bedtime regime (washing her face fifty times with her Erno Laszlo soap, showering, flossing, exfoliating and moisturizing). Maybe, she thought, things will work out. She knew he would never officially leave his wife. But she secretly hoped that he might one day commit himself to a more permanent relationship with her. What she wanted more than anything else in the world was for Harry to come and live with her.

Amanda sat in the hired car outside the gates of Ford Open Prison feeling a little bit like an extra in an episode of *The Bill*. Any moment now a door would open and Steve would emerge and walk to the car. She looked across at Annie and smiled encouragingly. She had fretted over whether or not she should bring her daughter, but in the end she had decided, somewhat selfishly, that she needed a buffer between herself and her husband.

Annie's apparent delight, in the days since she had

heard of her father's release, had depressed Amanda. She had fondly supposed that her daughter was as happy as a unit of two as she was. She thought that Annie, too, had put Steve behind her. She felt guilty about these feelings and, as they sat together in the back of the car, she reached across and cuddled Annie.

At ten minutes past eleven several men emerged from the side door. Sad, shabby creatures, Amanda thought, who looked furtively around for their own families. Then, some five minutes later, Steve appeared.

The change in him was dramatic. Amanda had, of course, visited him regularly, but seeing him outside, in the harsh sunlight, she was struck by the way in which his fall from grace had actually physically altered him, diminished him.

When she had first met him it wasn't just his wealth and charisma that had drawn her to him. He was wonderfully attractive. He had naturally blond hair, worn rather long, brilliant blue eyes and a boyish grin that, even after she had discovered how dissolute and corrupt he was, could still turn her stomach over.

But now his physical charm and presence were dramatically reduced. The blond hair was cut very short and had faded to a dull mousiness. He was thinner, more lined, less confident, and the grin had gone. For the first time in their relationship Amanda felt a pang of pity for him.

Annie was ecstatic. She had opened the door and run out to meet him and he, seeing her again, stopped and held out his arms.

'My Princess,' he said as he caught her and walked her to the car.

It was just like Steve, Amanda thought when he greeted her with an inappropriate and passionate kiss, to act as if nothing had really changed in the last three years.

As if he had just returned from a prolonged business trip abroad. In many ways he was a typical example of the ill-fated eighties entrepreneur. All he had ever had was front.

Annie dominated the conversation on the way home, enchanting her father with her cleverness. Amanda was quiet and nervous on a number of counts. Firstly she knew that her husband would be horrified by the circumstances in which they were now living; secondly she suspected that the press might be waiting for them; and thirdly she was terrified at the prospect of having to cope with a three-year build-up of testosterone in a man as sexually aggressive as Steve.

He almost cried when he entered the flat. For a moment it seemed as if it symbolized to him, more than his own imprisonment, the loss of his riches.

'But there must have been something better than this. I can't believe it has come to this. What about that flat that I leased for George Walters, or the penthouse the company bought in your mother's name, and the cottage I let that friend of Chris's have on a bloody peppercorn rent all those years? And what about the big house in Surrey and the property on the Isle of Wight? Christ almighty, there must be something left, or Johnny Britten has got something to answer for.'

'As a matter of fact, Johnny Britten is answering to a number of fraud charges at the Old Bailey right now,' Amanda said.

Steve was horrified. Clearly the news of his close friend and financial adviser's professional demise had not reached him in prison. Amanda wondered, as she watched her husband's face collapse, if Johnny Britten might have some knowledge of the famous missing Minter millions.

'You can't blame Johnny for this, Steve. It was my

choice. I suppose I could have fought to hold on to one of the properties, but I just wanted a new start and anonymity. I had this idea that it was better to rebuild from nothing, to earn my own way rather than to cling to what we had. Anyway, everything but the few pieces you can see here went to the official receiver. But it's not so bad. In an odd way I have become rather fond of this place, and so has Annie.'

'Well, I can't live here. It's worse than the place I just left,' said Steve angrily. 'And for God's sake, Amanda, her name is not Annie. It's Anoushka.'

There was no point attempting to explain to him that in their new life Annie was a much more appropriate name. Nor was it possible, at this delicate moment, to point out to her husband that his credit rating was not good and that any idea he might have of checking into Claridge's or renting some fabulous Mayfair apartment was now pure fantasy. Particularly since the arrest of Johnny Britten.

'Steve, unless you have some other source of income that has been kept secret from me for the last couple of years, the only money we have is my salary: £15,000 a year. It just about keeps us going here. I've been rather lucky. Debbie next door has to get by on income support.'

He looked at her in astonishment. They had a row, then, about how he had always given her everything, how he had provided for her, how he had achieved the impossible from a starting point of zero. It was like the arguments they had in the last days before his trial. Steve was still, Amanda realized, in denial. He still believed that he was a successful man, that he could lift a phone and order up whatever he wanted, that he could speak to a few friends and summon up another fortune.

'Steve, don't you understand, it's over, gone,' Amanda screamed.

The force of his anger was frightening. He looked at her savagely and then slapped her round the face so hard that she fell to the floor. And then he walked out.

Annie tearfully tended her mother. Sat her up and put ice from the fridge on the rising bruise on her face.

Later, when Amanda had recovered, she concentrated on Annie. Bathed her and comforted her and, against her better judgement, assured her daughter that all her father was suffering from was the pent-up emotions of a man who had been imprisoned for something that he did not do. It was an old line that she had agreed with Steve to pursue, out of pity for her daughter, whenever their situation impinged on Annie's life.

When she had finally gone to sleep, and Steve had not returned, Amanda drank the dregs of a bottle of white wine that had been in the fridge for weeks and lay down on the sofa in the sitting room, fearful of what might happen next.

He came back shortly after midnight. He was drunk and tired and obviously depressed and guilty for the way he had lashed out at her.

'Everything will be all right, darling, you'll see. You leave it to me,' he said as he kissed her, thrusting his tongue down her throat and pushing his hand up her skirt as if she were some cheap one-night stand.

She was wary of him now. There had always been, in their relationship, an element of fear. In the good days he had imposed on her a punishment-and-reward system that she had learnt to accept. If he got cross with her, was unfaithful, deceitful or let her down in any way, he would, within the next few days, present her with some gift that would assuage his guilt and make her feel, although she didn't approve of it, as if a price had been paid for the hurt she had endured. But in those days he had never hit her. There had never been any physical aggression apart from the occasional overenthusiastic sexual reunion.

Cornered now, she responded as if she were a cheap one-night stand and allowed him to manoeuvre her into the bedroom. He began to undress her, watching her intently in the glowing lamp light as he did so.

'You're so beautiful, you were always the only woman for me,' he said as he unclasped her bra and caressed her breasts.

She actually wanted him now. She remembered how good they had been together in the past and, anyway, it had been ages since she had indulged her taste for casual sex. What was happening now was not unlike a pick-up. It was as if they were strangers to each other and not two people whose lives, for over ten years, had been intertwined.

'Come on, come on,' she urged him as she began to remove his jeans. Then she noticed that the erection that she had felt as they had moved into the bedroom had subsided, that he was no longer aroused. Her hands moved down to work on him, but she could not make him hard enough to enter her. She took him in her mouth but he still could not get an erection, and suddenly he was angry with her again. He pushed roughly at her breasts and tightened the grip of his hands around her neck as if to show that even if he couldn't fuck her he still had power over her.

'Bitch, bitch,' he shouted as he released his grip and began to shake and slap her. 'I know what you are, you are a whore, a cheap tart.'

The abuse, both physical and verbal, seemed to go on

forever. Then he collapsed, crying in her arms and she gently rocked him to sleep.

Although she cried when she waved Carl through to the Departures lounge at Heathrow, Nicola was in no way dispirited. In fact, she was feeling more positive than she had ever been before in her life.

She had secured the necessary investment for the European launch of Manifold, within a couple of weeks she would be reunited with the man she believed to be the love of her life, and by the end of the year she and her colleagues at the Malestrom Foundation would be fabulously rich. Not that money had ever been the motivation for Nicola. She genuinely believed that Manifold was the sociological equivalent of discovering the cure for a hitherto terminal illness. In fact, she thought that it was potentially even more important than finding the answer to AIDS or any of the other life-threatening problems that still faced mankind.

There were only one or two things left to do in England, she thought as the taxi took her back to her hotel. She must make contact with her family and, rather more urgently, she must help the four friends who had been to her, throughout her life, more important than that family. In her suite she prepared, for the following night, one of the most important presentations for Manifold that she had ever given. She had invited Juliet, Georgia, Caroline and Amanda to a farewell dinner. But it would be much more than that. Nicola was going to offer them the opportunity to change their lives. More than anything else, she wanted to give them the chance to achieve the happiness she herself enjoyed.

SEVEN

Nicola had arranged for dinner to be served in the sitting room of her suite. A large circular table, beautifully decorated with fresh flowers and little gifts at each place, dominated the room. She was determined that the evening was going to be special, on more than one level. She felt unaccountably excited, almost as if she were a teenager again hosting a forbidden party for her friends in her parents' absence. She had even put on a new dress quite different from anything she had owned before. She had gone out shopping with Carl before he had left and he had dragged her into shops she had never dared enter before to buy the kind of clothes she had never seen in her usual haunts (Jaeger and Simpson's). And somehow, with his approval, she felt wonderful in the white linen-and-Lycra scooped minidress that he had chosen to contrast with her brilliant red hair.

Georgia, who arrived first, was also transformed. She had lost weight, so much weight that her fabulous face – with the slanting violet eyes and the Cupid's bow mouth – seemed almost prettier than it had when she was eighteen. In fact, she looked so much more like the girl they had envied in the Lower Fourth that Nicola teasingly asked her if she was having an affair.

'Nicola darling, is that likely? No, I just had another crisis with Richard, one that finally made me realize what I was doing with my life, and I've made an attempt to regain something of what I used to be. I spent three weeks with my mother ignoring political pleas from Richard and emotional demands from the children, and it was wonderful. I've lost two and a half stone –

I can now buy stock size 12 – and the other day a man whistled at me. Admittedly he could only see me from the back – and I've always had rather good pins – but it brought back memories.'

'And Richard, has his attitude to you changed?' Nicola asked.

'I'm sorry about that night at dinner, darling. Richard was unpardonably rude. But right now – with the election just ten days away – he's displaying the political equivalent of cupboard love. And I'm going along with it for the moment. But he might find that he doesn't just lose his ministry, his sexy researcher and the ministerial Daimler after the election. He might also lose me,' Georgia said. 'And how is the delicious Carl? I do hope he's joining us tonight. He's the only man I have ever encountered who could fit into one of our girls' dinners.'

'He went back to the States last week. I've been tidying up a few details for the European launch of Manifold and I'll be flying out to meet him for the US launch next week.'

Caroline arrived at that moment, and the two women fell into an awed silence at the sight of her previously boyish body swollen by approaching motherhood. Not that her style or her ridiculously young face had been altered by her pregnant state. Her hair was as short and blonde as ever and she was wearing one of her outsized men's shirts beneath a stark square-necked pinafore dress.

'Darling,' said Georgia as she hugged Caroline emotionally and laid a hand, half enviously, on her extended stomach, 'you look like a schoolgirl in trouble. Like a tiny teenager who made a mistake. Has the sickness finally gone? And is everything organized at the Portland?'

'I can't thank you enough, Georgia. It's all wonderful. And they've been marvellous at work, too. I shall hang on as long as I can, though, so that as much of my maternity leave as possible will be after the babies are born. With twins that could be almost any time.'

'And Nick?' said Nicola rather tactlessly. 'How is he adapting to the prospect of being a parent?'

'He's in denial. I think he regards me as schoolgirl in trouble as well, or at any rate a woman who made a terrible mistake. He doesn't talk about it, doesn't look at me, sleeps on the sofa and writes less than ever. But he's still there.'

Nicola opened the first of many bottles of champagne and poured out three glasses.

When Amanda arrived Nicola noticed another transformation. Only in Amanda's case it was worrying. Her face was pale and drawn, and beneath heavy foundation it was possible to distinguish a dark bruise on one of her cheeks. Nor was she as glamorous as Nicola had expected. In place of her usual short, tight shift and stilettos she was wearing a pair of wide-legged trousers, a plain white shirt and some flat loafers.

'Steve has become absolutely ridiculous. He wouldn't let me come out in my Alaïa frock, or a frock at all. He has become absurdly jealous of other men seeing me looking what he calls "provocative",' she said noticing Nicola's surprise at her appearance. 'He's even taken to criticizing my make-up and I've been forced to trade my pillar-box red lipstick for something more discreet.'

'And discretion, darling, was never your trademark,' said Georgia.

Juliet was, as ever, the last to arrive. She looked impeccable in one of her little suits, but there was about her a certain restraint except when it came to the champagne. She drank it, Nicola thought, far too eagerly.

They finally sat down to dinner at 9 p.m. The food was delicious, although no one was particularly hungry. Caroline had reached that stage in pregnancy when indigestion and heartburn take over from morning sickness. Georgia was obviously serious about her diet and, along with her sister, was in any case more interested in the champagne.

'Only 73 calories a glass, darling, and a wonderful diuretic,' she exclaimed.

At the end of the meal Nicola rose to her feet, tapped a silver spoon on her champagne glass to silence their chatter and began to address them almost as if, she thought later, they were clients or investors or members of the press.

'You probably don't remember, but at that dinner at Juliet's – when we were celebrating my return – we started to talk about the perfect man. I think we called him the Stepford Husband –'

'Of course I remember,' interrupted Juliet. 'In fact, I brought him with me. Our composite Stepford Husband, our prototype for the perfect man. He's in my handbag,' she squealed.

'Well, the thing is, Juliet, well, everyone, the thing is that our Stepford Husband need not be a fantasy, a hopeless dream, he could be a reality.'

Her friends shifted awkwardly in their seats, unsure exactly what it was that Nicola was trying to tell them.

'I don't want to sound self-important or over-confident, but I do believe that what I have done – well, rather, what I have been a part of creating – is going to offer women the greatest liberation of all. If you can spare me a few minutes, I'd like to show you what I mean,' she said as she picked up the remote control for the television that was positioned to one side of the table.

'What you are about to see is, to use an old cliché, nothing short of a miracle. The introductory video for Manifold and the proof that the Stepford Husband can be a reality.' She flung a switch and directed her friends' attention towards the screen.

The Malestrom logo – the old male sexual symbol with the arrow transformed into a heart – dominated the screen for a moment accompanied by some rousing classical music that none of them could quite place. Then a dignified male American voiceover introduced the project and the camera panned to some very serious-looking laboratories.

Georgia, who had consumed a deal of champagne, couldn't quite make out what the man was saying. Something about a revolutionary product that could help men – and mankind – achieve a greater peace of mind and potential. How they had done exhaustive research into male hormonal imbalance, chromosomal disorders and genetic engineering, and into the new smart drugs, and how they had gradually developed Manifold, a miraculous formula with limitless possibilities for the treatment of a number of common male problems.

There followed a lot of complicated scientific data, theory and diagrams that floated over Georgia's head. Then it began to get a little more interesting.

'Three years ago, when the first series of experiments were deemed successful, we began our human-research programme. We took a number of men – volunteers with specific problems taken from within the penal system – and monitored their reactions to Manifold,' the commentary said. At that moment the camera moved down a line of about fifty men – of all ages and all physical types – before closing in on one face.

'Oh look, it's Carl,' squealed Georgia.

It was indeed Carl. In fact, for the next few minutes Nicola's lover dominated the video.

'Twenty years ago society wrote me off,' he said. 'I grew up in a deprived family in a deprived area and in a depraved society. I can't remember a time in my childhood when I wasn't involved in crime of some kind. I committed my first act of violence when I was twelve. By the time I was fifteen I was hardened to the world around me, addicted to drugs and involved in a netherworld where morals, principles and any code of common decency were regarded as aberrations. I had my first criminal conviction – for street mugging – when I was thirteen. As I grew older, so the crimes became more serious. Violence became a way of life. At twenty I got life. For killing a woman. It was a terrible thing. I still have no excuses. It doesn't matter that she was a prostitute, that I thought I loved her, that she had robbed me of my money and my drugs, that she had betrayed me. I murdered her. Ending her life probably should have finished mine.' He paused for a second and the camera panned back to expose the contrast between the present-day Carl and the twenty-year-old criminal with a conviction for murder he was recalling.

'I'm still not sure how it was that they came to pick me as part of the programme for testing Manifold. There were many, many volunteers simply because we believed that taking part might count when we came up for parole. I think that they wanted men who apparently had no regrets – and, believe me, in the seventeen years I had spent in prison I had not suffered a single moment of guilt or shame for what I had done. Looking back, I can see that in many ways I regarded my crime as a sort of achievement. It proved what a hard man I was. There was some kind of distinction, in prison, in being a killer. I regarded the perpetration of violence as manly, as part of the way all real men were. I didn't want to change. I was, if you like, the last person who would have wanted Manifold to work. A perfect specimen for their experiment.'

The screen switched back to some earlier footage of Carl. At least it must have been Carl, although the facial expression – even the facial features – seemed quite different. He was cold, hard, aggressive and swaggering, talking – at the outset of the drug programme – about his crime.

A nervous shudder swept down Caroline's spine as she watched him. It simply wasn't possible that the man they had all found so charming, so *simpatico*, so sensitive and perceptive, could ever have been the man they now saw on the video.

The serious American male voiceover took over Carl's story against a changing visual background of his progress. It was astonishing. Within days of his first exposure to Manifold he was visibly altered. Within months he was, quite literally, a new man. The commentary told of his dramatic academic achievements, his fantastic rehabilitation and his new-found contentment.

When Carl's testimony was over the camera panned down to another, younger man who told a similar, dramatic story about his earlier life and his astonishing progress on the Manifold programme. Nicola fast-forwarded the tape to the final presentation of the drug. The same serious voiceover explained that the programme was not just one drug for one man, but a series of drugs that could enhance the life of every man.

'Men suffer from as many emotional, physiological and psychological problems as women. Contemporary statistics reveal an increase in male depression, in the potential for violence, in declining virility. As a result we are a society in crisis. Yet curiously no drug company has addressed those problems until now. The Malestrom Foundation has created nothing less than a miracle product. Manifold is a brilliantly engineered smart drug that can offer the men of America the opportunity to achieve their full potential.'

At this point, as the commentary became even more extravagant in its claims and more evangelical by the moment, Nicola switched off the television and looked at her friends enquiringly.

'Well, what do you think?'

'I'm not sure,' said Caroline. 'It sounds a little like HRT for men.'

'It's much more than that. It's not just about testosterone, it's far more complex, although much of the original work – done as you saw within the American penal system – involved the problem of aggression and violence in young men, which meant a lot of hormonal fine-tuning. But the drug – or rather the drugs – isn't just a hormone-replacement or repression therapy. It's much bigger than that: it can help men to overcome many other behavioural problems. It's been a great uncharted area – the male psyche. Much research has gone into making women more manageable, but nothing has been done before to alter chemically male behaviour. I wanted you to see the tape for several reasons. Firstly because, as my dearest friends in the world, I wanted you to understand about Carl, and secondly because I wanted you to realize how terribly important the work I have done is. It's simply revolutionary.' She finished with a smile.

'But darling, how can you be sure that Carl is, well, reformed?' Georgia asked cautiously.

'My God, if you had seen Carl when I first met him, you wouldn't have to ask that question. The footage we used in the tape was quite mild compared to some of the sessions we had with him. He was an animal. Yet curiously I always sort of knew that there was something else there. Of course, I don't have to tell you that my only initial interest in him was scientific. As he said, he was the ultimate challenge. And seeing the real man emerge as Manifold took a hold was just the greatest experience of my life. I felt like a kind of female Professor Higgins moulding my own Pygmalion. Only in reverse. I took this man, whose education had been minimal, a man who had been so badly abused as a child and who had gone on to abuse others in his early manhood, and I turned him into the man of my dreams.'

'Your Stepford Husband . . .' muttered Juliet thoughtfully.

'As a matter of fact, we are going to marry when the launch is finished. Sometime towards Christmas. Carl designed and made the ring for me himself. It was, he said, a real labour of love.' Nicola held out her hand, revealing a tiny and quite exquisite band of gold.

'But how can you be sure that he won't revert. Can the drug have a permanent effect on behaviour?' Caroline asked.

'No, Carl will probably have to remain on the medication for a while. But we are cutting back slowly with no obvious signs of any regression.'

'It's an incredible concept, Nicola. I mean, if you can eradicate the aggression of men without any side-effects, I suppose you could ultimately eradicate war.'

'That's possible but unlikely. It would be nice to slip some Manifold 1 into the water system in the Balkans or the Middle East, but I doubt that could ever happen. But certainly in America it is being taken very seriously as a possible answer to the increase in young male urban crime. We are hoping it will become a mandatory part of the rehabilitation programme within the American penal system. And no, there are no side-effects. Men on Manifold don't grow breasts or anything like that, although there are suggestions that it might help with baldness, which, of course, will make it even more attractive to older men. The only other side-effects are a renewed interest in life and contentment,' Nicola said with another warm smile.

'But isn't it a little bit like neutering a cat? The chemical equivalent of two bricks on their balls?' asked Amanda.

'Oh no, because it doesn't in any way affect sexual performance. Except positively. Manifold 3 was specifically created for men with problems of infertility or impotence.'

'Darling, you are going to make millions out of this. I don't think there is a man of my acquaintance – including our men – who couldn't do with a little fine-tuning,' giggled Georgia.

'Well, I might as well level with you all,' said Nicola. 'That's the third reason why I showed you that tape. I want you to have what I have got. The money I'll make will be nice, I dare say, but this whole thing has been much more of a mission than a means of making my fortune. I can't tell you how distressing it has been for me to see you all trapped in such difficult relationships. You are all such special, wonderful women, and yet not one of you is happy. Not one of you has the man she deserves. Not one of you has a Stepford Husband.'

'Oh, Richard could be worse,' said Georgia quickly. 'I mean, he might not be faithful but he loves me and the children, I really think he does. And he has provided for us.'

'We're playing the ultimate truth game tonight,' said Nicola. 'And, however much you might deny it, Georgia darling, Richard is not a nice man. He's manipulating you now because of the election. He is an insensitive, unimaginative, emotionally retarded and selfish man.'

'Nicola, I simply can't take this. I think you've gone mad. I'm sure that Carl is wonderful and what you have done for him is marvellous, but, for Christ's sake, Richard isn't a murderer. He isn't even aggressive and yet you seem to be leading up to a suggestion that Richard needs a good dose of this ridiculous drug you've developed. Frankly I've had enough of this evening.' Georgia got up and searched for her handbag.

'Sit down, Georgia. I'm not suggesting that Richard is a potential criminal in need of the kind of rehabilitation that Carl went through. I'm just saying that if he were to take Manifold 2 just once a week, he would turn back into the man you married. I'm offering you the future I thought you wanted,' Nicola said as she handed Georgia the gift-wrapped package that had been placed on her side-plate at the dinner table.

'Richard really isn't that bad,' said Georgia, tears streaming down her face.

'Since it's the truth game we're playing,' Juliet suddenly interjected, 'I think you should know, Georgia, that Richard is more of a bastard than anyone here thought. He even fucked me when you were in hospital having Tom.'

Georgia sat back down and held her head in her hands. Suddenly the evening had gone terribly wrong for her.

'I don't want to hear, Juliet,' she screamed.

'And why do you think that Richard set me up in my business? It certainly wasn't an altruistic gesture, or even one meant to keep me quiet about our affair. It was so that I could organize things for him. Make sure everything was kept quiet. A nice little flat for the latest secretary. The odd girl I could send his way. He's corrupt, mean, deceitful and cruel. Not that much unlike my Harry, actually.'

There was an embarrassed silence, before Juliet continued: 'In some ways I blame Richard for what happened to me. He didn't just fuck me, he fucked me up. I didn't love him or anything, but I was obsessed with him when I was your skinny, plain little sister and you were the Deb of the Year. It seemed to me then that you had everything and I had nothing. And over the years Richard realized how I felt. He bided his time, flirting with me now and again in order to keep my interest up. He didn't pounce for years, he knew the moment. Just after my marriage collapsed, when I was at my most vulnerable. I know I shouldn't have done it, I know it was wrong, but he just played on my insecurities, and before I knew it I was in bed with him. It didn't last long but it changed me. Hardened me and put a block between me and you, Georgia. I'm so sorry but you have to know, you have to see what he is.'

Georgia was softly sobbing, her head still clasped between her hands.

'Of course, I've been punished,' Juliet continued, 'because now I've got my own Richard. A man who uses me, abuses me, treats me with contempt and goes off with other women. And the thing is, Georgia, I love Harry and I would do anything to make him love me. I keep remembering how Carl was that night at dinner, how he listened to all of us, how he talked to us and yet how attentive and devoted he was to Nicola.' She looked eagerly at the gift-wrapped parcel that lay on her own side-plate.

'Make sure he takes one tablet a week,' Nicola said as she passed the parcel to Juliet. 'When we started out the research we were working on patches and a kind of

Pill-type arrangement whereby the volunteers would take one each day and know if they had forgotten. But it was all too complicated for them, and we simplified things and ended up with the One-a-Week Manifold. Since Harry isn't looking for early parole, he probably won't volunteer to take it. I know it's unethical, but it's better if he doesn't know. If the positive effects of the drug just creep up and make him the man you want.'

'Is it my turn now?' said Amanda.

'If you want,' Nicola answered, 'or maybe it's Caroline's.'

Caroline had been sitting quietly through the scene between Georgia and Juliet, occasionally fiddling with the gift that Nicola had left on her side-plate.

'Nick and I have a whole different set of problems. He doesn't cheat on me, he doesn't hit me, he just ignores me. I don't believe any drug in the world could cure what is wrong with him. Could a drug make him finish his novel, fall in love with his wife again, accept his responsibilities and love the children we are expecting?' she asked despairingly.

Nicola moved over to Caroline and put her arms round her.

'I can't promise all that, obviously, but Nick is a classic Manifold 4 type. And what have you got to lose, Caroline? You are the one person here with the most to gain from Manifold. You could give up on Nick or you could give him another chance.'

'But it's so, so . . . underhand. I mean, suppose the situation were reversed and Nick fed me some drug that would turn me into the devoted little woman . . .'

'You don't need a drug. You've been his devoted little woman voluntarily for ten years. But God, Caroline, I'm not here to coerce you all into putting your men on the programme. I'm just saying here it is. This is what it can do. It's perfectly safe, there are no known side-effects. Make your own decision. Think of the way your lives are going and think how that might change. Think of the babies,' Nicola said, reaching down and touching Caroline's swollen stomach.

'I know I'm preoccupied by the idea of the castrated tomcat,' said Amanda, 'but I can remember when I was a little girl my mother explaining to me that my cat had to have a little operation that would make him "happier". And in a way it did. He got fat, he was very docile, he never caught a bird or got involved in a fight, he purred a lot and sat on my lap. But he was never the same, never as daring, as funny, as full of character as he was before she took him off to be "done".'

'Do you really imagine that we would have got a drug past the Food and Drug Administration if it turned men into fat, fluffy eunuchs? The whole point of Manifold is that it balances things out. It doesn't emasculate men, it improves them. Brings out in them qualities and emotions they might have been denying. Enables them to live fulfilled lives. How is it with you and Steve now, anyway?' Nicola asked Amanda who, even beneath the heavy foundation, visibly blushed.

'Bloody, fucking difficult, thank you very much, Nicola. He's jealous, resentful, controlling, obsessional, depressive and incapable of making love to me. Instead, as you can see from my face, and my body if I had worn a dress, he makes hate to me. But that is my problem, not yours. And I must say, I think you've got a fucking nerve moving in on us like this – patronizing us with your perfect life and your ridiculous solution to our problems. How bloody dare you, Nicola?'

'I just wanted to share something very important with you. I didn't mean to patronize you. I love you all. I just want you to be happy.'

'And what do you know about men? Before Carl you never really had a proper relationship,' said Amanda. 'You might be able to see through to their genetic make-up, to their chromosomes, but do you really understand the very nature of the beast? Isn't all this a little dangerous and worrying, mucking around with the order of things? Isn't it all a bit sinister? Rather like that medical research the Nazis did in concentration camps. Let's change the make-up of man. Let's chemically reconstruct man. Let's make him more user-friendly, more docile, more like my poor, dull, old cat after he lost his balls. How can you be sure, after just three years' testing on a bunch of criminals, that this thing won't have some disastrous side-effect? Christ, Nicola, the Malestrom Foundation and all it's doing sounds like feminist fascism to me.'

It was Juliet who made the peace. Juliet who opened another bottle of champagne and toasted Manifold and Nicola. Juliet who jokingly placed everyone's gift-wrapped sample of the wonderdrug in their respective handbags, saying that they could throw it away in the morning if they wanted.

They finally left, in a fleet of cabs that Nicola had ordered, at 1 a.m. Georgia still wouldn't look or talk to Juliet, Amanda was still furious, and Caroline was just simply exhausted. Alone with the debris of the evening, Nicola decided that she had made a mistake. It had been arrogant and patronizing of her. But when they had been at school – throughout their lives so far – they had shared everything with each other. Was it so wrong to want to share Manifold with them?

EIGHT

It took Caroline until the weekend to pluck up courage to give Nick the first capsule of Manifold. The whole business went against her principles, but then so had Nick. In a way she saw this as a form of revenge. He deserved it. In the weeks since she had broken the news of her pregnancy to him she had moved, emotionally, miles away from him. His reaction, as predictable as it was, had woken up a resentment in her. She now found herself criticizing facets of his character that she had always previously admired.

His 'dedication' to his art now seemed like a sad delusion, his old all-encompassing love for her like sheer self-ishness on his part; his mood swings were no longer viewed as further evidence of his artistic temperament but as bloody-mindedness, jealousy and – when she really thought about it – a deeply felt resentment of her success. She couldn't even understand now what she had originally found physically attractive about him. His face seemed permanently set in a scowl, his colouring seemed to have faded and there was, she hated to admit, a rather acrid and unpleasant smell about him. As if he no longer bothered to wash or put on clean clothes.

She would probably have walked out had it not been for the two creatures now kicking hell out of her tummy. Nicola's gift, which came with careful instructions, was opportune.

On Saturday night she cooked him some *chilli con carne*, a particular favourite of his. Nicola had assured them all that the contents of the capsules was tasteless, but she wasn't taking any chances. There was a moment in the kitchen, just before she opened the bright yellow capsule, when her conscience reared up and almost stopped her from going ahead with her plan. But when she heard his grunted request for a lager, shouted from the sofa in front of the television, she took the capsule apart, emptied the powder into his food, mixed it in and carried his meal, together with the lager, to him on a tray.

She was rather relieved that he didn't thank her. She was not sure how she would have felt if he had looked up at her, made eye contact, and said something like, 'Just what I fancied.' Because today he was eating just what she fancied. And despite the heat of the day, he ate the lot, wiping the plate clean with a piece of bread.

She had a terrible dream that night in which Nick turned into a dear little old granny hopelessly devoted to the babies but grotesque in some indiscernible way. She woke up with a fright and thought that perhaps she had heard him being ill. But when she crept into the sitting room he was curled up on the sofa sleeping as soundly as usual. There was no turning back now.

Juliet had no qualms at all. Nicola had offered her a way of achieving something that she wanted more than success, more than that black-and-white Ralph Lauren suit, more than the loss of two more inches from the top of her thighs. More, even, than regaining the love and respect of her sister Georgia. Nicola had given her the means to realizing her ultimate dream – control over and commitment from Harry.

The only problem would be in luring him to her home, or out to dinner, and successfully managing to get him 'on the programme', as it were. She was being very strict with herself at the moment. Waiting until he called her rather than leaving her usual string of messages at his office, on his answerphone and on his mobile. It was difficult controlling the urge in her to find out where he was, when she could see him, but she managed it because she had this secret knowledge of how things would be after Manifold.

She was prepared for every eventuality. She had filled the fridge with Harry's favourite bits and pieces so that she could do the deed if he turned up one evening unannounced and she had worked out, in a practice run at lunch with a potential new client, how she could slip the contents of a capsule into a plate of food without her dining companion noticing.

She convinced herself that it couldn't do the man – a surly and particularly mean millionaire – any harm and might do some good. And, funnily enough, two days later he rang up and gave her the account for the worldwide rentals for his entire corporation. Coincidence, of course, but amusing none the less.

On Friday night Harry finally called. He was just finishing at the studio, could she join him in half an hour at Kensington Place for a quick bite? She trembled a little after she had put down the phone, not out of nerves but out of excitement. Within ten minutes she was out of the house, fully made up, carefully poured into a new pair of jeans, and on her way.

They arrived within seconds of one another and Harry, for once, looked approvingly at her, kissed her even. It went entirely according to plan. It was even easier than it had been with her lunch partner because just before the food arrived Harry nipped to the loo, and in one sweeping movement, moments after the waiter had left the food on the table, she slipped the contents of the capsule into his pasta, adding a little black pepper and parmesan for effect.

The only snag was that Harry wasn't that hungry and

left at least half of the food. Juliet must have tensed a little when she realized he wasn't going to finish his pasta and immediately Harry picked up on it.

'Juliet I'm tired, overtired actually, and if you are going to instigate one of your scenes, then I think I'll leave now, alone.'

Beneath the table she slipped her hand across to his lap. It wasn't the kind of gesture that Juliet would ordinarily have sunk to in a public place, but desperate times called for desperate measures, and a little sensual squeeze seemed to do the trick. Harry smiled again.

At home she poured the contents of another capsule into his coffee. He drank it all. Still, she thought as she led him up to bed, it didn't say anything in the instructions about exceeding the stated dose. And besides Juliet was impatient for the drug to take a grip on Harry. An overdose would make him hers that much quicker.

Georgia, when she finally put her tears and defensiveness behind her, was altogether more straightforward in her approach. With just a few days to go to the election she told Richard, in no uncertain terms, that he needed a little B12 vitamin boost. In some areas of his life, at any rate in the kitchen and the medicine cabinet, Richard allowed Georgia absolute control. He made a bit of a fuss about swallowing the big yellow capsule, but then he always did.

'You'll be a new man in no time at all,' Georgia said without a hint of irony as her husband was swept off for yet another door-to-door, meet-and-greet-the-people tour.

She was inordinately pleased with herself that day. She had managed to climb back into a pair of hopelessly outdated jeans from her deb days. As a matter of fact, she thought as she felt the firm outline of her bottom and the top of her thighs, it was when she was wearing these very jeans that HRH had first taken an interest in her all those years ago.

She rather doubted that Manifold would make any appreciable difference to Richard's behaviour. And she absolutely knew that if he were to turn into a Stepford Husband, she wouldn't want to stay married to him. But she was so angry, and so hurt by his betrayal of her with her own sister that the idea of him turning into a dear, malleable man held a certain appeal. It would be the ultimate role reversal. And, my goodness, she was going to enjoy rejecting and humiliating him.

Amanda had fully intended to throw her own gift-wrapped pack of Manifold straight into the bin. But when she got home after that extraordinary evening with Nicola she became involved in such a violent scene with Steve that she forgot her intention and left the pack at the bottom of her bag.

Steve's behaviour was becoming more intolerable with every passing day. His possessiveness was now bordering on the paranoid and affecting Amanda's livelihood. While in the old days he had taken great pleasure in the admiration that other men gave his wife, he now felt threatened by the idea of her – in her regulation stilettos and short skirts – brushing up against other men in the workplace. He insisted on taking her to work each day and picking her up. Once, when he saw her walk out of the swing doors of the building with a male colleague she barely knew, Steve had launched at the man with his fists.

It was obvious he was in crisis. Amanda guessed that he had planned, post release, to get hold of some of his missing money with the help of Johnny Britten. But with his main adviser in the middle of a fraud case, and with every other avenue of earning a living now closed to him, he was dependent on Amanda. And he simply could not bear it.

Every night he would go out drinking and return to attempt some sort of sexual reconciliation with Amanda which would inevitably end in physical violence.

On the fourth morning after she had discovered the truth about Carl and the Manifold programme Amanda finally decided that she, too, had nothing to lose and a great deal to gain. Steve came up to her in the kitchen as she was making the tea and put his arms round her and said how sorry he was. She smiled at him.

'Christ, my head hurts,' he said sheepishly.

'Here,' Amanda said, holding out to him a yellow pill and a small glass of water, 'take this. It's the latest thing for a headache. Nicola says it's an absolute cure-all.'

He swallowed it, kissed her tenderly and thanked her. What the hell, she thought, taking Manifold wouldn't kill him. But not taking Manifold, if he carried on the way he was right now, might well kill her.

NINE

Nick couldn't understand where the idea had come from. He had been sitting, as usual, doing his book research during the afternoon repeat of *Coronation Street* when it suddenly came to him that there was something wrong with the plot. Mavis was acting uncharacteristically and it was simply unthinkable that Jack and Vera should ever be pictured, as they were now, in a cosy clinch. Who the hell was writing the script this week? Christ, he could do better himself.

Then something else clicked into action in his hallowed brain and he remembered a friend of his who worked for Granada television. It only took a phone call and then an afternoon of intense thought and a day of solid writing. At last the years of work on Mancunian dialogue – mastered for as yet unwritten sections of his great work of art – was put to some use. Nick *was* Rita. He was in the Kabin selling magazines and chatting to Mavis when Deirdre dropped in for a copy of *Best* and a gossip about Des's new girlfriend. He was transported. The writer's block that had been weighing down on him for the past three weeks lifted and he couldn't press the keys fast enough. He was behind the bar in the Rover's with Raquel serving Percy a slow pint of Newton & Ridley's finest when Alma burst in with the news that the café was on fire. It was a bit dramatic for The Street but then Nick realized that if the producer was to understand his capabilities he had to make an impact. By heck, he thought as he packaged his script up in an envelope and ventured out in the dead of day to post it (something he hadn't done in months), I'm on to summat here. And all the way home he whistled that wonderful theme tune.

Of course it wasn't serious work. It wasn't The Novel. But it might bring in a little money and alleviate the strange stirrings of guilt he had been experiencing in the last week or two whenever he glanced across the room and caught sight of Caroline's increasing girth. Naturally he didn't say anything to her about it, although, again, he had been sorely tempted in the last week to talk to her. He had even, that morning, raised his head and grunted goodbye when she had slipped out of the flat at 8.15.

Perhaps he was coming down with something, he thought as he made his way into the kitchen for a nice cold medicinal Budweiser.

Then the oddest thing of all happened. Nick decided to drink the lager from a glass. Which was as uncharacteristic as Jack and Vera Duckworth publicly kissing in the Rover's. Nick always drank straight from the can or bottle (or whatever Caroline had left in the fridge). He never drank from a glass. And then something even stranger happened. In the process of looking for a glass he noticed the pile of dirty dishes in the sink and, before he had even had time to think, he had turned on the hot tap, squirted some Fairy liquid into the water, grabbed the brush and begun to wash up.

He even wiped the lot dry and put it carefully away in cupboard and drawer. Finally, he polished a tall tumbler, carefully poured in the lager and sipped it, with a great feeling of well-being, from the gleaming glass.

All this happened, he decided later, in a flash. It was almost as if he was sleep-walking. As if he was not quite in control of his body or his faculties. By the time *Neighbours* came on at 5.30 he had slipped back into his usual state of dazed depression. When Caroline arrived home he had forgotten it had happened at all and was, as she came through the door, back drinking lager straight from the can. He didn't even manage his usual grunt of greeting. Instead he belched very loudly.

There was something at the very back of Harry's mind that he wanted to remember. Something or someone, he couldn't make it out. For most of the day – even when he had been shooting the stills of that stunning new Flake girl – he had been preoccupied. When they had finished, and she had laughingly suggested he might like to unwrap and eat her, he looked at her as if she had landed from another planet and pushed her quickly out of the door with a detached smile of thanks. Most unlike him, really.

Perhaps it was someone's birthday, he thought, or the anniversary of some event from his childhood. It was almost as if he were haunted by something. An image, in sepia or black and white, of a woman. But he wasn't sure who. His mother? His grandmother? His sister? In the end he decided it must be Juliet. Well, it wasn't the Flake girl or the model he had been on location with the previous week. Or his assistant. Or any of the other women who wandered in and out of his life.

He rang Juliet and suggested that they meet that evening. He felt oddly, well, romantic. Not himself at all. And on the way to her house he bought a big bunch of pale pink roses and some pink champagne. She came to the door in a statement T-shirt, jeans and a lot of make-up. Perhaps she thought he liked her like that. He took her gently in his arms, wiped the lipstick from her mouth, took down her hair and asked her, in what she could have sworn was a French accent, to come upstairs. He picked her up and carried her up to her bedroom and laid her, very gently, on the bed. Then he turned his attention to her wardrobe – that image flickering through his mind again – until he found what he wanted. A long, floral voile dress that buttoned up the front.

With gentle hands he undressed her and, when she was naked, slipped the dress over her shoulders. The final touch for this curious fantasy of Harry's was the roses. He shredded the petals all over the bed, stuffing them down the front of her dress and squashing them against her body. Then, very slowly and very carefully, he made love to her, the scent of roses overwhelming them both.

'Oh, Harry!' said Juliet.

'Oh, oh, oh . . .!' said Harry.

It was then, in the midst of orgasmic ecstasy that Harry realized it wasn't Juliet's name he wanted to shout. It was at that precise moment that he remembered who it was that had been haunting him all day: Annabel. Ridiculous, he thought, I must be losing my mind. Annabel was his wife. The mother of his rarely seen (and rather plain) daughter. A woman he had neither desired nor thought of for some twelve years. Why, Annabel would be over forty now. Beyond a stage of life that could possibly interest Harry. And even though they had never divorced (Harry's masterpiece), he could not imagine why, as he lay next to a replete and apparently sleeping Juliet, it was Annabel he was still thinking about. Annabel in a long, flowery frock. Annabel wafting past him smelling – as she always did – of crushed, fresh roses.

A week, as they say, is a long time in politics. This time last Wednesday Richard had been part of the British Government. A senior member of a Tory administration. This Wednesday he was the Shadow Secretary of State for Social Security. And curiously, despite the loss of the ministerial car, the status, the privilege and even the salary, he felt rather good about the whole thing.

He had been in the House all day clearing out his rooms and sorting out his papers and now, at just six, he decided to go home. To Georgia. He felt a little light-headed. Perhaps, he thought as he came out of St Stephen's Entrance and made his way towards Parliament Square, it will hit me later. Perhaps in a few days I will suddenly feel dreadfully upset about losing my power, my influence, my chauffeur and very probably my pushy little researcher.

For now, though, he couldn't give a damn. And then, as he walked towards the Embankment to find a taxi, something very odd happened. A filthy, reeking tramp pushing a supermarket trolley filled with old bits of wood and empty bottles came up to Richard and said, in slurred tones, 'Can you spare a shilling for an old man down on his luck?' Richard had spent a fair amount of his political career stepping carefully over the flotsam and jetsam of life. He had always firmly believed that you made your own luck. That people who ended up sleeping on the streets, dependent on charity hand-outs or the social services got what they deserved. It had been his previous policy, on encountering any kind of social deprivation, to either ignore the person or offer some sort of advice such as 'on yer bike'.

But there was something about this man that held Richard's attention. And somewhere inside he experienced a feeling that he could only assume was compassion. Then he found himself searching through his pockets for some loose change and emptying the money into the grimy hand of this stinking stranger.

'Here you are my good man,' he said.

The tramp, looking down on the assortment of coins, seemed disappointed.

'Mean bastard,' he shouted abusively at a startled Richard.

It occurred to Richard then, as he did a most uncharacteristic thing and walked towards the Tube station, that he should have offered the man a ten-pound note. But he had been confused by his request for a shilling. 'Thank goodness we've got a Labour Government,' he said to himself as he bought a ticket and went down into the depths of the Underground for the first time in twenty years. 'They'll make sure poor men like that have somewhere to live and some dignity in life.'

When he reached Paddington and the train for home he had forgotten the whole incident. By the time he got to his station, and discovered that Georgia had forgotten to meet him, he was his old disgruntled self again.

At 2 o'clock Steve stirred from his chair by the television. If he was quick, he could clear the place up before he collected Anoushka from school. It took him ten minutes to find the place where Amanda hid the Hoover and another twenty to run the machine round the meagre floor space of their home. He found himself rather enjoying the challenge of tidying up. He scrubbed the bath and sink, washed the kitchen floor and even managed to Sparkle up the windows.

That done, he set off for school via the little local network of shops – all of which betrayed signs of the times and the kind of location they were living in – big metal grilles covered every inch of the doors and windows, and large, predatory dogs sat warily on the pavement outside. He had this idea that he might cook a good old-fashioned toad-in-the-hole like his old mum used to make. He bought some batter mix and some big sausages and some potatoes and a fresh cream cake for pudding. Then he walked down to the school gates to wait for his daughter.

For some odd reason he didn't feel resentful today. He didn't mind that he wasn't driving the Merc to pick up his Princess from Hill House. It didn't bother him that he was standing amongst a group of dowdy, down-market mums and dads. He even got talking with Debs from next door and the two of them walked the children home via the swings and sat chatting, while the kids played.

By the time that Amanda got home he had managed to fix the meal. Not quite as mum used to make it but tasty enough, he thought. Annie – suddenly she seemed more of an Annie to him than a Princess Anoushka – laid the table and the three of them sat down to eat. Amanda didn't eat much, to his disappointment. Nor did she seem that impressed by the way in which he had tidied up the flat. She was pale, detached and, he thought, a little nervous.

'You must be tired, love,' he said. 'I'll put Annie to bed and then make us a nice pot of tea.'

Later, when he went into the bedroom and saw Amanda sitting at the dressing table, he stood behind her and gently brushed her hair. It was part of the ritual of their old life. Amanda's extraordinary hair had been, for him, her most erotic zone. He had liked, in those long lost days, to sit and arrange her hair around her naked shoulders. It had been, between them, a signal that he wanted to make love. He could feel the tension within her disperse. Taking her in his arms he kissed her, sensually, sensitively, full on her mouth.

Tonight, for no reason he could comprehend (unless it was a return to their old erotic pattern), he was able to make love to his wife. It didn't last long – he came almost as soon as he had managed to enter her – but it released something in him, even if it didn't quite satisfy her. And in the warm, afterglow of love he began to talk. He told her of his regrets, his realization of the foolishness of his ways. He even told her how much he valued what she had done. How he had come to understand why she had chosen to do this, to start again in this place.

In fact, he couldn't stop talking that night, much to Amanda's evident annoyance. At 2 a.m., as he was telling her of his burning new need to contribute something positive to society, he noticed that she had fallen asleep.

Carl was relieved the day was over. Manifold had been launched, amid much media interest and general razzmatazz, in a vast baseball stadium complete with cheerleaders and a 100-piece band all wearing sparkling costumes emblazoned with the Malestrom logo. As one of the central exhibits, Carl had been called upon to address the press – in much the way he had in the launch video – about the extraordinary transformation that had overtaken him once he had begun the Manifold programme.

A giant wall of screens above and around him displayed before and after shots – the 'animal' of Nicola's recollection next to the calm, academic, sensitive, contemporary Carl. The whole event had the feel of one of those big born-again Christian conventions. There was certainly a deal of evangelism from Nicola and the rest of the mainly female team who had conceived, tested and perfected the drug, Carl had thought wryly as he had watched their bright-eyed zeal.

When the main press conference ended he was again called upon – along with half a dozen other prime Manifold specimens – to do a series of TV and radio interviews. Tonight the team were to have a celebration dinner with important potential clients, politicians and media celebrities. There would be more pressure on Carl to be the Manifold Man.

He lay down on the bed in his hotel bedroom – Nicola and he, for form's sake, had been booked into separate rooms for the launch – and closed his eyes. He needed to have some space, some calm, or he might, well, he wasn't sure what he might do.

It was Nicola's fault. It had been her idea to gently phase him off the drug. He had been quite happy on the maximum weekly input of Manifold. In fact, he thought now, he had been happier than he ever had been in his life. But in the last weeks, as the dose was lowered, that happiness, that deep contentment, had begun to evaporate. At odd times of the day and night he would find himself – as he was now – anxious and disturbed. And there were the dreams. Awful flashbacks to the way he had been before he had met Nicola. Moments, in the dead of night, when he would awake and think that he was back in captivity. Worse was the growing feeling that although he was a free man again, he had entered into another, more sinister, kind of captivity.

It was that feeling that had prompted him to question the whole concept of Manifold. He wanted to be his own man, not Nicola's ideal of what a man should be. He wanted to recapture some sense of his own self – not the murderer, the drug-taker or the thief – but some semblance of his old emotions, his old ambitions, his old needs.

For now he was playing along with the Malestrom Foundation. But his heart was no longer in the project – he was not even sure if his heart belonged to Nicola. Moving off the bed and through to the bathroom, he took his latest carton of capsules and taking one, very carefully, pulled apart the two ends, emptied the contents down the sink and then put the two halves together again.

It was important, right now, that Nicola should not know the effect that the reduced dosage was having on his behaviour. He would make a great show tonight, after their dinner, of taking one of the empty capsules. He needed to feel alive again. He needed to be himself. He needed to get off the damn programme. He was sure he could handle the consequences. His past difficulties, he thought to himself, were caused by the grinding poverty and ignorance in which he had grown up. The real him, the post-Manifold man, had no need to behave in that way. He was certain that he could control himself. That there would be no going back to his old ways. But equally, he was now sure, there was no going back on the programme. He would be the real Carl, not a diluted, malleable, model man. He smiled to himself in the mirror as he left the bathroom and said out loud, 'Will the real Carl Burton please raise his hand?' Then he raised his left arm up high in the air and brought it down again, with all the pressure he could summon, on the empty packet of Manifold.

TEN

Nick woke up early in the big comfortable double bed. In the last few days he had quietly abandoned the old sofa and returned to sleeping next to Caroline. In fact, a curious turn-about had occurred in their relationship. For nowadays it was Nick who wanted to talk and communicate and Caroline who was always too tired to listen. He looked across at her sleeping body and found himself pulling the duvet up over her swollen form. As he did so he thought he saw a movement from within her womb. The kicking of one of my babies, he thought tenderly. A wonderful warm feeling overwhelmed him and he leant across and gently touched her stomach.

Caroline awoke with a start.

'Oh Nick, you frightened me,' she said.

'You must stay calm,' he said softly, 'even before they are born babies pick up on the moods and feelings of their mother.'

'How do you know?' she asked blearily.

'I've been reading up on it.'

'What do you mean?'

'I've been doing some research. I went to the library and got out some books. I've been making notes. It really is the most astonishing thing, pregnancy. Did you know, for instance, that at twenty-five weeks a human embryo can be affected by the music it hears outside the womb?'

She looked at him doubtfully.

'Look, Nick, it's Saturday and I want to sleep in. Do you think we could discuss the pros and cons of pregnancy at some other time?' she said a little irritably.

'But, Caroline, haven't you forgotten something?' he said with his new, ever-present, sincere smile. 'We're due at parenting classes at the NCT at ten.'

She looked at him with what, from his side of the bed, appeared to be contempt. It worried him that she seemed so uninvolved in their pregnancy.

'Nick, I'm having the babies at the Portland. They'll probably be premature, they'll probably be born by Caesarian section. Is there really any point my going through another one of those awful sessions?'

'Look, Caroline, the more we know the easier it will be for us to achieve a natural delivery. Nigel was telling me that when his sister had twins they had them at term in a special birthing chair the NCT have helped develop. No gas and air, no drugs, no epidural, nothing.'

'Nick, it may have escaped your notice, but it isn't you that is going to achieve any kind of delivery. It's me.'

'A couple of months ago all you wanted in the world was for me to show an interest in our babies,' he said with another one of those dazzling smiles.

She froze for a second and then smiled herself.

'All right, then, just one more session.'

He couldn't exactly pinpoint the moment at which he had come to terms with the idea of parenting. He had, he realized, been rather absent-minded in the last few weeks. He had been forgetful and vague and rather removed from what he had always judged to be reality. Nigel had said he was probably experiencing psychosomatic symptoms that were quite common and which, apparently, could often result in the father feeling labour pains.

It was certainly true that Nick had come to see Caroline's pregnancy as his as well as hers and that he had begun to assume a kind of aura of contentment that was common in expectant mothers. He would talk about 'their' pregnancy, 'their' delivery and 'their' symptoms. He had even, at great expense, bought a solid-silver frame for the picture he now treasured most in the world – the slightly dog-eared Polaroid of his babies taken at the scan he so regretted missing. And his conversion to the prospect of fatherhood wasn't the only difference in his behaviour of late. Since being accepted into the pool of *Coronation Street* scriptwriters he had become incredibly productive. The producer would forward him the storylines and he would write round them. Sometimes he didn't agree with their ideas but, unusually for Nick, he had learnt to bite his tongue and do as he was told. And so far they were thrilled with his work.

He had been rather distressed by Caroline's reaction to his news. He had thought that she would have been pleased by his success. But she was rather tight-lipped and resentful. She even accused him of 'selling out' his talent.

'Christ, Nick, stop talking in a Mancunian accent. You're a middle-class north Londoner not a bloody working-class Northerner,' she said one day.

'But don't you see,' he had replied, 'this is what you always wanted. I'm getting to a stage where I will be able to support you and our babies. If I can get a contract and a few more jobs on the go, we will be in a position where you could give up work and be a real mother.'

From the expression on her face he got the distinct impression that the idea of being a real mother wasn't foremost in Caroline's mind.

'But what about your dream, Nick? Those ideas you had that would change the face of the literary novel. Can *Coronation Street* really compensate for that? What I used to admire about you was the fact you were so, well, high-brow. That you had such strong principles about your work. That you wanted to challenge your readers to reach upwards and not offer them, on prime-time television, the lowest common denominator,' she said passionately.

'But Caroline,' he said, that saccharine smile distorting his face, 'I've discovered that people are more important than art. The fact that I can move thirteen million people through those characters, Christ, that's incredible. And if I can make them happy, isn't that worth it?'

She muttered something then that he couldn't quite hear.

'Darling,' he said, 'I think you should rest a little bit more. I'll get dinner tonight and you can put your feet up. Tell you what, I'll run you a nice hot bath while I get things ready, OK?'

She had this way of looking at him lately that worried him. As if he were mad in some way. Or as if he were not him, Nick, but someone she didn't really know or understand. He went into the bathroom, had a wee and then put on the taps for her bath, throwing in some expensive Prenatol oil he had bought for her that week.

Minutes later, as he was chopping up onions for the spaghetti bolognese (the first dish he had learnt to cook from scratch), there was a terrible scream from the bathroom. Fear overwhelmed him. What was wrong? Had she fallen? Were the babies all right?

'Christ almighty, Nick,' she screeched. 'You even put the loo seat down. You had a wee and then remembered to put the loo seat down!'

It must be her hormones, he thought as he went back to chopping the onions.

Harry's obsession with Annabel, at least that old vision of the Annabel of twenty years ago, was threatening to overwhelm him. He couldn't keep his mind on his work.

In fact, he had become rather bored by his own rather limited field of photography. Searching through his cupboards for old pictures of his wife he had noticed how much more sensitive his work had been in those days. His influences then had been men like Cartier-Bresson. His dreams – in the early days of their marriage – had been to create work that was technically brilliant but would also be a warm, involved social statement about the real world. Not Smirnoff calendars and Cadbury's Flake girls. Success and his split from Annabel, he now decided, had ruined him.

At first he was content to pretend that Juliet was Annabel. His fantasies, which seemed to please but puzzle her, became more and more nostalgic and precise. He had bought her a number of thin, flimsy frocks of the kind that Annabel had always favoured. Quite unlike anything that Juliet had ever worn or admired. He had made her change her own favoured perfume – a rather sophisticated Guerlain scent that she had always worn – to a raw concoction made of crushed roses. He had even riffled through her underwear drawer throwing out her entire collection of Calvin Klein cotton crop tops and briefs and replaced them with plain white knickers. Bras were forbidden.

Annabel, in the golden days of his youth, had possessed tiny pert breasts that were always freed from the constraints of underwired, uplifting, artificial aids. Her nipples – rose-pink like her scent – had often been visible beneath the flimsy fabrics of the antique dresses she had worn.

His evenings with Juliet – almost every evening now was an evening 'in' – followed the same pattern. She would answer the door dressed as Harry had commanded and would draw him into the house for the kind of meal (also pre-ordered by her lover) that she had never thought to serve. Vegetarian food full of pulses, organic vegetables and home-grown bean sprouts (Harry had even bought her a sprouter) or fresh soups, wholemeal breads and vegan cheese. In fact nowadays rather than dropping into the fifth-floor deli at Harvey Nics Juliet would pop into places like Cranks, where Harry's new tastes were more readily satisfied.

After the meal they would go up to the carefully prepared bedroom. Petals would be strewn up the stairs, into the bedroom and across the Indian bedspread that, thanks to Harry, now dominated the room. Then he would make love to her in a very affectionate and passionate manner, kissing and caressing every inch of her rose-scented body and whispering, in French, what Juliet assumed must be tender terms of endearment.

But although this strange courtship was, at least for Juliet, rather endearing and gratifying, for Harry it was never quite right. He would find himself, when he woke in the mornings next to his lover, looking across, hoping that the body he would see was Annabel's.

One day, overwhelmed by his need to see Annabel again, he decided to find her. He spent a week tracking her down, talking to old friends and contacts who might know her whereabouts. Eventually he discovered that she was living in a little village in Cornwall. Unchanged, the word was, from the old days. His heart soared when he heard that. Maybe, he thought, it wasn't too late to recapture what they had. To get back to the simple life they had enjoyed when they were free-living loving hippies in the seventies.

There were moments, nowadays, when Richard found himself looking at Georgia with a new interest. It wasn't just that she had lost weight and regained some of her old allure. It was more than that. It seemed to him that he was a lucky man to have her, and his family. He couldn't for the life of him understand why he had never realized this before.

In fact, there were moments when he would be overcome with what he could only describe as retrospective remorse. With more time on his hands he had become more involved in their day-to-day life. He hadn't stayed a night in Lord North Street since before the election. And sometimes when he was involved in the little domestic challenges that he had come to enjoy – a Waitrose shop in Henley, for example – he would remember how badly he had behaved in those last mad years of Tory power.

He hadn't spoken to Louise for weeks. She had resigned from her post immediately after the election and had aligned herself with a younger Tory hopeful, much to Richard's relief. He had begun to think that really the person he most wanted to be with was Georgia. Understandably she was still a little cold with him. After all, he had been abominably rude when she had found him with Louise at the House. But he was confident that he could win back her trust and affection, although he was aware that it might take time.

He didn't attempt to cross the divide in the marital bed. He didn't want to push things. But he would find himself doing little things for her that, he now thought, were probably more satisfying than sex. He would buy her silly little gifts and leave them under her pillow. He would find himself thinking about her wherever he went and looking for something that could, in some small way, begin to make up for his previous bad behaviour. He bought her books he thought she might like, he bought flowers – not the old kind he used to snatch from outside petrol stations or get some aide to send through Interflora – but huge bouquets of bridal roses or terribly expensive out-of-season bunches of gardenias or camellias that he carefully chose himself in expensive shops.

On her birthday, a date that in the past he would have forgotten had it not been for the eagle eye of his constituency secretary, he arranged a special treat. He took her away for the night to the Chewton Glen Hotel and presented her, after a long romantic and intimate dinner, with a beautiful eternity ring. Georgia had cried.

'It's too late, Richard,' she had said through her tears, 'too damn late.'

'But darling, it isn't!' he said. 'It's not too late, it's, well, it's a new beginning. You and I starting again. I never stopped loving you, I just got caught up in that frightful political arena.'

'I don't mean that it's too late in your political career, Richard, I mean too late in our lives. Too much has gone wrong.'

It was then, well, a little later when they were alone in the draped four-poster in their suite, that Georgia told him that she knew about Juliet. She had, she said in an unsteady voice, made up her mind when she realized the depth of his deception – on the night that Juliet revealed her affair – that their relationship was over. That was why, she said, tears sparkling in her eyes again, the ring had come too late.

They talked all that night. It was, for Richard, a bit like an all-night sitting on an important bill. Only it was much more important than any damn political contest because he believed in what he was fighting for – his wife. And for once it wasn't a great oratory show – well, he could hardly resort to the kind of posturing he used in the House in an intimate hotel room with an audience of one. For once Richard spoke the truth. Or at least what had, of late, come to be the truth. His shame was evident even to Georgia. And sometime towards dawn she forgave him and he took off her wedding ring and replaced it with the diamond-encrusted eternity band that he had chosen so carefully. Then they made love so cautiously, so tenderly, so sincerely, that, at the end, they both wept in each other's arms.

Professionally, though, things were not going so well. He had begun to find his new job tiresome in the extreme. Defending decisions made by his predecessors in the former Tory administration was becoming increasingly difficult for him. Indeed, more and more he would find himself nodding in agreement at what his opposite number – the new Labour Secretary of State for Social Security – suggested. Some of his old chums were rather surprised by the change in him. His old reputation – as an ebullient, hard-line Conservative loyalist – had changed. He was beginning to be referred to as a 'wet'.

One day, in the middle of a heated exchange in the House, he found himself heckling his own side and cheering on the Government spokesman. But thankfully, in the general uproar no one, not even Madam Speaker, noticed. Worse, he had begun to lie to the whip and would find himself voting for the Government on key issues such as the minimum working wage and the repeal of the Education Act.

Georgia was sympathetic to his political change of heart – she had always hated him in what she now termed his 'Portillo Period' – but she didn't think his fantasy plan of walking across the floor of the House and declaring himself a socialist was a good idea.

'But Winston Churchill changed parties, darling,' he said.

'Richard, you'd lose your seat. Can you imagine the local Party accepting such a strange turnaround?'

He decided to take his wife's advice to bide his time

and look for other outlets for his new feelings of altruism.

'Get involved in some charity work, darling,' she said.

It was in the course of this, while doing a little research into the Howard League for Penal Reform, that Richard remembered, with some shame, his old friend Steve Minter. Had Minter come from his own background it would not have been quite so easy to drop him when his empire crashed. But as Steve was a self-made man without the network of contacts that Richard and his old school chums had established, there was no need, at least at that time, for loyalty.

Now he felt a little different. He decided to visit him in Ford Open Prison only to discover that he had been released on parole and was back living with Amanda. He called him, rather sheepishly, from the House.

'Steve?'

'Yes.'

'It's Richard James, here, Georgia's husband. I wondered if you might like to meet up one evening for a chat,' he said tentatively.

Steve was thankfully rather keen, didn't seem to hold a grudge, and jokingly suggested that they ought to meet up in rather the way that their wives did.

'Let's get Nick Evans along and Harry, too, and have our equivalent of a girls' dinner,' he said.

Richard loved the idea, which was odd, really, because the four of them had never previously had much in common apart from the deep friendship of their partners. But he contacted Harry who seemed rather more talkative and amiable than he had in the old days, and he even rang Nick who, to his great surprise, readily agreed to come to supper at the House the next week.

★

Steve was especially pleased to hear from Richard. Not because he had any particular affection or respect for the man – at the height of his own success he had been rather shocked by the corruptibility of such a seemingly powerful political figure – but because he needed all the help he could muster in order to achieve his new ambition.

It was his probation officer that had set him thinking. Steve had become very close to David King in the months following his release from prison. The two of them would talk for hours about anything and everything. And when, one day, Steve had confided a new need to make amends for the excesses of his past, David had suggested he might like to retrain as a social worker.

'But surely my prison record would stand in my way?'

'Not necessarily. There are all kinds of areas of our work in which your experience could be very helpful to others. Have you thought of training as a counsellor?'

Within days Steve had found a six-month course in counselling and stress therapy that would accept him. He did not have to disclose his record, nor did he need any qualifications. All he needed was the money for the course, and with Richard's recommendation – backed up by David King's reference – he was sure he could get a grant. It was curious, but even before he had embarked on his course he had become a kind of counsellor to the troubled people on their estate. A number of the mums from Annie's school had begun to confide in him and he would find himself, most mornings after the school drop, offering advice over coffee to a stream of worried women.

'The thing is, Steve,' Debbie said one day, 'I've never come across a man like you before. You understand how I feel. The blokes I know are all like Dean. They don't talk to women, they screw them, beat them up and impregnate them. The last thing they do is listen to women or offer them any support. The only support a woman gets round here is income support from the Government. We get nothing from our men. And generally we've come to expect nothing from them. But you, you're not like other men. It's like you're a different species . . . like you're the, well, the ideal man.' She looked across the kitchen table at him with tears in her eyes.

It was odd how often women said that sort of thing to him nowadays. He'd certainly never had a reputation as a sensitive, caring type in the old days. Particularly with women. He supposed the change in his attitude must have been prompted by prison. It had obviously had a more profound effect on his character than he had thought at the time. Because it was true that nowadays he did care about people. He did want to help them with their problems. He did sympathize with these women, he understood the dreadful burden of their lives.

Yet two years ago, maybe even six months ago, he wouldn't have given them a second thought. The old Steve would have dismissed them all as dreadful low-life slags who drained the State and threatened the well-being of society.

In fact, the old Steve hadn't even liked women he couldn't condemn as low-life slags. He couldn't relate to successful women in business and he had a particular horror of feminists. There was something unnatural, the old Steve had thought, about women who imagined that they could ever achieve equality with men. He'd never really even considered Amanda as anything approaching an equal. He'd worn her on his arm as a kind of sexual status symbol, but he had never really related to her, understood her or been faithful to her. She was just something else that his money had bought.

But now he saw her as an individual rather than some

extension of his own ego. And curiously as he had begun to value her she had become increasingly alienated from him. She was, he thought ironically, about the only woman he couldn't talk to or reach. She had been promoted at work, had escaped from the temp circuit and had taken on a junior management post that seemed to dominate her life.

He suspected that she wanted more than he did. That maybe it was she, and not him, who secretly hankered after the old days. She was ambitious and eager to move on. More and more when she returned home from work in the evenings to find he and Annie doing homework and cooking supper, she seemed like an outsider to their world. But he was confident that he could win back her affection. Once he was working again – once he had completed this course and was able to earn his own living – he would regain her respect. Meanwhile at least their love-making had resumed its old importance in their life together. More than anything else he wanted to prove to Amanda that he was the perfect husband.

Carl couldn't remember where he had picked up the girl. She was, he thought as he looked down on her sleeping form lying on soiled sheets in the sordid room, probably under-age. Not that it had been her age that had drawn him to her, it had been her red hair. An almost exact match to Nicola's.

She was, he realized now, probably an addict. Her pallor, the shadows under her eyes and the scabs up her arms exposed her as a tragic victim of her times. Not that he had felt any sympathy for her a few hours ago when they had negotiated a fee for the whole night. It had been worth the money. Tying her up, pretending she was Nicola and savagely fucking her had put him in touch with some part of himself that he had lost.

She didn't mind him being rough, she was used to it. Expected it, even.

It had been so good to be in charge again. To look down on someone else with the kind of contempt that had, even after Manifold, generally been directed at him.

She had done everything he had asked. Allowed him to indulge every awful fantasy that had entered his head in the past few weeks. How could he ever have imagined that he could be fulfilled by someone like Nicola? Their dull couplings were as nothing to the raw rucking he had inflicted on this bitch. This was real sex. This was the real Carl. But the night he had paid for wasn't over yet. He pushed the whore over so that she was lying face down on the bed and he entered her anally. She didn't react, didn't stir even, as he pummelled in and out of her. All the contempt he now felt for Nicola he took out on the inert body of this sad stranger. He had no shame. This was what women were for, after all. This was what he had always known they were for. Women weren't meant to think, to achieve or to find ways of controlling men. They were meant to fuck.

All his life women had been in his way, women had prevented him from being what he wanted. All his life women had tried to contain and control him when all they were really fit for was fucking.

'Fuck you, Nicola,' he cried as he came, his hands tightening round the neck of the girl. 'Fuck you, Manifold.'

It was so good to be in control again. So good to be a man.

It was only then that he questioned the stillness of the woman beneath him. Pushing her over on to her back, he noticed that she had been sick into the pillow and that she was not merely asleep but unconscious, the only sign of life being an occasional rasping, rattling breath. Livid red marks stood out around her neck where he had grasped her as he fucked her.

He started to shake her again and again.

'Come on, you stupid bitch, wake up.'

But she didn't stir. Sometime in the night they had taken some stuff together. She had been stoned when he had picked her up and it looked as though she had overdosed. The marks on her neck didn't mean anything. It was nothing to do with him if she chose to kill herself in the course of a night's work.

Nevertheless he was momentarily frightened. He spent an hour making sure that nothing could link him back to this place. He flushed the used condoms down the loo, wiped clean any surfaces – including the skin of the girl – that might hold his fingerprints and stripped the sheets from the bed, put them in an old carrier bag and, very cautiously, let himself out of the room down the dark back stairs and out into the sleazy back street. No one saw him. Several blocks away from the girl's room he threw the bag into an incinerator shoot. Then he went home to catch up on some sleep before Nicola arrived back from Chicago and he would have to switch himself back into perfect-man mode.

ELEVEN

Richard met his guests in the vaulted, echoing central lobby of the House of Commons and escorted them through to the members' bar overlooking the Thames. Steve Minter's arrival caused quite a stir. His face was imprinted on the memories of many of the Tory members – although it was generally unrecognizable in the circles in which Minter now mixed – and the fact that he was dining with Richard was further proof, if it were needed, that something was very wrong with the Shadow Secretary of State for Social Security.

Curiously right from the start they got on. Richard was relaxed and generous with his guests, and by the time they made their way to their table in the members' dining room they were much like their female partners might be on one of their regular nights out. Nick was rather gratified by the interest they all took in the progress of Caroline's pregnancy (rather more interest, he thought darkly, than the woman herself seemed to be taking).

'It's odd, you know but at first I was really unhappy about the idea of being a parent,' he said. 'I'd always said that I didn't want children. But when I felt my babies kicking and when I saw that picture from the scan I was just overwhelmed. You'll think me mad but I actually cried. I was overcome. The magnitude of the whole human creative process overwhelmed me. For the first time in my life I felt, well, fulfilled. Now I honestly think that I am more involved in the day to day progress of the babies than Caroline.' His face lit up with a huge, transforming smile.

'Children,' said Richard, 'are God's own gift. Perhaps one of the best things about having lost my former power is having time for the children. Tom and I went away for a couple of days fishing last week and it was wonderful to be able to talk to him properly. There is nothing as rewarding as watching your children growing up to be happy, healthy and confident little people.'

'My God, I envy you Nick,' said Steve. 'I'd give anything to have another child. But twins, how bloody wonderful. Sadly I don't think Amanda shares my views. While I would gladly turn into a happy old homebody with loads of kids she's suddenly been hit by ambition. Children are the most precious gift. And believe me, in the last couple of years I have learnt exactly what is precious in life.'

'I'm frightfully sorry, old chap, that I wasn't more supportive of you in those difficult times,' muttered Richard.

'In rather the way that I used to think that people make their own luck, I think I made my own misfortune,' Steve said. 'Of course, it did hurt that many of the people who had been my friends in the good days disappeared in the dark times, but I couldn't really blame them. I have no doubt that at that time I would have behaved in the same way had one of my friends hit the kind of problems that I faced. I was only interested in success and successful people.' He looked across at Richard, offering him a warm, sincere grin.

'So no regrets, no resentments?' asked Harry.

'Well, I admit that when I got out I was bloody angry about Johnny Britten. And furious that he hadn't sorted things out for Amanda and Annie. But now I think it was all for the best. We needed to start again. I don't want that life any more.'

'And the fabled missing Minter millions?' pursued Harry.

'If I knew where they were,' Steve said with another sincere smile, 'I'd give them away.'

'It's curious, you know,' said Harry in thoughtful mode, 'how one changes one's aspirations and values in life. Lately I've been rethinking my own life and all the things that I once held to be precious – my Aston Martin, my antiques, my reputation as a society snapper, my model girlfriends – no longer seem to have any importance or relevance in my life. Or rather, in the life I want to live.' He paused for a moment, looking round the table at the other men before adding, 'and that's without the sobering effect of three years in Ford Open Prison.'

'Do you suppose that our change of values has something to do with the sea change going on in the country, with the new Government?' asked Nick earnestly.

'The thing is that I feel so very content now,' said Richard in a puzzled way, 'whereas before I was always searching for something that would, I imagined, bring me contentment – a new woman, a new job, a new ambition. I have now discovered that everything I needed was there all along. But I just couldn't see it. I had lost sight of what was really important to me. My wife, my children, my home.'

'God, Richard, I couldn't agree with you more,' said Harry. 'I feel as if the last few years of my life have had no meaning. Does it sound strange if I say that all I want now is to get back to the simple life I rejected all those years ago?'

'It doesn't sound odd,' said Steve, 'but I imagine it will be difficult to achieve.'

'Can I confide in you, chaps?' said Harry emotionally.

'Of course,' they echoed back at him.

'I've decided to go back to my wife. Back to Annabel. Do you know that until about a month ago I hadn't given her a thought in bloody ages? But then I began to think about the way our life together had been, how pure she was, how simple and satisfying our life was. Before I was overtaken by sodding success and my not inconsiderable lust for other women,' he said with a regretful laugh.

'What about Juliet?' Richard said nervously.

'Can you honestly imagine Juliet wanting to share a simple life? Besides it isn't just a nostalgic fantasy that is drawing me back to Annabel, it is my faith. I suddenly remembered that I had promised to be with her in sickness and in health, for richer for poorer until death do us part. My God, you all think I'm mad,' he said, looking round at them.

'Far from it, Harry,' said Richard. 'I think you're talking like my kind of man. Do you know something? All those years that I was rabbiting on about "family values" I had no conception, no idea of what I was talking about. It was just another vote-winning political concept. I never applied it to my own life. Do you know, Harry, that I even screwed Juliet, my own sister-in-law, at a time when I was publicly preaching about family values? What kind of values did I have, eh? Although I suppose you could say I kept it in the family. When I think back I am just overwhelmed with shame.'

'I am sure I could match you shame for shame,' said Steve jovially. 'It was not uncommon, in the last days of the Minter empire for me to lock myself away with three or four call-girls and a load of cocaine. Never gave Amanda or Annie a thought. I was only into self-gratification and self-aggrandisement. It didn't mean anything, but then nothing meant anything. And the turning point wasn't really prison. When I got out of

Ford I was like a man possessed. I thought I had lost everything, not just my fortune and my dignity. I even took to beating Amanda. I was, well, I was an animal. And now I am just horrified by the thought of hurting Annie or Amanda emotionally or physically. They have a far greater value to me than those Minter millions.'

'I don't think that I can quite equal you guys on physical excess and bad behaviour. But, Christ, looking back I'm every inch your equal when it comes to self-indulgence,' said Nick, shaking his head with regret. 'I was so consumed by self. My talent, my potential, me, me, me, me. I was never unfaithful to Caroline, but, my God, I was a mean belligerent sod. I sneered at what she did. I refused to communicate with her, I took the money she earned and I gave nothing in return. Nothing on this earth was more important than my fucking talent. And suppose I had written that great literary novel? Would it have changed anyone's life, would it have moved anyone but me and – if I was lucky – a few equally pretentious critics on the broadsheets? When I think now of the way in which I have the power and the means to move so many millions of people I am just overwhelmed with humility. Talent? Isn't it a talent to give people what they want, to take them out of their own lives and into the lives of others? I'm sorry if I sound like some pathetic evangelist extolling the virtues of good popular culture, but, my God, it means so much to me now. People are so important. Nearly as important as family, as my babies.' Tears were clearly visible in his eyes.

It was, Richard said later, an extraordinary meeting of minds. By some wild coincidence – perhaps by some divine intervention – each of them had reached the same conclusions about life at the same time. Harry had found his faith again and, hopefully, his wife. Richard had discovered compassion, fallen in love with Georgia and abandoned his overweening political ambition. Steve had lost his empire but gained a new life, an aim, and the love of his family. Nick had abandoned his self-ish dream of artistic perfection and found unpretentious success and the fulfilment of impending fatherhood.

There were other striking similarities about the four men. To people who had known them for a long time, they were as physically transformed as they were morally regenerated. They had a similar glow about them. There was a brightness about their eyes, an eagerness about their expression and, most noticeable of all, there was, on every one of the four faces, an almost ever-present smile.

They felt so at home with each other, so at ease in their common company, that it was almost as if they were akin to one another, as if they were family. To a stranger they might even have appeared as brothers, despite the differences in their appearance. There was something unnervingly similar and familiar about them all. They were, Nick said, like mental clones of each other.

Towards the end of the meal, enlivened by a little alcohol (although much less than they might have consumed at a more conventional men's dinner), they each described their perfect woman.

'She's soft, and sweet and gentle and womanly,' said Richard. 'She's pretty – my goodness, I had forgotten how pretty – and she is supportive and loving and good.' He paused and smiled. 'She's Georgia, of course.'

'Even when I was unfaithful to her Amanda was my perfect woman,' said Steve. 'I loved her strength, her beauty, that lustrous hair, that passionate body. I am not sure that I am her perfect man any more, or that I ever was. But she is my woman even if winning back her trust and love might take a lifetime.'

'I never doubted Caroline, but I gave her such a difficult time, I was so uncommunicative and morose that I believe she now doubts me. There never was any other woman for me. And never will be,' Nick said. 'I think my great challenge now is not to be just the ideal father but also the ideal husband.'

'My goodness, if anyone had said to me a year ago that I would find myself sitting with a group of men admitting to being monogamous, I would have thought they were insane,' Harry said. 'But that was then, and this is now. We all know Georgia and Caroline and Amanda but none of you know Annabel. She's petite and pretty. Covered in little freckles that match her long, wavy auburn Pre-Raphaelite hair. Lean legs and small high breasts. Terribly feminine in the real sense of the word. Wears proper dresses and smells of flowers. Sweet, shy and virginal . . . If you can describe the mother of your child as virginal,' he added solemnly.

There followed the only silence of the evening. Each of the men, with an identical expression of tenderness and warmth on their smiling faces, quietly thought of their chosen partner.

'God, I've enjoyed myself tonight,' said Richard a moment later as the lights dimmed in the dining room and the four men, now the only people left, prepared to leave. 'Why have we never done this before?'

It was, they thought individually as they made their way back to their separate homes, quite unlike any evening any of them had spent before. Harry and Richard had often attended 'boys'' dinners together, but they had never really exchanged an idea. They had swapped lewd jokes and crude confidences, but they had never really communicated with each other. They had got hopelessly drunk and struck obviously macho poses because, heck, that was how men behaved when they were together. But they had never really TALKED.

There had been times, too, in Steve's past when an all-male get-together would produce the kind of behaviour he now so utterly rejected. Stag nights with scarlet women, blue movies and white powdery substances. Even Nick had, in his student days, spent evenings with the lads crawling from pub to pub in an incoherent senseless stupour. But none of them had ever experienced anything like the closeness and the depth of conversation that they had all enjoyed that night. Steve had wondered, before they said their farewells, if their women experienced a similar uplifting feeling when they had their dinners together.

They all agreed that they would meet up at least once a month, Nick volunteering to cook them spaghetti at his place in four weeks' time. As they parted they each stopped and, in the most natural, affectionate but asexual manner, kissed each other on both cheeks.

TWELVE

Nick was sitting on the parquet floor with a cushion stuffed up his shirt practising the breathing exercises.

'One, two, three, four, five, exhale. One, two, three, four, five, exhale,' he chanted before slipping into his panting routine and then moving on to the nursery rhyme he had chosen for their labour. 'Jack and Jill went up the hill to fetch a pail of water – hold one, two, three, four, five, exhale – Jack fell down and broke his crown – hold one, two, three, four, five, exhale – and Jill came tumbling after.'

'Bravo, Nick,' said Denise, the class tutor. 'I only hope that Caroline will be as good as you. Will she be able to make the next session?'

'Well, it's difficult for her at the moment,' said Nick rather sheepishly.

It had been a bit galling to be the only partnerless future parent at the NCT class. Particularly the only male partnerless parent. But he had learnt a lot. He was certain now that he could handle the labour with the minimum of hospital interference. That he could achieve a natural delivery with nothing more drastic than, if the worst came to the worst, a little gas and air. His greatest wish was to make Caroline more aware of the importance of a natural delivery. But she remained unconvinced.

On the way home he dropped in at Safeway to do a big shop. He had, of late, become something of a picky shopper. An odd obsession about additives, pesticides and the hidden dangers of processed foods had begun to overtake him. He was trying to cut back the babies' intake of damaging junk food and hormone-soaked meats.

He filled his trolley with a variety of fresh organic fruits and vegetables, free-range eggs, corn-fed chicken and a number of herbal teas. He was also trying to wean the babies – well, Caroline – off caffeine and had secretly replaced all the tea and coffee cannisters in the flat with decaffeinated alternatives. So far she hadn't noticed. When he got home he carefully unpacked his purchases and put them away, in the process discovering that the kitchen was in need of some radical reorganization and spring cleaning.

Two hours later he sat down and ate a quick sandwich with a glass of naturally carbonated mineral water. Before he settled to write his latest script he thought he would just go through what he referred to as his bottom drawer.

Underneath the big double bed he had hidden, in the deep drawer, all the things he had so far accumulated for the babies. A dozen plain white Babygros, two dozen towelling nappies (if he had anything to do with it, his babies would not be using those environmentally destructive disposable nappies), several neutral-coloured (lemon yellow and pastel green) jumpers, a dozen pairs of little multicoloured socks, five cotton baby blankets (of the kind that could not be damagingly inhaled by an infant) and an assortment of little hats (babies can lose 90 per cent of their body heat through the top of their heads).

It gave him enormous pleasure to sort through these things and to refold them carefully and place them back in the drawer. He was very nearly ready for the birth. He had placed an order for a double buggy, two baby chairs, two Moses baskets and a baby bath at Peter Jones. Superstition prevented him from collecting them until the twins were safely delivered.

By some wonderful bit of luck the most recent script lines in The Street had involved a pregnancy and birth, which had allowed him to use his new knowledge and indulge his own excitement at what was happening in his own life. He spent the afternoon happily writing, slipping, as he did when he was really absorbed in The Street, into his Mancunian accent.

When Caroline came home at seven he was still furiously typing away at his terminal.

'Had a good day, darling?' he asked her with a cheery smile.

'All right,' she muttered sullenly.

'I've cooked us a delicious casserole for dinner. Why don't you sit down and relax and I'll bring it to you on a tray?'

It looked very much as if Caroline would be able to carry the twins to term. But the strain of the collective weight of her babies was beginning to show in her face and the way in which she moved. She was due to leave work at the end of the week and, although this should have been a relief to her, Nick was aware that she was wary about being at home.

'Only four more days to go, darling, and then you can really get some rest before the birth,' he said as he put the tray down on a table by the sofa and turned on the television. 'It's my script tonight,' he added enthusiastically as the theme tune for The Street echoed through the room.

He sat down next to her with his meal and spent much of the next half hour speaking the words out loud in an awful imitation of the familiar characters.

'Darling,' he said when the credits had left the screen and the ads took over, 'you haven't eaten all your food. Didn't you like it?'

'It was delicious, Nick. It's just that my appetite seems

to have disappeared,' she said, forcing a wan smile on to her worried face. 'If you don't mind, I think I might have a bath and go to bed. Conserve my energy.'

'Loss of appetite is perfectly natural at this stage,' Nick said authoritatively, 'and of course you're tired. Go on then, love, go and have that bath.'

While he was clearing up in the kitchen he thought he heard her call out. He went to the bathroom door but before he could knock and ask her if she needed anything he realized that she was talking to herself. She was laughing hysterically and then sobbing a little and laughing again and then, most curious of all, he heard her say quite clearly, 'God save me from the Stepford Husband.'

The divide between Richard's new private beliefs and his public position was getting wider with every passing day. After all those years in power the party was finding it difficult to adjust to life in opposition. There were those amongst them who believed that the way forward – the way back into control – lay in moving further to the right. Prime Minister Blair's ruthless renovation of his own party had been successful, had certainly appealed to the electorate, but it was clear that already certain sections of the population were worried about how the Labour Government might change their lives.

A lot of Richard's colleagues – those hard-liners that he had once so heartily agreed with – believed that the way forward was in a dramatic attack on the way in which the new Government were encouraging and extending the welfare state. Which meant that Richard, as Shadow Secretary of State for Social Security was meant to toe the party line and prepare to savage 'state spongers' at Prime Minister's Question Time.

Of course, Richard hadn't got to the top of his

profession by adhering to his own principles, even in the days when he still had them. But now it was different. He had been given a speech, written by the ghastly party hopeful for whom Louise now worked, that was so offensive to those dependent on the state that it frightened him. How on earth could he stand up and speak these words with conviction when his heart now belonged on the other side of the dispatch box?

Richard was known as something of an orator. As one of the only people in the party capable of putting across a bunch of clichés as if they were inspired new ideas. But on this occasion, as he stood nervously in front of an expectant and rather full House, it was scarcely possible to hear the words he was saying, let alone understand them. Indeed, Richard made a nonsense of the speech, choosing to leave out the most callous chunks of rhetoric, replacing them with uncustomary pauses and inaudible asides. Such was the embarrassment of his colleagues (many of whom whispered amongst themselves about the state of Richard's mental and physical health) that the only response his words provoked was silence. No heckling from across the House, not even an unkind jibe from Dennis Skinner.

'You will forgive me,' said the Secretary of State for Social Security in reply to Richard's incoherent speech, 'but I am not sure what the Honourable Member was trying to say. Could it be that some members of the Opposition are so ashamed of the results of seventeen years of Tory rule that they no longer have the courage of their previous convictions?'

The Labour back-benches loved this, applauding their man with such enthusiasm that Richard blushed scarlet and, in full view of the television cameras, scrambled out of his seat and on out of the Chamber. The scene, and Richard's untimely exit, was repeated on the early evening news, the *Nine O'Clock News*, *News at Ten* and *Newsnight*. Worse, it provoked a series of editorials in the next day's papers that questioned the behaviour not just of the Shadow Secretary of State for Social Security but of the entire Shadow Cabinet.

Richard knew that it was probably the end of his career in politics. But he didn't much care. Georgia supported him, wept with him when he got home that night and told him that whatever he decided to do she was behind him.

He didn't resign, nor was he immediately removed from his position. Instead there followed a cooling-off period in which Richard was asked to take a rest and prepare some sort of defence for his peculiar behaviour in the House.

For some time Richard had been actively following his wife's advice by involving himself in a number of diverse charity works. He had decided that he didn't just want to sit on committees or find his name on the letterheads of recognized charities. He wanted to get involved at grass-roots level. Get his hands dirty, as it were. It was, he quickly discovered, far more rewarding to do something that could directly and physically help the disadvantaged than to get caught up in the administration or the fund-raising of some gigantic charitable organization.

Two nights a week he was a volunteer on a soup run for the homeless organized by a small group of young people he had stumbled across on his way home from the House late one night. He had been so impressed by their selfless devotion to the people they tended that he had approached them and offered his help. Thankfully they had no idea of his identity, and indeed part of the joy in the work came through the anonymity.

Dressed in his old gardening jeans, a big Guernsey

sweater and a paint-spattered anorak, he would help man the van that followed the same route every night. At first he was rather shocked by what he saw. There were young people, middle-aged people, old people and not, as he had always imagined, just men. There were a great many women, some of whom, he noted with great sadness, were not much older than Emily or Tamsin. Talking to them proved an education for Richard. Helping them went some way to alleviate the guilt he felt for the arrogant and insensitive way he had treated these people in his political past.

But ultimately, perhaps inevitably, it was this very work that was to be his political undoing. A reporter from the *Daily Mirror* got a tip-off that a senior Tory politician was working with the homeless, and within days a startling and shocking picture of Richard, grotesquely dishevelled with his arms draped round a drug-crazed young girl, appeared on the front page beneath the headline 'Tory Hands Out To Homeless'.

After a long talk with the Leader of the Opposition (he couldn't now understand what it was he had ever seen in Portillo) he agreed to stand down from his post and to announce that he would be giving up his seat in the House. The smile on his face, now an almost permanent feature, grew wider as he wrote his letter of resignation. For the first time in his life he counted himself a happy man.

Harry had decided against contacting Annabel prior to his arrival in the small Cornish village of Boscastle. It was best, he thought, simply to turn up on her doorstep and throw himself on her mercy. He was in such a state of excitement that for the last few miles of the journey he could scarcely keep his grip on the steering wheel. Throughout the five hours it had taken him to reach

Cornwall he had been playing memories in his mind and on the car stereo. Tapes of their favourite bands that had taken him back to their youth.

He was a little disappointed by the rather un-attractive municipal car-park in the village and by the number of ugly tourists that were wandering around. But his fantasy of the place that Annabel would have chosen to live perfectly matched the reality. It was a small, pretty, slate-roofed cottage that looked down over the rocks to the sea. The garden was overgrown in a romantic way and the front door was painted a delicate shade of blue.

He knew she must have changed. He didn't expect her to look exactly like the pictures that littered his studio and haunted his head. He knocked very carefully on the door and stood, spellbound, as it was opened and a woman – with long, wavy hair – looked out at him. It couldn't be Annabel, she was too young and too tall. It took him a moment to realize that it must be his daughter, Amber, named after the particular shade of hair that she shared with her mother.

'Yes?' she said in a rather cold tone of voice.

'Is Ann – I mean, is your mother at home?' he stuttered.

'Who wants her?' Amber snapped.

'Tell her it's Harry.'

'Harry who?' she said, totally oblivious of his identity.

'Amber, I'm your father.'

She let him in, then, although her hard expression did not change, and led him through to a dingy, purple-painted back room decorated with stars and moons and a great deal of dusty, Victorian furniture. At first, in the darkened room, all he could see was the back of a small woman with long hair. My goodness, he thought as his heart leapt within him, she still has the hair and the clothes and, most poignant of all, the strong smell of crushed roses.

'Annabel,' he said.

When she turned round he could see the changes that time had made on her. The colour of her hair was not quite so vivid and much of it was streaked with grey. Her body was thicker and her breasts had lost their pertness. But curiously the reality of the older Annabel did not in any way dampen his ardour. Rather, he found himself longing to put his arms round her to protect her.

She didn't say anything for a while. She just looked at him.

'I suppose you've finally decided that it was time we divorced,' she said, glancing wearily past him at the retreating figure of Amber.

'No,' he said.

'Well, it's a little late to start establishing visitation rights. Amber is nineteen now,' she said with a bitter laugh.

'No, I've come to see you, Annabel. I mean, of course I want to see Amber, and talk to her and get to know her. But the last thing on my mind is a divorce from you. Look, I've brought some pictures with me.' He put down a parcel of photographs on the purple tablecloth that covered the round table between them.

She looked down at them and, for the first time, she smiled. It took him most of the day to persuade her of his sincerity. He might not have pulled it off had Amber been staying. But she was merely visiting her mother from Exeter University. Her antagonism towards her father was tangible. She looked at him as you might an alien. But she didn't interfere and, after an hour or so, she departed for Exeter in her little 2CV.

He was very cautious. Very careful not to rush things. When they were alone Annabel made them both something to eat and they sat and talked and looked at one another. Harry couldn't believe his luck. He had known that Annabel was not living with a man, but he had no idea whether she was romantically involved. There had, she told him in her soft voice during the course of the evening, been a few men, but Amber had always been her main priority. 'And Amber has never liked men,' she said with her strange Madonna-like smile.

She earned her living nowadays as an illustrator. She had converted one bedroom into a studio where she worked on her tiny, exquisite pictures of flowers and wildlife. She had, she told him gently, just enough money to live as she wanted. It was at this point, as the clock on the mantelpiece struck ten, that he asked her where he might stay in the village that night.

'Harry, you can stay here,' she said, and in the soft light of candles that illuminated the room she was as lovely and as entrancing as she had been on their wedding night.

She led him upstairs into her bedroom. She had held on to the big mahogany bed that they had slept in when they were first married. She had even kept the Indian bedspread on which they had lain and loved so many times.

On the bedside table there was a bowl of rose petals. She looked up at him and unbuttoned the thin, long voile dress she was wearing. He didn't focus on the body, it didn't matter that the breasts had sagged and that the skin on her stomach was loose. He just looked at her face and lost himself in her eyes. They made love for most of the night. She had an energy and a ferocity that he didn't remember. She was accomplished and experienced and as clever with her hands and tongue as any of the women that had followed her in his life. But he didn't give much thought to her love-making skills. He didn't give much thought to anything. He just let the smell of the roses overwhelm him and noted, as he fell into a deep and satisfied sleep, that at last he had come home.

Steve closed his eyes and held hands tightly with the people on either side of him in the circle.

'I care, I care, I care,' he chanted in unison with the others.

He was almost at the end of the weekend encounter group that was the climax of his counselling course. It had been a revelation to him. He had, he thought as he opened his eyes and looked at the people in the circle with him, learnt almost as much about himself as he had about helping other people. Later today he would be awarded the Council of Counselling Certificate that would secure his future.

With Richard's help and David King's encouragement he had managed to get a post within a practice of GPs. He would be working with people with all manner of problems – depression, drug addiction, mental illness. And despite the magnitude of the job he was taking on – and the relative speed with which he had trained – he had no doubts about his capabilities. He was, as their course tutor had said, a natural. People liked talking to him. At home on the Featherwell Estate he had become the man to whom everyone turned. His advice, his sensitivity, his honesty and integrity had made him, at last, a man to look up to.

Of course, it was difficult for Amanda or any of the people who had known him in the old days to accept the change in him. He had, he realized now, been a monstrous person when he had power and money. He had treated everyone in his life with the same callous contempt. And in his desperate bid to scale the social ladder he had neglected his own family (although he had set his old mum up in a nice little bungalow in Southend, he had never bothered to visit her, and the shock of his arrest had prompted the heart attack that had killed her just weeks after his empire collapsed).

He had been the ultimate eighties man who believed that everything and everyone had a price. He even regarded his wife and child as just another commodity. But he was a new man now. He wasn't that Steve Minter – clever, corrupt and cunning. He was Steve Minter MCC (Member of the Council of Counselling).

He had to wipe away a tear when they presented the certificates, even though he was rather surprised that some of the people present – several of whom he had privately judged to be deranged and socially inadequate – had managed to pass the final postal examination.

He spent most of his journey home that evening fantasizing about how things would be. How he would be able to take over as bread winner, how Amanda would be able to give up work and be a proper wife and mother, how Annie would benefit from a more normal family life. How, ultimately, they might add to that family and transfer to one of the little maisonettes on the other side of the estate. But Amanda did not seem to share his enthusiasm, let alone his fantasies. She looked at his certificate with a sceptical expression on her beautiful face.

'Why can't you be happy for me? Why can't you accept that I have changed?' he demanded after Annie had gone to bed that night.

'Oh Steve, I understand that you have changed,' she said. 'It's just that I don't think you understand why you have changed. And whether that change is really for the good . . .'

'What do you mean? For the first time in my life I feel,

well, content. I am about to start doing something positive for other people. I love you, I love our daughter. What more do you want? What more could I want?'

'What happened to your spirit of adventure, Steve? What happened to that part of you that loved taking risks, that loved to gamble on people, places and things? How can you, Steve Minter, be content with so little?'

He was hurt by this outburst. He couldn't understand why she couldn't be happy for him, with him.

'Darling, Amanda, please be happy for me. Please be happy with me,' he said moving over to the dressing table to begin the ritual of the hair-brushing.

There were tears in her eyes when he carried her over to the bed and began to make love to her. Sexually he knew that he had not changed, except for the better, and at the moment of climax he asked her the question again: 'Please be happy for me, please be happy with me.'

'Oh Steve,' she groaned, 'I wish I could.'

Carl was becoming a more and more accomplished actor. When he was with Nicola he was exactly the man she wanted. What that frightful English politician had described as a 'fancy new house-pet'. Of course, at the time that the man had made the comment Carl hadn't understood what he meant. But now, finally off the programme, he could see what Nicola had turned him into. Worse, he realized that Nicola and her colleagues at the Malestrom Foundation were not content to convert a few men into poodles. They wanted a nation, no, a whole world of mice-like men.

He now believed that he, and he alone, was the hope for mankind. Lord knows how long it would take them to make Manifold as acceptable and as widespread a drug as penicillin or paracetamol. Meanwhile he must play along with Nicola. She must not suspect anything.

To that end, this morning, he brought her breakfast in bed complete with a red rose in a little silver vase. And when she had eaten her croissant and sipped her coffee he leant over her and made love to her the way she liked (and not the way he had lately discovered he preferred). Later when she had showered and dressed he drove her to work.

'What are you going to do today, honey?' she said, stroking the back of his head in a way that made him want to bite off her hand.

'Oh, I thought I'd put in some work on my MA and send off some applications for a couple of posts I like the look of,' he said, smiling broadly back at her.

She kissed him full on the mouth as she got out of the car and it was all he could do, as he drove away, to stop himself from spitting back at her. He had no intention of working on his MA or of applying for any job. He wanted to find out more about Manifold and Malestrom, and he decided to go home and look through Nicola's private correspondence.

Nicola had always been very careful to keep her study at home locked. Not once in the years that they had been together had she allowed Carl into her inner sanctum. He laughed out loud when he thought of the implications of that, and how it contributed to the idea of him as a 'fancy new house-pet'. He could imagine her telling her colleagues, 'Of course, I don't allow Carl in the study, but he can come in and out of the rest of the apartment as he likes.'

The first thing he did was call a locksmith. It was pretty easy to convince the guy that he had mislaid the only key to his goddam study. Half an hour and sixty dollars later he was inside the room methodically going through her files. Of course, none of the really important confidential work would be at home. But there were bits and pieces that offered him some idea of the extent to which Manifold was to be marketed worldwide.

The most frightening thing about the whole concept, he had recently decided, was that it appealed to the vanity of most men. All that crap about increased sexual potency and career potential. And once they had tried the stuff they would be hooked simply because they would believe that they were happy. When he looked back at the pictures of himself in the early days of the programme he was shocked by that blank, smiling expression that transformed his face and the faces of the other volunteers. He shivered at the thought of a million men – a zillion men – smiling their way through the Manifold programme.

He had to do something. He had to think of a plan that would expose Manifold for what it was – a sinister plot to control men conceived and developed by a group of hysterical feminists. But what shocked him and motivated him most that day, as he hunted through the desk and filing cabinets in Nicola's room, was the letter he found from her friend in England.

Dearest Nicola,

I am so sorry that I got so emotional on that last night. I was simply in denial. I couldn't see what Richard had become. And I couldn't see what you were offering me. But a few days after you left, overcome by anger, I think, I gave him the first capsule. (I told him it was Vitamin B12!)

Suffice it to say that now, six weeks on, he really is my Stepford Husband. He isn't just the man I used to love, he's more than that. He is my perfect man!

Last week on my birthday he gave me the most beautiful eternity ring and we made love properly for the first time in ages. I can't believe how sensitive, and caring and, well, SMILEY he's become in such a short time. He even did the Waitrose shop the other day and tried to cook me supper!

But it isn't just his attitude to me and the family that is transformed, it's his attitude to the whole world. He wants to give up politics, he hates what he had become, and he has such compassion and kindness for everyone he encounters. It must sound silly, but he thinks like a woman but remains a man (perhaps that was the aim of Manifold?).

Thank you, thank you, thank you. I think we are both happier now than we have ever been before in our lives.

Love, love, Georgia

P.S. Could you please, please send me some more Manifold – I couldn't bear to run out!
P.P.S. I've even forgiven Juliet!
P.P.P.S. The funniest thing of all is that all four of the men have become best friends. They even get together for supper like a bunch of girls! Can you imagine Richard and Steve and Harry and Nick (who's now the most frightful baby-bore!) talking for hours together and chatting on the phone every other day?

Although the idea of that dreadful politician turning into a 'fancy new house-pet' himself rather amused Carl, it also frightened him. Because the moral implications of putting men on Manifold without their knowledge or consent gave Nicola's work a whole new dimension. It was then that he started to work out his masterplan. It would take him a while to organize the details, but by the time he and Nicola were due in England for the European launch of Manifold in a couple of months everything would be in place.

He spent the rest of the day carefully photostating everything he thought might constitute evidence and then putting everything back in place. For the next month he would have to remain Nicola's own Stepford Husband, her tailor-made man. When she got home he gave her that long fixed smile that had been so easy when he was on the programme but which, right now, was frighteningly difficult to sustain.

THIRTEEN

Nick's pains were coming every four and a half minutes. He was trying very hard with his breathing, singing his rhyme and panting as loudly as he dared but it made no difference. He felt as if his body would burst open with the pressure of the pain. For some reason Caroline did not regard his symptoms as in any way equal to her own. In fact, for much of the last couple of hours she had been screaming and ranting at him, crying out for drugs, epidurals, anything to alleviate the agony of her contractions.

But Nick was resolute. If he could cope, she could cope.

'JACK AND JILL WENT UP THE HILL – one, two, three, four, five, EXHALE,' he chanted at her. 'Come on, darling, it really helps.'

'Nothing can help me, Nick, NOTHING,' she groaned, 'except perhaps death.'

Even though he could hardly stand up by this time, he was not going to give up, although somewhat reluctantly he did agree to her having some gas and air.

'COME ON, DARLING, YOU CAN DO IT – remember, inhale, hold, one, two, three, four, five, EXHALE,' he pursued.

'FUCKING JACK AND SODDING JILL WENT UP THE BLOODY HILL . . . Oh no, no, no, I can't stand it. Get the nurse, Nick, get the nurse,' screamed Caroline as an alarm sounded from some machinery in the corner of the room.

It all happened pretty fast then. A man in a pinstripe suit came in and talked very softly to Caroline, an anaesthetist was called, a screen was put up and, within twenty minutes everyone was scrubbed up and ready for the Caesarian. Except, that is, for Nick.

'But I told you I wanted a NATURAL delivery,' he shouted at the surgeon.

'Do you want what is best for your babies?' the man replied in smooth patronizing tones.

'Of course I do,' Nick replied tersely.

'Then I suggest that you wait outside.'

Nick wasn't going to be banished from the birth that easily. Three minutes later, dressed in a gown and mask, he was back in the theatre. But as the surgeon raised the scalpel to make the discreet bikini-line incision there was a terrible commotion.

'Stop! Stop! Hold it there!' shouted Nick. 'I forgot the camera.'

He managed to capture the most moving moments on his brand-new zoom-lens Sony Camcorder. The emergence of the first blood- and amniotic-fluid-covered baby – a girl – and three minutes later the emergence of another, marginally smaller, baby – a boy.

'Jack and Jill,' shouted Nick ecstatically.

The camera, the latest, state-of-the-art model bought especially for the occasion, even captured the sound bites of the medical staff who, frankly, had never come across a man as obsessive as Nick before. And it picked up the low moans of Caroline as the surgeon sewed her up (a process that took far longer than the delivery) and the effects of the epidural – which lowered her temperature – overwhelmed her and she turned blue from the cold and the blood loss and the sheer emotion of the occasion.

The paediatrician, who had been present throughout the operation, had checked and weighed the babies and pronounced them in rude health – Jill weighing in at 5lb

7oz and Jack at just 5lb 1oz. Nick was openly sobbing when they handed him one of the babies. The tears that streamed down his face were captured for posterity by a helpful nurse who held the camera while he nuzzled his first-born and then his second-born.

Caroline slept for what was left of the rest of the night, but Nick sat, alert, and watched over the two clear-perspex cots in the corner of her room. Every time one of them muttered or moved or cried out he would grab the camera to record the moment.

He was still there in the morning when the nurse came in to try and get the babies on the breast. Nick held Jack to Caroline's left breast while the nurse held Jill to the right. Caroline was too weak to hold either of her bundles of joy.

'Why don't you go home now and have a sleep, and let all the relatives know the news,' the nurse suggested helpfully.

But Nick had no intention of leaving his babies. He made the calls on a phone they wheeled in for him, exulting in informing the grannies and grandpas, the uncles and aunts and, of course, Georgia, Juliet and Amanda. Georgia was especially thrilled and passed the phone over to Richard.

'Congratulations, Nick!' he boomed down the phone. 'Us boys must get together and celebrate.'

Later that morning, when Caroline eventually managed to get up and struggle to the loo, Nick finally fell asleep in an upright chair at her bedside with one hand reaching into the pink cot and one hand reaching into the blue cot, an expression of deep contentment on his face which, even in sleep, was fixed in a beatific smile.

'What have I done,' she muttered out loud as she passed him.

*

Richard was revelling in unemployment. And while, of course, he had no immediate money worries Georgia had expressed a little concern about how they were to maintain their lifestyle without his income.

'But Georgia darling,' he said softly, 'why on earth would we want to maintain THAT lifestyle? I've been thinking that there are so many ways in which we can cut back on our expenses. I mean, darling, for a start we don't need a nanny any more.'

And it was true, they didn't. Richard had taken over the school run, had volunteered and been accepted as Tom's class rep on the PA and spent all his time, after school each day, helping the children with their home-work and arranging activities for them.

'What's more, old girl, I'm not sure that we need the Hendersons any more either. I mean, I daresay Mrs H could still put in a few hours' cleaning and such, but it's not as if we need staff now.'

And again, it was true that they didn't. Richard had become dreadfully domesticated. He had reorganized the running of the big old kitchen and had drawn up, on his own initiative, a two-week food rota that was chiefly made up of the dishes he could now cook – mostly pies and simple pasta meals. He was even threatening the livelihood of Bob the old gardener with his new plans for an extended vegetable garden, which he had every inten-tion of digging himself.

'Darling, in some ways we could be self-sufficient. I'm planning on growing all our own potatoes, marrows, sprouts, greens, spinach, and I'm looking into the possi-bility of keeping a few chickens. And maybe a goat or two.'

Indeed, there were moments when Georgia herself began to feel a little redundant.

'But, Richard, this isn't *The Good Life*. Even with the

cut-backs you suggest we'll need to establish some form of income. And besides you'll soon get bored with tilling the earth and tending the chickens. Isn't there something else you could do? Take a directorship from Uncle Freddie or do something profitable but part-time in the City. That's what all the other ex-ministers do.'

'Well, darling, I'm not all the other ex-Tory ministers. I can think of nothing worse than having my name on the notepaper of a merchant bank or a big corporation. I want to get away from all that. If I did anything now, it would have to be something completely different. Do you know what I like the idea of? Teaching,' he said.

'Well, I suppose you could become an Oxbridge don or something. Or perhaps you could make a name for yourself public speaking on the international lecture circuit. Or write your memoirs. Lady T made an absolute fortune that way.'

It was then that it hit Richard. He was in the perfect position to write the first totally truthful political memoirs. He had, of course, kept diaries throughout the most important years and, with the hindsight he now had (not to mention the change of heart he had experienced), they could be turned into a riveting and terribly damaging book. Every moment that he wasn't working in the garden, cooking, tending the children or talking to one of his new chums on the phone he spent dictating his memoirs into a tape recorder. Georgia was positively relieved by the idea of a huge publishing advance, although Richard himself was, for once, not motivated by greed but by a need to put the party in its place – History.

Harry could not remember ever feeling quite as distressed as he had been in the days following his reunion with Annabel. He had risen early on the morning after their first glorious night of love-making and had nipped downstairs to prepare her breakfast (something he had done from time to time in the early days of their marriage). But when he returned to the bedroom with the little tray she was not as delighted as he had expected. In fact, she was irritated and argumentative. A different woman from the night before.

'For God's sake, Harry, are you still here?' she said, emerging from beneath the rather grubby sheets (he now noticed) looking considerably older in the morning light.

'Of course I'm still here. I'm here for all eternity, my darling,' Harry said affectionately.

'What?' she said as if she had woken up and found a stranger in her bedroom.

'I'm back, darling. I'm your husband again. I should never have stopped being your husband. And I promise I will never, ever leave your side again.'

'What are you talking about, Harry?' she said in such an aggressive manner that he was momentarily taken aback.

'I'm talking about us, Annabel, you and I and our future together,' Harry said, a tone of desperation entering his voice.

'What future?' she said.

'*Our* future,' he persisted.

'I can tell you about my future, Harry, but I really don't want any part of yours. I think you misunderstood last night.'

'You mean, it didn't mean anything to you?'

'It meant a fuck for me and not a particularly good one at that,' she said with a coarseness that shocked him. 'But obviously you thought it was something else.'

'But surely you wouldn't have taken me into your bed if you, like me, didn't want us to be together again?'

'I quite often take men into my bed – better men than you, Harry – whom I have absolutely no intention of being with for longer than it takes for me to come. Which sometimes can be a matter of seconds and sometimes a whole night.' Annabel paused for a second. 'Last night it never actually happened, although I don't suppose that you noticed. Now if you don't mind, Harry, I've got a lot of work to do and I want to get on with my life, not yours.'

'But last night you said that there was no one else. Last night you led me to believe we had a future,' he said, his eyes brimming over with tears.

'Last night, Harry, I was stoned out of my mind. I obviously made a mistake. Clearly you are mentally unbalanced. Why would you want a future with me after all this time? Harry, we barely had a past together, why would we have a future?'

He was weeping loudly now, holding his head in his hands. He couldn't believe that this woman – a woman that he would not ordinarily have looked twice at – should be rejecting him so cruelly.

'Harry, I've managed perfectly well on my own for the last God knows how many years, why on earth would I want to live with you now? It suited me when you walked out. You were a bore. An affected bore. You had an ego a hundred times bigger than your talent, and living with you was driving me insane. I never wanted to be a little woman. I was quite happy being a mother, but I was never cut out to be a wife. It was marvellously convenient for me, all those years, to be officially married but hundreds of miles apart from you. And it would suit me very well now if you would get the hell out of here and go back to London where you belong,' she spat.

'Is there no way I can change your mind?' he managed to ask between sobs.

'No,' she said curtly. 'Now just get out.'

He went downstairs, unable to accept what she had said. All the plans he had, all the dreams of leading a simple life with his precious wife were shattering before him. He sat down on a chair in the kitchen, a feeling of utter desolation overwhelming him.

She went mad when she came downstairs, dressed in some unflattering wide-legged trousers and a jumper that revealed the outline of her sagging breasts. Through his tears he could now see that she wasn't the woman he remembered. She was older, fatter, coarser and altogether different from the vision that had lodged in his head these last few weeks.

'Harry, will you please fuck off,' she said, pushing past him to put on the kettle for some tea. A wave of her rancid breath hit him and he shuddered a little.

'I'm going,' he said quietly.

His last view of her from his car was of her broad backside bending down as she picked up the milk bottles from the porch.

He drove back to London in a dream. Seven times on the journey he rang Annabel on his mobile. And seven times she slammed down the phone on him with a brief but hearty 'FUCK OFF, HARRY'.

Steve was experiencing a few difficulties in his new job. He had no problems getting people to tell him what was worrying them, but he had dreadful problems getting them to stop. He was supposed to time each referral strictly. He was supposed to cut them off after exactly one hour and make another appointment for the next week. But with some of his clients it was terribly hard to do. In fact, very often after a trying day at work Steve quite literally took his problems home with him.

There was Joyce, who suffered from post-natal depression, even though her youngest child was now eight. There was Mavis who had agoraphobia, and Linda who was addicted to Night Nurse. Then there was Charlie, who had a phobia about worms; George, who was struggling with his sexuality (and on one occasion with Steve's); and Maria, who suffered from religious dementia (she had a stigmata on her left hand).

Some evenings in the meagre Minter flat four or five of Steve's clients would sit down to supper with the family. It was, Amanda exploded one night, a little like living in a Care in the Community hostel.

'It's only a matter of time, Steve,' she screamed, 'before one of them goes completely off their rocker and murders us all.'

In fact, if Steve wasn't being worn down by his over-dependent clients, he was being worn down by his overly independent wife. Amanda had been promoted again at work and had received a substantial pay rise. She was now obsessed with getting out of the Featherwell Estate, a place that had lately, at least for Steve, come to seem like home.

She had found some run-down Georgian house in Stockwell that she wanted to buy and renovate. He had been to see it with her and he had to agree that it had potential. But to him it seemed like going back to their other life. The one he no longer craved. It was another sign of the growing difference between him and Amanda. She was now actively – often aggressively – aspirational, while he was very much content with his lot. Well, the Featherwell Estate and his new friends and his needy clients. Besides he didn't want to uproot Annie, who had adapted so well to her new environment. And how did Amanda think that they would be able to get a mortgage on that great big place?

'Quite easily, Steve,' she said contemptuously. 'I'm earning a great deal more now, and with my bonuses and commissions I'll have no problem meeting the mortgage payments. Of course, if Steve Minter is happier living on a notorious, scummy estate surrounded by a load of dead-beat misfits, then that's fine. I'll do this on my own.'

'But I keep telling you, Amanda, I'm happy now. I'm content. I was never content in the old days. Nothing satisfied me. The more I acquired, the richer I got, the bigger the house, the more impressive the yacht, the more coke I crammed up my nose, the less happy I became. I always wanted more and more and more. And now, finally, when I've got rid of the need for all that crap, when I have finally discovered what is important in life, you want to drag me back into that world. A Georgian house, a new car, then what, then what? I am happy where I am. It might not be much. It might not give me the status I once longed for or the money or the power. But it's all I want now.'

She looked at him for a few moments with a puzzled expression on her face.

'Do you know who you are beginning to remind me of, Steve?'

'No, who do I remind you of?' he asked defensively.

'You remind me of Tigger. My old tomcat with one battered ear from fighting. My poor old Tigger whose sense of adventure and spirit of freedom eventually got too much for my mother. You remind me of my old tomcat Tigger. After he was castrated.'

It was his turn to look at her with a puzzled expression on his face.

'What on earth do you mean, Amanda? Are you suggesting that because I'm happy, because I like my new life and am not screwing every woman I meet in the way

I used to, I am in some way emasculated? Didn't we make love last night? Didn't you cry when you came?'

'God, I'm sorry, Steve, I'm sorry. I don't know what I meant. Of course, I don't want you to go back to what you were. I just want to be able to move forward again. Featherwell was fine for us. It helped me and it's helping you. But we can't stay here for ever.'

She moved over to him and put her arms round him, and he held her tightly to him for a moment.

'Just give me a little more time,' he said, smiling at her, 'and we'll do it together. We'll move on together.'

'I don't want the old Steve, really I don't. You can't begin to understand how much I don't want the old Steve back,' she said as she put her head on his shoulder. Then, looking up at him, she added, very softly, 'It's just I'm a little scared of the new Steve.'

Carl felt as if he had lockjaw from smiling so much during his day at the Malestrom Foundation headquarters. He had been called in for a routine briefing on the European launch which had provided him with a legitimate reason to penetrate the building.

His plan was quite simple. After his meeting he would find somewhere safe to hide until the staff left at the end of the day. Then, with duplicate keys to Nicola's office (carefully copied at the weekend) and the pass codes he had discovered in her study at home, he would be able to complete copying the most important data on Manifold. He had told Nicola that he was flying to Seattle for a job interview that afternoon. She didn't expect him back till late the following day. It hadn't been difficult to work out the safest place to hide. After all, Carl was familiar with the lay-out of the building and only too aware that with a staff that was 98 per cent female the least likely place for him to be found was in the men's room on the first floor. Why, even the security officers at Malestrom were female. This was the last place they would look.

He waited until 11 p.m. before he attempted to make his way up to the suite of offices that Nicola and the other key members of the team occupied on the fifth floor. It was unlikely that anyone would still be there and he knew for certain that the cleaners wouldn't arrive until 5 a.m.

It took him two hours to copy all the material stored on Nicola's computer. And a further two hours checking through the rest of the system for anything he might have missed. He was frightened by what he found. The Malestrom Foundation was growing faster than he had imagined. Since getting FDA approval – something he was certain had been achieved through suspect means – they had made moves and done deals in some fifty countries. Europe was completely tied up. Australia was on course. Within a year, Carl reckoned, most of the men in the civilized world would be grinning, Manifold-addicted model males.

At 3.30 a.m. he carefully let himself out of the office and made his way back down to the men's room on the first floor. There was a drop of about twelve feet from the window in the disabled toilet. He checked very carefully before he braced himself and jumped on to the soft earth at the back of the building. His left leg hurt a bit and his right hand – where he had reached out to protect himself – was a little grazed, but otherwise he was OK. Most importantly he had everything he needed in the soft-leather British briefcase that Nicola had given him for his birthday. He'd pulled it off.

His heart was beating so loudly it echoed in his ears and he felt a sudden surge of excitement. He'd beat those bitches if it was the last thing he did on this earth. But now, he decided, he deserved a reward. Two blocks from the Malestrom offices he grabbed a cab and made his way into the network of streets that would provide him with the kind of action he wanted. It took him half an hour to find a redhead, a real redhead like Nicola. She was young, he really liked them young, and fragile-looking. He liked women he could look down on in every way and this one was perfect.

The whole night, he insisted, on his terms not hers. She was desperate, he could tell, and the offer of so much money made her agree to anything. A place she knew where no one would see him, whatever he wanted.

He was more careful that night. He wore very fine surgical rubber gloves and although he tied her up and slapped her around, he didn't make any mistakes. He gagged her to stop her from screaming when the fucking got really hard. It was like he was getting his own back on all the goddamn women in the world. He hated them. He hated the fact that he needed them. Most of all, he hated the idea that women could ever, ever imagine they could control men in the way that Nicola thought she controlled him.

Nicola's biggest mistake was in picking Carl for the programme. What she had imagined was chemistry was, in fact, the hatred for women that oozed from every pore of his skin. Women had always meant trouble for Carl. As far back as he could remember they had abused him, shat on him and betrayed him. There had been a time, in the first year of the programme, when he had seen women differently. But he now understood that it had been a chemically induced madness. Women had always been the enemy. Making love had always been about making war. Women should know their place. Lying beneath a man while he fucked out what brains they had. Or in this case just fucked the life out of the cheap slut.

At midday, when he had got away from the tenement

block the bitch had taken him to, he checked into a cheap hotel and took a shower and slept for a couple of hours. Then he went to a big computer store and copied everything he had got, carefully putting his originals in one large bubble bag and the copies in another. The originals he put in a safe deposit box at his bank. The copies he sent by registered mail to Richard in England along with a carefully worded letter.

Dear Richard,

Be very careful with the enclosed. It is very important that you put these discs in a safe place. Do nothing else until I contact you. Say nothing to your wife. Please trust me.

Carl Burton

FOURTEEN

It hadn't taken a lot of persuading to get Nick away from the Portland for a night out – or rather a night in – with the boys. At first he had been reluctant to leave the twins – well, Caroline seemed so very detached from her children – but the thought of showing the guys the video of the birth and describing the details of the delivery appealed to him and, in the end, he offered to give them supper in the flat. After all, babies aside, it *was* his turn.

He cooked a chicken pasta dish he had thought up himself and served it round the rickety kitchen table with a couple of bottles of that Italian wine he and Caroline had discovered in Umbria.

'Nick, this is delicious,' Richard said. 'What exactly is it?'

'Diced breast of chicken, one chopped large onion, six finely sliced mushrooms all bunged together with some seasoning in a pan. Then you add a 500ml carton of *crème fraîche*, some parmesan and a packet of fresh penne. Concocted the recipe myself.'

'Marvellous, I'll add it to our supper menus,' said Richard. 'The kids loved that last recipe you gave me.'

'I've got a great quick supper recipe for moussaka,' interjected Steve. 'On the table in twenty minutes. I'll give it to you if you like.'

Harry was the only one who wasn't much interested in swapping recipes that night. Indeed, the others were rather concerned by his expression. For while he still smiled when he caught anyone's eye, there was a sadness about him that was disturbing.

'Harry, you have hardly eaten a thing,' Nick said gently. 'Is something bothering you?'

'It didn't work out with Annabel,' Harry said, horrified to realize that at the mere mention of her name his eyes were filling with tears. 'The dream turned sour.'

'Harry, it was all a long time ago. She was bound to have changed,' said Richard softly.

'The thing is that when I arrived I thought I'd come home. She seemed the same. Oh, her hair was streaked with grey and there were laughter lines around her eyes and she was not as lean as I remembered. But she seemed to have the same values, the same lifestyle that I wanted to recapture,' Harry said.

'Was she involved with someone else?' Steve asked.

'No, it wasn't that. Although clearly there were other men in her life. No, the dreadful truth is that she didn't want me except briefly that night in her bed. She didn't want to share a future with me,' Harry said, his voice slurred with sorrow.

'Do you know something?' Nick said. 'It's a bloody woman's world.'

'Women,' said Richard, 'I'll never understand them. Don't get me wrong. I love Georgia. But in so many little ways I am aware that she doesn't want what I want. She doesn't really listen to me. She doesn't seem to need to talk in the way I do.'

'It's like that with Amanda, too,' said Steve, a little too passionately. 'I mean, I come home and I want to tell her about my day, discuss what has happened, sit down and properly communicate with her. And she's either too tired, or too distracted or too involved in watching the news or some bloody documentary or other.'

In fact, women, particularly their own women, dominated their conversation that night. It was an odd departure for them all, but they didn't see it like that. In the past women had only cropped up in conversation in smutty asides or in raised-eyebrow referrals to 'her indoors', 'the little woman' or 'the wife'. In the past should any of the four men have found themselves in all-male company they would have talked about politics, sport, work or the state of the nation. The state of their relationships had never previously bothered them. But tonight each of them sought to unburden on the others their own particular problems.

But first, immediately after the penne had slipped down their throats, they were treated to Nick's interpretation of the birth. Curiously Richard was transfixed. His youngest child Tom was born by Caesarian section, but he had little memory of the process. He did vaguely recall spending a lot of time on the payphone in the corridor outside the operating theatre, but he could not remember any detail of the delivery. He had been aware, at the time, of a swelling male pride at the fact that, at last, he had pulled it off and sired a son. But of the emotion of the event, or even of the mechanics, he had no memory.

'My God,' he said as Jill emerged, attached to a straggly bloody cord, 'it's nature's bloody miracle, isn't it?'

'She came out crying,' said Nick emotively, 'and then two minutes later her brother emerged.'

Harry could hardly bear to watch. In place of the nostalgic love that he had nurtured for Annabel he was now experiencing a terrible guilt. He hadn't even been in the hospital on the night Amber had been born. He had been rumping some model he had met that afternoon. They didn't manage to get a message to him for over twenty-four hours. Perhaps that's why I never really bonded with my daughter, he thought now. Perhaps that's where I went wrong. If only, he thought as he watched the video of Nick beaming at the camera with first one and then the other of his babies, I had been there.

Children had never held any fascination for Harry. He had never felt a twinge of affection for Amber and he had been actively hostile to Juliet's son Sam. He regretted that, too, now. And, lately, he had begun to regret his desertion of Juliet. Why, in those long voile dresses she was almost the essence of the young Annabel (particularly when she smelled of that rose scent). He made up his mind to get to know Sam better. To rebuild his bridges with Juliet. There was such a need in him nowadays to nurture, to be a part of a couple, maybe even a family.

Steve, too, was absorbed by the video and Nick's running commentary. He had found Anoushka's birth repulsive. Indeed, although he had been present and had feigned an emotional response to the sight of his newborn daughter, the whole event had left him cold. And, for nearly a year afterwards, unable to make love to his wife (although not, he remembered, unable to make love to other people's wives).

After the video had finished Nick showed them into the little boxroom that was to be the nursery. He had decorated it all himself. Every detail was perfect. His friends squealed with delight at the collection of soft toys, at the tiny clothes and the pretty mobiles that hung over the cots.

Harry, Steve and Richard had each bought a gift for the babies. Richard had popped into a little shop in Henley and had chosen a terribly expensive tiny pink outfit for Jill and a terribly expensive tiny blue outfit for Jack. Harry had bought each of the babies a classic teddy bear, one with a floral ribbon round its neck, the other with a blue-and-white gingham kerchief. Steve, on a rather tighter budget, had bought each of them a pair of tiny baby trainers that, when unwrapped, prompted an exclamation of 'aaah! how sweeeet' from Nick.

'Do you know something,' Nick said when they were all relaxing in the sitting room, drinking a third bottle of wine. 'I experienced this real pang of envy during the birth. I wanted to have those babies. Does that sound mad? I even experienced most of the symptoms of labour – excruciating contractions every couple of minutes. When I said earlier that it's a woman's world, that's what I meant. All those years when I thought the only real achievement in life was in creating a great work of art I was wrong. The greatest achievement in life is in creating a baby.'

'I think I understand how you must have felt,' said Harry. 'It would be wonderful to be one with another human being, your baby. Fatherhood is somehow one step removed, isn't it? Not the same thing.'

'Do you suppose,' said Steve eagerly, 'that what we are suffering from is a kind of reverse of penis envy? Vagina envy?'

Richard laughed out loud at that, although deep down it was something he, too, had experienced of late.

'Nick, you are right. It is a woman's world. Not that they see it that way,' Steve went on. 'All I really want in life now is to make Amanda and Annie happy, and maybe make up a bit for my past by doing something positive for the future. But Amanda just won't accept that I am happy. That everything I want in the world is on the Featherwell Estate. She's urging me on to more and I can't seem to convince her that if I return to those old ways – bigger houses, business responsibilities and so on – I will be lost.'

Richard looked across at his friend and offered him a warm sympathetic smile.

'Georgia is the same. Worrying about the unimportant things in life – money, mortgages, school fees – and oblivious to what really matters to me now. People, family, friends,' he said.

Then Harry led the conversation back to his own distress over his disastrous reunion with Annabel.

'Do you know, I still can't quite believe that she rejected me. I don't think that any woman has ever rejected me before. My God, it hurt. And the funny thing is that because of what she did to me I've started to question the way I treated women in the past. And not just Annabel. I feel terribly bad about Juliet. Richard, have you seen her recently?'

'She came down last weekend with poor little Sam. She was looking a little pale and thin. Not at all her usual designer self. She was wearing the strangest sort of floral frock – the kind of thing my mother might have worn – and scarcely any make-up at all.'

'Was she very unhappy?' Harry enquired.

'Well, she's never very happy when she's got poor little Sam in tow. Poor little bugger spent the whole summer holiday with his paternal grandparents. Juliet hadn't seen him for months. And then, of course, she and Georgia had a lot to sort out after the revelation about my affair with her. It was a weekend of soul-searching, I can tell you. But in the end I think I convinced them both how ashamed I was of my past behaviour. She's very cut up about you, Harry.'

This news cheered Harry. He had a happy facility for rewriting his own fantasies and dreams. And just lately he had a new picture haunting his head. It was of Juliet, lying on her bed half in and half out of a long, floaty dress.

'I think I might look her up. Try and make amends,' he said. 'It's high time I divorced Annabel and settled down again.' He finished with a glowing, hopeful smile.

'Good idea,' his friends echoed in unison.

'The funniest thing happened the other day,' Richard said, his beamy face briefly adopting a serious expression. 'This package of computer material arrived from the States. Nothing that would work on my old Amstrad. And with it there was a note from a man called Carl Burton. At first I had no idea who he was, but then I remembered he was that boyfriend of Nicola's. The one I took such a dislike to. Curious note it was, too. Something about keeping the contents safe and secret. Apparently he and Nicola are coming over next month for the launch of that drug she's involved in.'

'You know, I was thinking that he wasn't so terribly awful,' Harry said. 'I mean, he wasn't what you would call a classic hunting, shooting and fishing sort of man, but I think he meant well.'

'Perhaps you are right,' said Richard. 'Although I think I was rather rude to him. He seemed a little, well, effeminate, didn't he?'

Which brought them back to the now endlessly fascinating subject of women.

'Do you know, I always saw Nicola as a kind of spinster,' said Nick. 'I was convinced she didn't like men. I don't mean that I thought she liked women in that way. I just got this feeling sometimes that she despised me.'

'It wasn't just a feeling in my case,' said Richard. 'It was a fact. I found a letter she had written to Georgia once and the tone of it was really nasty. I don't think that she thought that any of us were good enough for her friends.'

'She was probably right,' said Steve. 'I was an absolute bastard to Amanda. But not any more. Heavens, I'd say that nowadays Nicola might even approve of us. My God, isn't it odd how much we have changed? We might almost be the kind of men Nicola herself would have chosen for our women.'

It didn't occur to them that they had become Carl clones. That their own preoccupation with relationships, emotions, babies, recipes and idle gossip was in any way strange or sinister.

'I think I'll invite them to Gallows Tree House for a weekend when they come over for the launch. Then Nicola can see for herself what decent, sensitive chaps we really are,' said Richard as he kissed Nick on both cheeks and made his way happily out into the night in order to be in time for the last train home.

Harry offered Steve a lift back to Lambeth in his cab.

'Isn't the Featherwell Estate a bit out of your territory?' Steve said nervously.

'Not at all, it's a pleasure.'

'I can't tell you how I value these evenings together,' Steve said as he bade Harry farewell.

'Me too,' echoed Harry as he embraced his parting friend. The cab pulled away from the kerb and the jeering crowd of youths who loitered outside the ghastly concrete blocks that had become Steve Minter's new empire.

FIFTEEN

Nick had hired a breast pump from the NCT so that Caroline could express milk and he could help to feed the twins. But so far, since his family had come home, it didn't seem as if she was producing enough milk.

'Nick, you know I really think it would be better if I could give them some supplementary SMA,' she said despairingly one day after she had spent an hour and a half trying to feed an angry, hungry Jack.

'Breast is best, Caroline,' said Nick confidently. He might have given in to her ridiculous scheme to cheat him out of a natural delivery (he still hadn't established why the hospital had performed a Caesarian), but he certainly wasn't going to give in on this. 'It's terribly important that the babies are breast-fed. Not just because they take on your immunity to illnesses, but also because statistically it has been proven that babies who are fed on breast milk grow up to be more intelligent, well balanced and healthy. Breast-fed babies achieve more in life and are less prone to allergies. Not to mention the cot-death factor,' he said decisively before adding, 'You are just going to have to try harder, darling. Drink more fluids. Eat more. Work at building up your milk.'

He had noticed that he was much calmer than his wife when he was with the babies. They were more likely to settle if it was him that fed them with a bottle filled with her milk than if they were put to her breast. This gave him an odd sense of satisfaction. He loved feeding them. He would sit down in the old feeding chair and revel in the eye contact of his tiny charges.

But it wasn't just in the feeding of the babies that Nick

was emerging as the dominant parent. He was far more adept at changing them, at bathing them and at bringing up their wind and soothing them. What is more, the first great milestone of their lives – the moment when they smiled in recognition and not in wind – was witnessed when they were five-and-a-half weeks old by Nick rather than Caroline. There was no doubt that he was what Penelope Leach described in her book *Baby and Child* (which he sometimes sat reading for hours), the twins' 'primary carer'.

Caroline was clumsy and nervous with her children. She was, too, abstracted and in low spirits. Probably a touch of post-natal depression, Nick thought, whereas, he was suffering from post-natal elation. He had never felt happier, more content and fulfilled in his life.

He tried to put aside a couple of hours a day for writing, but Caroline was so dependent on his help that it was very difficult to get much done. She spent most of the day in bed, was eternally tired and hadn't managed to get dressed since she had come home. He, meanwhile, was doing all the cooking, washing, cleaning and most of the caring for the babies. She would only let him out of her sight for brief periods – when he had to go shopping. One day he returned from a half-hour trip to Sainsbury's to find her locked in the bathroom sobbing while both babies screamed hysterically from their cots in the nursery.

'For heaven's sake, darling, what were you thinking?' he said as he warmed up a bottle of expressed milk for Jack and put Jill to his wife's dripping breast.

'I was just frozen. I didn't know what to do, and the noise, I thought the noise would send me mad. I wanted to . . . I wanted to shut them up,' she said, tears streaming down her face and on to her naked breasts.

'Pull yourself together, Caroline,' Nick said sternly.

'Salt is very bad for babies. Your tears are running into Jillie's mouth.'

Nick had fondly imagined that the birth of the babies would bring them closer. But it seemed that it only served to highlight the differences between Caroline and himself.

For him the babies came first. Of course, he still loved and cherished his wife, but his priorities had changed. The rest of the world – apart from his close male friends and one or two members of his immediate family – had ceased to exist. All his energy, all his attention were focused on Jack and Jillie. Which was, after all, natural. The way it should be for a parent. Whereas Caroline seemed to be focusing on herself. She seemed to have become completely absorbed in her own world. Not that she communicated any of this to Nick. She was almost as uncommunicative now as he had been in the days before he had properly appreciated the importance of children and family. It was almost as if, he thought, she was jealous of the attention he gave the children.

Sometimes he laughed to himself when he thought back to the time when he had been so convinced that he wanted to remain childless. He had even inserted a 'no children' clause into their version of the marriage service (it had been very fashionable in those days to write your own marriage vows and it struck him now as rather ironic that all their friends who had written similar individually tailored vows had all since divorced). But then as someone had said – Harry was it, or maybe Richard? – there was none so zealous as the newly converted. And, my goodness, was Nick converted.

Indeed, he was so confident in his new role of father, and primary carer, that he didn't raise any real objections when Caroline suggested – just fourteen weeks after the birth – that she thought she might go back to work. Women nowadays, he had privately decided, didn't know what they wanted. Hadn't Caroline been crazed to have these children at the outset? And now, now that she had what she had claimed to want most in the world – her babies and his assured devotion as father and husband – what did she want? She wanted to go back to work.

He cooked a simple but delicious soufflé that night and brought her a tray to bed. He had been desperately trying to get her milk production up by supplementing her diet with the things that Penelope Leach suggested. But it was becoming clear that rather than producing more milk Caroline was making less.

'Darling, if you really think it's for the best, then maybe you should go back to work,' he said as he sat and watched her eat (if he left her alone she would only leave the food and compound the milk problem).

'I think I need to get out a bit, Nick. I think that I would feel happier if I was working again,' she said, managing a wan smile. 'And besides we need the money. I mean, it's not going to be very easy for you to work at home with the babies to look after, is it?'

'I don't think that money should be a motivation, darling. I'm sure that I will be able to do bits and pieces when the babies are asleep. I haven't dropped behind on my quota of scripts yet and I don't intend to, so there is no "having to go back to work". If you want to, though, I suppose you should,' he said in tones that hinted, at least to him, of disapproval.

Having made her decision, she found that her mood improved. She even managed to get dressed some days. The only problem was that her job was not quite the one that she had left. She went in for a meeting with her Creative Director and came home rather distressed by the news that she had been sidelined back to copy-writing. 'But at least I'm on the same salary,' she said.

Privately he was quite relieved when she went back. The children were now his own. The kitchen was now his own and the domestic order of the home was his sole responsibility. He liked it.

The babies thrived, he thrived. Only Caroline seemed in any way put out by the new arrangement. By the fact that her previously domestically inept partner had been transformed – as if by magic – into the perfect house-husband.

When news of Richard's book had leaked out – his prospective literary agent was very indiscreet – he was immediately summoned to a meeting in the House. There, surrounded by men he had once held to be his friends as well as his colleagues, he was summarily informed that he would never find a publisher for the kind of book he wanted to write.

'You will find,' said the Shadow Heritage Secretary, 'that the establishment is still true blue. Any idea of your finding someone prepared to take on your nonsense is unrealistic.'

'Then I'll publish it myself and be damned!' said Richard, smiling brightly.

'Look, Richard,' said the Leader of the Opposition, 'I think we ought to do some sort of deal here. Something that will benefit us both. I'm not sure that we treated you terribly well at the time of your resignation. We value you. You are an asset to the nation.'

'I'd like to be,' said Richard, 'which is one of the reasons I wanted to do the book.'

'Richard, your friends and your family are worried about you. There is concern that your sudden departure from public life has had a detrimental effect on your health and your mental well-being.'

'But Michael,' interrupted Richard with a sincere smile, 'I've never felt happier in my life.'

'I simply cannot believe that a man of your calibre and your previous ambition can be happy digging a vegetable garden and playing with his children. I want you in the Lords. It would have happened eventually anyway, but since there is a certain urgency about all this I have drawn up an announcement today. The Prime Minister was perfectly in agreement that your service to your country should be recognized with a Life Peerage,' said the Leader of the Opposition.

'Was he?' said Richard suddenly interested. 'Was he really?'

'Yes,' came the terse reply.

It had never been Richard's intention to give in to persuasion on the book. But the idea of being in the Lords was rather attractive. In a quiet way he could do what he wanted in the Upper Chamber. They probably wouldn't notice if he walked across the floor in the Lords. And it would make Georgia happy. She had, bless her, always harboured a secret desire for a title.

'Well then, maybe that would be the best thing,' Richard said, smiling at the men he now counted as enemies rather than friends.

Before he left the House he rang Georgia.

'Hello,' she said.

'Is that Lady Georgia James of Peppard?' he said.

'Sorry, darling, is that you?'

'This is Lord Richard James of Peppard. Put a bottle of champagne in the fridge. I'll be home to celebrate in an hour and a half.'

By the time he got home the announcement of his elevation to the Lords had made the news – albeit as a small item some way towards the end of the bulletin. Georgia was flushed with pleasure and pride. Richard opened the bottle and gave each of the children a tiny glass.

'To us,' he said.

'To you, Daddy,' shouted Tamsin.

It gave him such pleasure to share this honour – for even though Richard had lost his political appetite and radically rethought his principles, some part of him still saw it as an honour – with the people he cared about most. Every advance he had made in life hitherto had been made alone or with some secretary, researcher or worthless political sidekick. He had never celebrated any of his career advancements with his wife and his children. He got quite tearful at suppertime – he had prepared the chicken pasta recipe Nick had given him – and he and Lady Georgia retired early to their happy, comfortable nuptial bed.

Not that it was going to change him, he thought the next day as he was digging up the earth in the new extended kitchen garden. He wasn't going to return to his old habits. Later that day as he was clearing up his study and tinkering with ideas for his maiden speech in the Lords (something shocking and socialist in substance, he thought), he came across the packet that Carl Burton had sent him from America. Curiosity got the better of him and when he went into Reading to pick up some manure for the garden he popped into one of those computer shops and asked them if they had anything compatible with the discs.

He was, to a great degree, computer illiterate. He had never managed to master even the little word processor he kept at home. But one of the staff sat with him, put the discs in the right place for him and attempted to make sense out of the jumble of figures, statistics and business plans that made up what appeared to be the data of a company called the Malestrom Foundation.

It made no sense to him, and not much more to the computer whizz-kid sitting alongside him.

'What does it mean?' he asked.

'Well, it seems to be a lot of scientific and medical data about some sort of drug. A drug that clearly has a huge market potential,' the man replied.

'What sort of drug? A dangerous drug or some kind of revolutionary medical cure drug – that's it, is it something to do with AIDS?'

'I'm no scientist, sir, but I think that it is some kind of behavioural drug. From this file here it sounds as if it is something like Prozac.'

Richard was none the wiser, although a vague feeling of unease came over him. There had to be some reason why Carl Burton had sent him this material and that message about secrecy. As a kind of safeguard, and because he was in some way frightened for Carl, he had fresh copies made of all the data.

On the way home he wondered if it had anything to do with that superdrug that Nicola Appleton had been working on. The one that had just got FDA approval. But if that was the case, why would Carl, her devoted partner, have acted in such an underhand way? Unless he was involved in some sort of industrial espionage. No matter, he thought as he drove the car up the drive and off towards the side entrance to the kitchen garden, in a few weeks Carl could explain it all himself. Nicola and he were coming to stay for a weekend to celebrate the European launch of that drug, Richard's elevation to the Lords and the arrival of the Evans twins. He only hoped, he thought as he laid the manure across his precious vegetables, that the mangetout and the spinach would be ready in time.

The move from the Featherwell Estate to the dilapidated Georgian house in Stockwell set more in motion than the Minter family. Some bright spark at the local estate agents recognized Steve and within a day of their move a picture of their new home – which looked rather grand from the exterior – was plastered over the pages of the newspapers beneath hostile headlines that referred to him as a 'fraudster', a 'conman', 'a convicted criminal' and a 'disgraced financier'.

Steve supposed that he had been lucky to escape media notice for so long. But he also guessed that if he had stayed where he was, safely tucked away in their cosy concrete flat, he could have carried on with his life without fear of press intrusion.

There was a terrible fuss at work. Journalists plagued the practice until, with some reluctance, Steve was discharged from his post. Worse, a few of his patients – those with a considerable dependence on his counselling skills – experienced a traumatic reaction to withdrawal from his care.

Of course, it all made for good copy. How was it possible, said the stern editorials in the daily press, for a man with a prison record for fraud and theft to be employed by the NHS as a crisis counsellor and therapist? How could a man convicted of cheating ordinary people out of their life savings be advising the disturbed and the troubled at the tax-payers' expense?

Annie took it all quite well, although it did rather mar her transfer to her new school. And Amanda was, of course, sorry about the whole business.

'But, darling, at least you'll have time to do the work on the house. And Joyce, Mavis and George won't be joining us for dinner every night,' she said gaily when she heard the news.

She really didn't understand him. She really had no idea how important his 'little job' (as she had referred to it) was to him. Not that he was ever likely to get a 'little job' like it ever again. One of the papers had done a big exposé of the 'counselling racket' revealing, rather worryingly, that Steve's qualification was not worth the paper it was written on and highlighting the threat that unqualified therapists were to vulnerable people. They even had a picture of Maria's stigmata and a detailed run-down of her medical history which, even with Steve's inside knowledge, provided frightening reading.

No one was more critical of Steve Minter than the man himself. Whereas in the past his ego and his optimistic nature had somehow prevented him from too much guilty self-examination, he was now plagued with self-doubt. He was horrified, now, when he looked back on what he had once been. Part of the *Sun*'s coverage had included a damning résumé of Steve's most unpleasant excesses. The kiss-and-tell story of the Page Three girl he had been involved with for over a year and, worse, the censored pictures taken of him – at the height of his fame and financial prominence – with two rubber-clad tarts. He had, he understood now, been out of his head with the effects of the drugs and the equally intoxicating influence that money and power had on him. Heaven knows why Amanda had stuck by him. Or, indeed, why she still did.

A few days after the newspapers had been filled with his story a woman turned up on his doorstep. At first he had no idea who she was, although clearly she was the kind of female he had associated with in his previous life.

'Stevie darling,' she said as she pushed her way past him and into the thankfully empty house.

'I'm terribly sorry,' he said in a hesitant voice. 'This might sound terribly rude but I really don't recall –'

'You don't remember your Sadie?' she said as she looked round the crumbling interior of the house.

Sadly, he suddenly realized he did remember Sadie M (as she was widely known). She had been one of the girls he had seen on a regular basis in the year or so before his downfall. She was, of course, a professional or rather a semi-professional. Adept at getting Steve not only other women for his adored threesomes but also the illegal substances that were so much a part of his old life.

She came over to him and put her arms round him.

'Sadie's got a little treat for Stevie,' she said as she took off her coat to reveal a brief tight Lycra frock, worn, it would seem, without underwear, 'for old times' sake and maybe for the sake of times to come.'

Steve felt physically revulsed. It wasn't that she was ugly. She was slim, young and blonde. But she had about her an aura – perhaps just a smell – of corruption that sickened him. It was almost as if she was a symbol of the life he had once led. He realized that she hadn't come here for 'old times' sake'. She had come here because she sensed, she smelled, financial gain. Or maybe she had been sent here by one of his old underworld contacts to establish some kind of relationship with him, to get him back into his old habits. And, he noticed as she reached into her handbag for a small compact, one habit in particular.

'No, Sadie, I don't do that any more,' he said, pushing the compact filled with white powder back at her and spilling some of it on the bare floorboards.

'Christ almighty, be careful with that,' she shrieked and then quickly regained her composure. 'If you want, I could get a friend, too. Kathy's still around. You used to love Kathy . . .'

'No, really. You don't understand, Sadie, I've put all

that behind me now. I'm a new man,' he said, edging away from her.

'Have you found God or something?' she asked with an expression of suspicion on her hard little face.

'No, I've found myself, Sadie. I was mad, deranged when you knew me. And besides I don't have any money any more. Even if I wanted to, I couldn't afford what you're offering me.'

'That's not the word on the street,' she said.

'It's true. I have lost my fortune, there's nothing left. But I have discovered something that has a greater meaning, a greater value than money.'

'Yeah? Tell me about it,' she said sarcastically.

'Sadie, the only thing that is important to me now – the thing that is worth more than my lost fortune and status – is my new-found love for my family.'

He wasn't sure whether or not she believed him, but eventually she left, looking, he thought, confused and disgruntled. It wasn't just the press, he thought after she had gone, who wouldn't let him forget his past. And it wasn't just the press who couldn't believe he was a re-formed man. He was sure that there would be other people like Sadie from his past who would keep creeping back, trying to drag him back down in the gutter.

He decided that day that since he was obviously not going to be allowed to attempt to make amends to society by involving himself in helping others he might as well go back to his roots. He threw himself into the work on the house.

In the early days of the Minter empire he had started out in rather this way. Buying run-down properties – often with sitting tenants – renovating them and selling them on. Curiously it seemed as if – at least in the streets of Stockwell – it was again possible to make a profitable business out of buying and selling property. But this time it was a little different. It wasn't profit that was motivating him now, but some kind of aesthetic need to make the tumbledown house into a beautiful home. The renovations seemed to have awoken some creative urge in him. He began to buy magazines such as *Homes and Gardens* and *House Beautiful* in order to gain new ideas. The satisfaction that he got from simple – if painstaking – tasks like stripping the fireplace in the main living room and discovering, beneath ten coats of paint, a perfect marble base was so much greater than any of the fleeting and sordid pleasures of the past. And all the more rewarding because, at last, the fruits of his own endeavours could be shared and savoured by his wife and child.

It took an awful lot of will-power for Carl to manage to make love to Nicola nowadays. His resentment of her, and indeed of women in general, made it especially difficult for him to do the things he knew she wanted. And to do them with that winning smile emblazoned on his face.

'Carl,' she said one night after they had made love in a rather unsatisfactory manner, 'is something wrong? Is there someone else?'

'Darling, how could you think such a thing?' he said, smiling tenderly at her and pulling her closer to him. 'It's just that I am a bit distracted at the moment. I want to get the right job in the right location.'

'Is it Seattle that's worrying you? You know, I wouldn't stand in your way, Carl. That was never what I intended. If you want the job, you must take it,' she said, concern flooding her face.

'No, it's not that. I couldn't accept an appointment that would take me away from you,' he said as sweetly as he could manage.

'Then what is it, darling? I sense that you are not, well, that you are not as content as you once were. Why is that?'

Carl began to panic, beads of sweat started to break out on his forehead. She mustn't for a moment suspect that something had gone wrong with her prototype of the perfect man. He had to think quickly. He had to come up with an explanation for his apparent lack of smiley Manifold contentment.

'Don't get cross with me, darling, will you?' he said sheepishly. 'It's just that you have been so caught up at work recently that I have been feeling kind of left out. I can't seem to get close to you any more. I thought . . . I thought . . .' He paused for effect. 'I thought that maybe you didn't want me any more. That I had out-grown my usefulness.' Fear of being found out helped to bring tears to his eyes and Nicola believed every word.

'Oh darling, darling, you are more important to me than anything. Even more important than Manifold. You do believe me, don't you?'

'Let's marry *now*, Nicola? Not next year but now, this week, or next week. Quietly before we go to Europe?' he asked with deep sincerity.

'Yes, yes, yes, Carl,' she said and they embraced. 'But darling, there is one thing,' she went on. 'I want to put up your dose, just a little. You'll feel better about every-thing then, more secure. I can't bear the thought of you being unhappy. Insecurity, emotional withdrawal, these are signals that the reduced dose is having an adverse effect on you.'

She went into the bathroom and pulled out a new packet of One-a-Week Manifold. Then she poured him a glass of water and handed him a big yellow capsule.

'You're right, of course,' he said, smiling at her and

taking the pill in his hand. 'I'll go back on the regular dosage for a while. Everything will be fine, then.'

He held the capsule in the side of his mouth and made a big show of swallowing some water. And when Nicola got up and went back in the bathroom he quickly spat it into his hand and pushed it down into his jeans pocket. Thankfully the capsule had not dissolved. Later when she had fallen into a deep sleep he got up and carefully emptied the contents of each of the capsules from the new box down the sink. Then he went back to bed and tried to sleep. Eventually he fell into a fitful sleep haunted by dreams of a world dominated by red-headed women followed around by slavish, smiling, submissive men.

SIXTEEN

Nick was looking forward to the weekend at Gallows Tree House for a number of reasons. Firstly he was longing to show off the twins – now four months old and, if he said so himself, absolutely adorable. Secondly he was looking forward to spending some time with Richard, Steve and Harry (now happily back with Juliet), and thirdly he was keen to get Caroline away for a bit of a break.

Her moods were beginning to more than worry him. Her boyish figure was now almost emaciated and the delicate face had a haunted look – hollow-cheeked and wide-eyed. More disturbing, though, was the fact that she showed no interest in the children. In fact, she seemed to almost shy away from them when she returned from work. And it was clear that she got no more joy from being out of the flat than she did from being in it.

Meanwhile Nick himself was flourishing. He now had a six-month contract with Granada to produce a set number of scripts at a decent salary. His domestic life meant that he had to fit his writing round naps and bedtimes, but for some reason he had an almost limitless energy. Of course, he couldn't have pulled it off without a strictly-adhered-to regime. He had made up a vast wallchart in the kitchen detailing all the activities that now made up his day. Even at their tender age the twins were already involved in a number of educational programmes – Tumble Tots, Water Awareness Lessons, Baby Brains (a revolutionary new flash-card system for the under-ones) and Tiny Tunes music sessions. Then there were the NCT teas where his group – well, actually Caroline's group, had she ever bothered to attend – got together once a week in one or other of their homes.

This afternoon Nick was hosting the tea. While Jack and Jillie had their lunchtime sleep he had baked a cake (a very simple sponge recipe that Richard had discovered) and done a quick hoover-up round the flat. He tried to repress the competitive instinct that made him, whenever he got together with the other 'primary carers' (half of whom were mothers and the other half nannies), compare the progress of the other babies with that of Jack and Jillie.

'How are Archie's solids going?' he would enquire. Or, 'Can Daisy pull her head up off the pillow yet?'

He was privately convinced that his children were more intelligent and physically advanced than the others. Particularly when you took into account the fact that they had been born so much smaller than the single babies in their set. Naturally he concealed these feelings at the teas. In fact, he was very popular and had acquired the complimentary nickname from the NCT group of Dynamo-dad.

'Is there anything you can't do, Nick,' said Sally, mother of Daisy. 'I bet you could even bake your own bread,' she added as she tucked into the cake.

'As a matter of fact, I did think I might have a go,' said Nick, smiling confidently back at his new friends.

'In between writing a script, doing the washing, ironing, shopping, cooking and bringing up the babies,' said Sally with an envious sigh.

In truth Nick didn't just value these teas for the surge of pride he got from the comparative progress of his own babies, he also valued the teas for the opportunity they gave him to share the minutiae of his life with like-minded individuals. He was only too aware that

Caroline was bored silly by the day-to-day details of the babies' lives and that even the boys (Harry, Steve and Richard) sometimes got a little irritated by his habit of talking about the teething problems (weight gains, innoculations, stool consistency, wheat allergies and so on) of the babies.

At 5 o'clock, as the tea was beginning to break up, Caroline came cautiously into the flat, a look of horror crossing her face when she caught sight of the assembled mothers, nannies and babies.

'Oh! we were just leaving,' said Sally, ducking quickly out with Daisy under one arm and her buggy under the other.

'Don't go on my account,' said Caroline rather coldly.

'No, no, we always go home at five,' Sally said.

When they had all gone and Nick had brought Caroline a fresh cup of tea he tried to make her talk.

'I didn't expect you home so early,' he said. 'It's a shame you didn't meet them all properly. They are a great bunch,' he added cheerily.

'Nick,' she began cautiously, 'are you sure you are really, really happy with all this?'

'Happier than I've ever been in my life, although if you had told me so this time last year I would have had you committed,' he said jovially.

'I mean, you wouldn't have CHOSEN this life, would you?' Caroline persisted.

'Well, no, but then I would have missed out on so much. I had no idea of the pleasure children can bring,' he said, adding, as he looked down on his now bulging stomach, 'You could say I have grown into it.'

'What I mean is if you could go back to the way you were before all this, before I was even pregnant, would you want to?'

'I'm confused, Caroline. What are you trying to say?'

'I mean, if it emerged that I had in some sort of way forced you into all this, would you hate me for it?'

'Well, in a way you did force me into all this, and no, I don't hate you for it. If you hadn't got pregnant, I would never have discovered the meaning of the word contentment. What is it, Caroline? Is something bothering you? Because I get the impression sometimes that if you could turn the clock back, you wouldn't have got pregnant in the first place.'

'Oh no, Nick, I don't think that. But I do believe that in a funny sort of way we have changed places. I don't know what I want any more and I don't see any way forward.' She broke down then and he comforted her.

'Never mind, love,' he said softly. 'It'll all be all right and we've got this weekend at Georgia's to look forward to. That'll cheer you up.' He smiled down at her even though, from the expression on her face, he was not sure that anything could cheer Caroline up.

Richard and Georgia were having their first row since he had given her the eternity ring on her birthday. As far as he could work out the only thing that could have upset her was the efficient way he had set about organizing the forthcoming weekend. He had planned everything – the seating arrangements, the meals, the bedroom allocation and the entertainment. And Georgia didn't like it. She had come down to his kitchen garden in the middle of the afternoon to criticize his carefully laid plans.

'It's no good putting Carl and Nicola in the blue room. They'll have to share a bathroom with Nick, Caroline and the twins,' she said. 'And I particularly don't want to have Juliet and Harry mooning around together on the same floor as Emily and Tamsin.'

'I think it's rather nice that they are so much in love. But perhaps you are just jealous,' said Richard.

'I have never, ever been jealous of my sister.' Georgia suddenly realized what she had said and quickly qualified her remark: 'I have hated her with a deep and abiding loathing for going to bed with you. But I can't say I've ever been jealous.'

'I thought we weren't going to talk about that EVER again,' said Richard in a wounded tone.

'We just did,' said Georgia. 'And another thing: I really think that the menu for Saturday dinner is far too bloody pretentious.'

'Pretentious? You think my cooking is pretentious now do you?'

'Well, yes I do. I mean, I'm all for your having a go at shepherd's pie and spaghetti bolognese, but some of the things that you have been serving since you bought that Marco Pierre White book are just ridiculous.'

'Harry said my *ris de veau rôti aux amandes* was sensational.' Richard was seriously upset by her suggestion.

'Harry is almost as absurd as you are nowadays.'

'What is that supposed to mean?'

'Well, you're always on the phone to him or Nick or Steve. And those silly suppers you have. What on earth do you find to talk about?' she asked.

'The meaning of life, relationships, food, children, each other – what did you think we talked about, Georgia? Football and rumping?'

'Well, I think it's unnatural. In fact, I think this whole thing has gone far too far,' she said, her face flushing with anger.

'What whole thing has gone too far?' Richard said.

'Richard, you are always under my feet,' Georgia said irritably. 'And, Richard, you get on my nerves. And, Richard, you have become a stupid pastiche of New

Man. Fussy, finicky, boring, gossipy, oversensitive and dull. It's really rather funny how you have exchanged one form of shitty behaviour in the House of Commons for another – being up to your ears in manure in your vegetable patch at home. Heavens, you shouldn't be Lord James of Peppard, you should be Lord Fucking MUCK. And the worst of it all, Richard, is that you are so damn fucking happy you can't keep that stupid grin off your face.'

'But isn't that what you always wanted?' he shouted. 'For us to live happily ever after together? For me to be at home more?'

'Well, I thought it was but I'm beginning to think that I was much mistaken,' she shrieked as she bent down and picked up a large marrow and threw it at him.

'Just keep out of my kitchen garden,' he screamed at her as she walked back to the house.

'Just keep out of my kitchen,' she spat at him as she went in through the back door and slammed it shut behind her.

Richard fought back the tears. It was ridiculous how much she could hurt him nowadays. In the past, perhaps because he never really listened to what she was saying, her most vitriolic insults would have just washed over his head. Now they resulted in the tears that washed down his face. What was happening to him? Why was he so damn EMOTIONAL nowadays? He simply couldn't bear it when Georgia was cross with him. Already he felt guilty for being so argumentative with her. Already he was wondering how he could undo the damage, repair the rift that seemed to have opened up between them. Then he had an idea. He got the trug and carefully picked an arrangement of his finest veg. They looked a little like a Kenneth Turner window display.

Sheepishly he made his way to the back door, gently

tapped and went in. Georgia was standing with her back to him on the phone to someone, Amanda, he guessed.

'I can't go on with it, I really can't. I just wish I'd never done it,' she was saying into the receiver. There was a pause while whoever was on the other end of the line made some comment. 'You mean you're having doubts, too?' She turned round and caught sight of Richard smiling in an apologetic way. 'Look, we'll talk about it at the weekend. I hated the way things were before, but I'm not sure I like this much either. Anyway, sweetheart, I'll see you at the weekend and all news then. Richard has just come in. Bye then.' She put down the receiver.

'Who was that, darling? And what was it all about?' enquired Richard in placatory tones.

'It was Amanda, Richard. And what it was all about has nothing to do with you,' she said sternly. 'Well, it has and it hasn't. By which I mean that it would be better for all of us if you didn't know what we were talking about.'

He presented her with the trug of vegetables.

'What's this for?'

'I thought they looked rather chic and, more to the point, would make a wonderful potage for tonight. Or maybe a centre piece for the weekend?' he said brightly in his eagerness to win back her approval. 'My goodness, look at the time, I'd better get going or I'll be late for the school run.'

Grabbing the car keys, he kissed her briefly on the cheek and walked to the door. When he glanced in through the window he could have sworn he saw her pick up one of his prize courgettes and bite the head of it before dumping the entire contents of the trug in the rubbish bin.

★

When Harry had returned from Cornwall in such a terrible emotional state he had been too frightened to call Juliet. But the boys – well, Richard mostly – had convinced him that she would welcome him back with open arms. And indeed at first she had. She had even, without a word from him, opened her arms to him wearing one of those flimsy frocks and smelling of that intoxicating rose scent. They had gone straight to bed. In fact, much of their post-Annabel relationship was conducted in bed. A little too much, truth be known, for Harry.

For while Juliet appeared to have forgiven him for his strange infidelity ('Imagine it,' she had said to Stella, 'Harry running off with a fat, coarse woman ten years older than me!'), she simply wouldn't TALK about it. What is more, every time Harry attempted a proper conversation with her, some in-depth discussion of the way things were going and what they both wanted from life, she would initiate some sort of sexual activity.

'There's more to life than sex, Juliet,' he said a little irritably one day.

'Darling,' she said with a throaty laugh, 'there never used to be. At least for you.'

'I may as well tell you that I intend to divorce Annabel,' he said carefully.

'Well, not before time, Harry.'

'And although I am not in a position to ask you formally, I very much hope that, in time, you will become my wife.'

'Harry, oh darling, you want to get married?' she asked eagerly.

'I want a family, Juliet. I want to settle down properly and be the kind of man I wasn't all those years with Annabel. And there's something else: I think I ought to get to know Sam a little better. When can we see him?'

'Well, I suppose we could go down to his school on

Saturday and take him out to lunch. To be honest with you, Harry, I think it's rather disruptive seeing him during term time. But if you really want to . . .'

'I do. If we are going to be together as a family, it is important that he approves and is a part of that family.'

Their visit wasn't terribly successful. Sam was, as Juliet had so often said, a difficult and rather un-attractive boy ('It's the Burrows side of the family coming out in him,' she would say defensively to Geor-gia), and he had never much liked Harry (or for that matter, Harry suspected, his mother).

There had been a lot of cases, recently, of furious cus-tody battles between estranged parents and their chil-dren. Instances of daughters and sons being snatched away from one doting parent by the other. Sam's case was rather the reverse. Neither of his parents seemed to want to be with him. He had spent the whole summer with his stiff and formal paternal grandparents and most term time weekends – even exeats – on his own at school. His Aunt Georgia had invited him to stay with her for half term, but even this gesture, he thought, was pro-voked more by pity than affection. Besides his cousins, out of sight of their parents, bullied him mercilessly.

He was, therefore, somewhat confused by the sudden interest of Harry and Juliet (who was evidently attempt-ing to look more of a 'mother' in that long, drab, floral frock). In fact, Sam quickly discovered, Juliet was making more than just a visual attempt to be more of a 'mother'. She even kissed him when he got in the car.

'Yuk,' he said, 'you stink of something awful.'

Harry had laughed in the way that adults do when they are trying too hard to appeal to a child. Sam thought the whole outing rather sinister. They had lunch in a restaurant in the small market town near his school. But the conversation was stilted and awkward.

'So, Sam, are you good at sport?' asked Harry, smiling warmly at him.

'No,' he said.

'A bit of an egghead, then, eh?' Harry enquired with a laugh.

'No,' he said.

'Well, what do you excel at? Every boy has something he's good at or likes. Trains, stamp collecting, cars . . .?'

'Insects,' said Sam.

'Insects? A collection?'

'I collect them and either pin them or keep them in a formula of preservative. I've got over a hundred different species of domestic spiders.' Sam's face, for once, was showing some expression other than boredom.

'Well then, we can go to the Natural History Museum together,' said Harry eagerly.

'OK,' said Sam, not quite sure whether Harry's interest was feigned or sincere.

'In fact, if you are allowed out on Saturdays I could pick you up next week and take you there. How would that be?'

'Hopeless, Harry,' said Juliet quickly. 'We're at Gallows Tree House for the weekend.'

'Well then, Sam should be with us. Do you think your housemaster would let you out for the weekend?'

Juliet darted a warning look to Harry, but he ignored it.

'I've never asked before,' said Sam, flushing a little, 'but maybe if Mother was to write a letter . . . I know the other boys go home on non-exeat weekends,' he finished rather pitifully.

'That settles it, then. Juliet, you'll write a letter and we can detour on our way to Henley and pick up Sam. It will be a real family weekend,' said Harry, smiling benignly at Juliet and her son.

When they had dropped Sam back at school and were on their way back to town Juliet began to sulk.

'You know, Harry, it would have been so much easier next weekend without Sam. He doesn't get on with his cousins, I don't often get the opportunity to be with Nicola and I really don't want to spend all my time down there mollycoddling my son.'

'But Juliet, you have never mollycoddled your son in his entire life. Perhaps it's time you did. The poor mite is in danger of turning into one of those withdrawn, solitary types that end up fitting the psychological profile of serial killers,' said Harry.

'How dare you say something like that, Harry. You've no idea how hard it was for me when my marriage broke up and I was left with that boy. Besides there is no danger of him ending up with psychological problems. He already has his own psychotherapist.'

'He WHAT?'

'He's been seeing a psychotherapist since he was six. He's really very together. I simply will not let you try and lay a guilt trip about Sam on me. I did my best. He has problems that have nothing whatsoever to do with me.'

'Darling, darling,' said Harry sympathetically, 'I'm not blaming you for his problems. I'm simply saying that he needs a father figure in his life and a little more attention. Heavens, it's probably my fault that he is so isolated. I know that in the past I never took any notice of him.'

'In fact, Harry, it was you who suggested I send him away to school,' said Juliet. 'If I remember, at the time – and it was in those first idyllic months of our affair – you said that it would make a man of him. That boys shouldn't become overly dependent on their mothers.'

'God, did I? How shaming,' Harry said, concern flooding his face. 'The thing is, I've never given children much thought. And when I saw Amber so indifferent to me, so grown up and lost, I realized how terribly irresponsible I have been all my life. I want to make it up to Sam. And I want us to have more children, darling. God, you should see Nick with his twins. He's marvellous, he has such a deep bond with those babies it's really moving. I've changed, Juliet. I really want to commit, to put down roots, to be a good father and a devoted husband.'

Juliet went very quiet. Harry imagined that she was rather taken aback, touched, by his emotional outburst. He looked across at her and smiled.

'Have I shocked you, darling?'

'No, no,' she said, regaining her composure.

'I think we should live together all the time now. I'll put my flat on the market and move in with you until we find somewhere else. In the country, don't you think? Children should grow up in the country.'

She still didn't respond. She sat beside him, playing nervously with the rings on her fingers.

'What is it, darling? What's wrong? Isn't that what you always wanted?'

'It's just a bit sudden, Harry. I mean, a couple of months ago it was difficult to get you to commit to staying the night with me and all of a sudden you want to live happily ever after with me. Just like that.'

'So now who's frightened of commitment?' he said, smiling at her.

'It's not that Harry, of course it isn't,' she said. 'It's just so much to take in so quickly. You are crowding me. And I'm not sure I'm really that much of a country girl.'

'Oh darling, you've lived in that city for too long. And what with all that terrible business with Mark Burrows you've forgotten how to trust a man. But you can rely on me now. I'll always be there for you. I'll support you financially and emotionally.'

'But you know me, Harry, I'm really a very independent woman,' Juliet said with a nervous laugh. 'I don't think that I could ever be dependent on a man.'

'Not on a man, Juliet, on your husband,' he said confidently as he drove up outside his London flat. 'There's no time like the present, darling. Come up with me and help me pack up everything I need and I'll move in lock, stock and barrel tonight.'

'Darling, you know I've got to be up early tomorrow. I've got all that paper work to do before the auditors come in on Monday. Give me a couple of days to clear some cupboard space and then move in after our weekend with Georgia. How would that be?'

Momentarily the smile faded from his face.

'I want a new start, Juliet, now,' he pleaded.

'Look, Harry, it's just not convenient tonight. I'll get a cab home from here. You start sorting out your things. I'll speak to you tomorrow.' She kissed him on the cheek, dashing out of the car before he could stop her.

It was really, really silly but there were tears in his eyes as he watched her hail a taxi and disappear into the night.

'Ridiculous man,' he said to himself as he made his way upstairs. 'We've got the rest of our lives together. One night won't make any difference.'

When he got in he rang her and left a tender message on her answerphone and another on her mobile voicemail. When he hadn't heard half an hour later he rang again, worried that something might have happened to her. By the time he finally got through to her, at 11 p.m., he was almost hysterical.

'Juliet! Where have you been?' he screamed when he

realized it was not a recorded message but the woman herself.

'Harry, what on earth are you on about?' Juliet replied irritably. 'I've just played back my messages and they are all from you. For goodness' sake, I only left you a couple of hours ago. What do you want?'

'It's just that I was worried when I didn't get a reply. The most awful things were running through my head. And I wondered if you might be with someone else,' he said, his voice shaking with emotion.

'Harry, I popped into the office to pick up the accounts just as I said when we parted. My God, I'm not sure I can cope with this level of interest.'

'But you said you were going straight home in a cab. And you said it wasn't convenient for me to move in tonight. You're not telling me the truth, Juliet.'

'Harry, I'm tired, I've got a lot to think about. If you don't mind, I'm going to have a bath and get to bed now. Alone, Harry. As a matter of fact, I'm really getting to appreciate sleeping alone,' Juliet said shortly.

'I can't believe you said that, Juliet. Do you mean you don't want me to move in?'

'Look, Harry, as I just said I'm tired. I don't want some detailed debate on the rest of our lives right now. I want to go to sleep, OK?'

'No, it's not OK. You can't say something like that and expect me to say it's OK. The only time you really respond to me nowadays is when we are having sex. You never want to talk about the rest of our lives,' he whined.

'Harry, you are being absurd and overemotional about this. I'm going to put the phone down and have that bath and go to sleep. OK?'

'No, I said it's not OK. I want to talk about our relationship. Now.'

'And I want to go to bed. Good night, Harry,' she said, putting the phone firmly back on the receiver.

Harry rang her straight back.

'I said good night, Harry,' she said, slamming the receiver down again.

He rang again and this time got the answerphone: 'I'm sorry I can't get to the phone right now, but if you leave your name and number I'll get back to you as soon as I can.'

Even her mobile was blanking him tonight: 'Sorry, caller, but the Vodaphone you have called is switched off.'

He was stupid, stupid, stupid. Why did he have to ruin everything? Why did he go that bit too far? What was wrong with him, why did he need this constant reassurance from Juliet? Why had he become so very intense about his relationships? Why did his formerly rather perfect existence now look so dull, so lonely and so utterly, utterly pointless? Going into the kitchen, he opened the freezer and took out a pack of Snickers ice-cream bars and ate them one after the other. He wasn't hungry, he had never been the kind of person that took comfort from food, but tonight the only thing that could stop the depression and the exhausting self-examination was ice cream.

There wasn't a great deal in Harry's fridge or freezer. He hadn't been caught – as the other boys had – by the cooking thing. He still ate out most of the time so there was no reason to stock up at home. And he had never had a sweet tooth so there was very little to satisfy this strange new need for high-sugar, maximum-calorie consumption.

At the back of the bottom shelf in the freezer he found two cartons of Häagen-Dazs that were, he thought, several years old (left over, actually, from a sexy shoot he had done in which a model – he couldn't remember her name – had been photographed bathing in the stuff). When he had finished them he ate the remains of an old box of chocolates he found in the cupboard and half a packet of chocolate Hob-nobs. Finally, feeling more nauseous than he had ever been before in his life, he collapsed on his bed and fell into a sad, sickly, sleep.

Although Steve still quietly missed life on the Feather-well Estate and his counselling work, he had become more and more engrossed in the transformation of their new house. He had performed a positive miracle and gained a great deal of satisfaction in getting back to what he called 'brass tacks'. In putting in a new damp course, rewiring, revamping the heating and, finally, in choosing and carrying out the decorating (he was enor-mously drawn to soft peach tones and a range of pastel Designer's Guild wallpapers). He had even embarked on an upholstery course and had managed to recover an armchair and make some cunningly draped curtains.

Of course, Steve had always had what his mother called an 'artistic flair', but he had never made much use of it before and this new area of creativity delighted him. And he adored seeing so much of Annie. He had even befriended some of the other mothers at the school, al-though they didn't quite match the estate mums. Their problems were more middle class and they were not quite so keen to confide in him over a cup of coffee.

He was thrilled by the reaction of his friends and family. Harry had already promised him the commis-sion to 'do' the house he planned to buy with Juliet. Even Amanda readily admitted that he had a wonderful eye for interior design. His only worry was that his new-found talent and its possible commercial success might lure him back into his old ways. He recognized that if he applied himself to what he was currently doing, if he finished this house, sold it for a profit and bought another in need of renovation, he could probably make quite a bit of money. Nothing like what he had made during the property boom in the eighties, of course, but there were opportunities, and if nothing else Steve could see an opportunity.

And there were other compensations for having abandoned his idea of doing good works in favour of home improvement. It had made Amanda and Annie happy. Charity, he had reluctantly decided, probably did start at home. And even if he wasn't contributing anything to those less fortunate than himself, he was, at least, a more considerate husband, a more devoted father and, most peculiar of all, an inspired homebody.

One day, as he was carefully stencilling Annie's room (with a pattern of fairytale castles he had made himself), he had an unexpected phone call. Nowadays the only people who regularly rang him were Harry, Richard or Nick. But when he reached the phone it was a different yet familiar male voice on the other end of the line.

'Steve Minter!' the man said, obviously expecting instant recognition.

'Yes,' said Steve cautiously. 'Who is this?'

'It's me – Johnny Britten.'

'Johnny? Where are you?'

'I got off, Steve. Walked free from the Old Bailey this afternoon. I'm celebrating. Will you come and join me?'

Steve didn't know whether to weep or laugh. He had, prior to his release from Ford, wanted to hear from this man above all others. But now he was not sure he cared.

'I'm downstairs at Mezzo. Everyone's here, Steve. Come and join us, it's like the old days.'

'I'm not sure I can right now, Johnny, but maybe we could get together some other time,' he said stiffly.

'OK, mate. We've a little unfinished business. It's all in hand. You only have to say the word.'

'Do I, Johnny? I didn't get that impression when I got out of Ford and discovered that you hadn't kept your word about looking after Amanda,' said Steve coldly. 'All those years I kept you afloat and you didn't even have the decency to look out for her and Annie.'

'I tried, Stevie, I tried. But she wouldn't listen to me. She wouldn't even take my calls. She wanted to do things her own way and in the end I gave in. Look, we can't talk about all this over the phone. We'll meet – tomorrow lunch?'

They arranged to meet in one of Johnny's favourite haunts the next day. Steve felt completely confused about what he now wanted. He spent the rest of that day furiously working on the petit-point tapestry he was making as a surprise for Amanda while conducting a ruthless inventory of his life so far.

He didn't tell anyone – let alone his wife – about the call because he wasn't sure what he was going to do. He didn't really want any part of the monies that Johnny had carefully stashed away for him. Wealth would, of course, put him back in control of his life. But he didn't much care for the way in which the money had been accumulated. And he was simply terrified of falling back into the decadence of his past. Besides, how would it look to the rest of the world? He kept thinking in newspaper headlines. All those people who had put their life savings in Minter Investments. All those people who had lost out because of his own irresponsibility and greed. And anyway, taking on the money would probably mean having to live abroad and possibly losing Amanda and Annie, something he couldn't countenance.

But he met up with Johnny the next day and signed the necessary documents that would release – into an offshore account – his ill-gotten gains. It wasn't a great deal of money – nothing like the amount he had been worth before Black Wednesday – but it was more than the wildest dreams of most people, and particularly those people who had invested in his company.

Of course, he had no intention of doing anything about it until he had talked to Amanda, and it took him several weeks to get his courage up to do so. He knew that any mention of the fabled missing Minter millions would infuriate and possibly alienate her from him.

'Amanda?' he finally said one night after a particularly intense bout of hair-brushing and love-making (which had followed the presentation of his beautifully executed and antique-framed petit-point tapestry bearing the inscription 'Home Sweet Home', now hanging proudly in the hall).

'Yes, darling?'

'Supposing I suddenly acquired some money. Supposing I won the lottery. What would you do?'

'Well, at one time, not so long ago, it would have been the answer to my dreams. When you were inside in the early days and I was struggling to earn a living and look after Annie I would have grabbed the cheque and screamed with joy,' she said, looking carefully at him.

'But not now?' he asked.

'Well, now I've got used to earning my own money – let's face it, darling, I had no conception of what money was about in the old days – and I think it would take away a lot of my pleasure suddenly to be rich again. I rather like the thought that in a couple of weeks I'll have earned enough money to buy that button-back chair we saw at the weekend. I rather like the kind of deadly middle-class values I seem to have acquired. I now understand about the work ethic. It's enormously satisfying, particularly for a woman like me. Someone who was only ever a trophy wife. The fact that I can earn some money while you do up the house is just so, so good.' She gave a gentle laugh. 'And there's another reason I wouldn't want that money – the lottery or the Minter millions – I think I might lose you – my trophy husband – and I don't think I could bear that,' she added, avoiding his eyes.

'So there's no going back for you?' he said, kissing her gleaming hair.

'No, not for me. But what about you? Would you want to go back?'

'Me? Well, I can't say that I'm much taken with these middle-class values of yours, but I am acutely aware of the old working-class values that I lost in that crazy time. I think I'd give it away. Set up some sort of charitable trust and administer it myself,' he said, smiling at her.

They looked at one another for a long time.

'But that wouldn't be legal, Steve,' she said softly.

'You mean, as a convicted criminal I wouldn't be able to front any charitable trust?'

'No, Steve, I don't mean that. I mean the money isn't yours to give away. It's the property of the official receiver. It belongs with the people you took it from.'

He had always underestimated Amanda. She had, of course, heard about Johnny Britten's acquittal and had guessed that the money he was talking about was not a wild lottery fantasy but an awful and oppressive reality.

'What do we do?' he asked.

'We give it back. You go to the press – to someone sympathetic – and you tell them your story.'

'Do you think so?'

'Yes.'

'And then what?'

'And then, Steve, we get on with the rest of our lives.'

'But what will I do?'

'After a public stunt like that you could do anything. Anything, that is, but go back to being the old Steve Minter. You could write your memoirs, you could go to art school, you could develop this flair you have for interior design.'

'Do you really think so?'

'I know so,' she said, kissing him. 'My God, Steve, we are so much wealthier now than we ever, ever were.'

'I was thinking today,' he said as they lay in each other's arms, 'that I'd like to have a go at making one of those traditional American quilts for the bed. In rich reds and pinks with maybe just a touch, here and there, of yellow.'

Carl was, he supposed, now two people. He was the smiling, sweet, sensitive Manifold man when he was with Nicola, and when he was alone, in the sleazy streets he prowled, he was the reverse of everything Nicola loved. Of course, it was all her fault. If she hadn't put him on that damn drug, if she hadn't meddled with his psyche, he wouldn't have started all this business with the girls he picked up. He saw now that when Nicola had described him as an animal at the outset of the programme she had meant it. For he had, he now thought, been treated like those poor dumb animals that are used for cosmetic or medical research. He was like one of those chimps they had picked to send into space. He was the ultimate animal experiment.

Of course, she had managed to house-train him – turn him into Richard's idea of a 'fancy new house-pet' – but she never really saw him as anything other than an animal. Christ, she saw all men as animals. The whole concept of Manifold was all about changing the 'manimal' into a controlled and docile beast. He knew now that, however passionate she had seemed about her relationship with him, what really drove Nicola was her mission. To make a world of Manifold men.

She thought she was so clever, so superior to the creature she had moulded into her ideal mate. But she had made one very big mistake. She had let her animal – her tame little manimal – out of his cage. And when you gave the animal the key to his cage you were asking for trouble.

It had became a pattern. In the last few months Carl had taken to picking up at least one girl a fortnight. Always red-headed, always young and always a street girl.

It amazed him how long it had taken the police and the papers to notice that pattern. But now he had been given a name, in the classic style of serial killers. Now he was known in the media as the 'Red Avenger'. He was very careful. He had to be. Tonight would be the last time before their trip to Europe, maybe even the last time ever, and he must not make any mistakes. This time the girl wasn't really a redhead, although she had that pale freckly complexion that went with the hair. Perhaps, he thought as he negotiated the terms, she had dyed her red hair brown in order to escape the 'Red Avenger'.

They went, as he suggested, separately to the room she rented. He didn't prolong the moment. He didn't, as he had at the beginning, take all night to reach his particular climax. In fact, lately it had got so that the fucking was secondary to the other thing. He was only with her about an hour from start to meticulous finish. No one saw him arrive and no one saw him leave.

Nicola was asleep when he got home. Red hair streaming across the pillow. He woke her gently and entered her quickly. The only time he could effectively and easily fuck her nowadays was immediately after he had been with one of his street girls. The secret knowledge of what he had just done – of what her Manifold model man was capable of doing – gave him the erotic charge he needed in order to give Nicola what she wanted.

'Oh Carl,' she cried out when she came. 'Oh Carl!'

SEVENTEEN

Richard and Georgia passionately patched up their row the evening before everyone was due to arrive at Gallows Tree House. They had made love the entire night, something that Richard rather regretted since there was so much work to be done that day and he now felt tense and tired. Not that he regretted their reunion. Rather, he had carefully and sensitively organized it. Cooked a delicious dinner (something simple and unpretentious), flattered her a lot and presented her with a little gift in order to create the right mood for a long and meaningful talk. Their truce had been achieved by the careful division of both the house and the forthcoming weekend. Richard was responsible for downstairs – flower arrangements, seating plans and so on, while Georgia took responsibility for upstairs – bedroom allocation and so forth. Likewise Richard was to do all the cooking and organizing on the Saturday and Georgia on the Sunday. Friday-night supper – when the Evanses and the Minters would arrive – would be a shared responsibility. Nicola and Carl and Juliet and Harry were arriving early Saturday morning.

Richard was rather ashamed to realize that he was experiencing a growing feeling of competition with his wife. He had made a particular effort with the flowers and the table arrangements, creating, he thought, a highly original centre piece that included a great many of his kitchen-garden vegetables. What is more, his starter for the casual Friday-night supper was rather more impressive than Georgia's main course.

Richard's excitement at the thought of entertaining

his close friends and their partners made him a little jumpy. Nick and Steve – who had both cooked 'boys' suppers in the last few months – were hard acts to follow. He had even made a special effort with his clothes. Well, for some time he had been experiencing a need to express his new personality with some new clothes. He had spent so many years in Savile Row suits and Turnbull & Asser shirts that his new look – Ralph Lauren polos, jeans and Timberland shoes – seemed wonderfully liberating and different.

He had grown his hair, too. It was curious but he could swear that his previously thinning hair (trimmed at Trumper's every six weeks) was thicker and more luxuriant. That little bald patch that he had fought to hide for the last five years appeared to be covered in a new layer of thick, healthy hair. He had always had a secret desire to have longer hair, but he had been such a deeply conventional man for most of his life that he had never given in to the dream. One of the things he had always envied about Harry was the fact that in his profession long hair and casual clothes were acceptable. And now that his own shiny, salt-and-pepper locks were nestling over his collar he got a strange buzz from throwing his head back and feeling the hair bounce back. He had even toyed with the idea of a pony-tail but dismissed it because it would look like an upper-class, middle-aged affectation, particularly since his elevation to the Lords (he didn't want to look like the poor man's Marquis of Bath or as if he was just copying Harry).

Not that Richard had ever been or now was a vain man. It was just that he took a greater interest in the way he looked and had, as a result, invested in a number of male cosmetics that he might previously have regarded as, well, sissy. He had the entire Daniel Galvin men's hair-care range; he had the Aramis skin-care kit; he had several new bottles of aftershave and, as well as his B12 tablet (Georgia still made him take one of the big yellow capsules a week), he now swallowed a variety of vitamin pills that had become an important part of his current quest for self-improvement.

Indeed, Georgia had made a little joke about the fact that the cabinet in his bathroom now contained as many lotions and potions as her own. But she seemed to like his new look. Especially the hair. It was, she said, a throwback to their youth. Longer hair, for them both, had always symbolized a sexy sort of rebellion that neither had quite achieved when they were young. She liked the look of his body, too. For his birthday she had bought him membership at their local health club – the place that had helped make such a change in her own shape – in order that he might take some exercise.

Most mornings they would go into the gym together, quietly admiring the new firmness they saw in each other's legs, arms and torsos as they sweated and toiled their way round the machines. And now, despite his growing interest in food, Richard was, if he said so himself, a fine figure of a man (or, as Georgia said 'a fine figure of a New Man'). He was enormously relieved that day when the first of their guests arrived – Nick, Caroline and the twins in their newly acquired Volvo Estate with its in-built baby seats and state-of-the-art safety features. It took nearly half an hour to unload the baby accessories and luggage. Nick had even brought – in a special cool bag – enough of the organic home-made baby food he religiously prepared to last the whole weekend.

Then there were changing mats, two bouncing cradle chairs, two travel cots, an assortment of educational toys, a baby alarm, the double buggy and, as a concession to the fact that they were away, a big pack of Pampers disposable nappies (Nick had stuck to his environmentally friendly principles and used, at home, old-fashioned towelling nappies). All this took up so much space in the vast car that there was scarcely room for the three suitcases (two for the babies and one smaller carry-all for their parents).

Caroline and Georgia disappeared into the little downstairs sitting room (Georgia's parlour, Richard called it) for a chat whilst Richard and Nick unpacked everything and cooed over Jack and Jillie.

'Caroline couldn't wait to see Georgia,' Nick said by way of explanation of her quick abandonment of her children.

'Of course,' said Richard sympathetically. 'But perhaps when she relaxes a bit she'll show a little more interest in the babies,' he added encouragingly.

Nick had, on more than one occasion, confided in Richard. Indeed, the 'boys' (as they now constantly referred to one another) were only too aware of the problems Nick was having in interesting his wife in the day-to-day life of their children.

'Sometimes,' said Nick despairingly as he changed Jack's nappy, 'I feel like a single parent. With Caroline it's just work, work, work. It's almost as if we don't exist.'

'Well, you know, some parents take longer than others to adjust to the whole business. I know people who couldn't relate to their children until they were two or three. Hell, Nick, listen to me – I'm someone who didn't relate to their children until they were much older than that. I didn't really enjoy being with Tamsin, Emily and Tom until this year.'

'Yes, well, that might be perfectly normal for a man – particularly a man with the kind of workload you used to have – but it's unnatural in a woman. Besides it isn't just the twins she doesn't relate to – it's me.'

'How do you mean?'

'Christ, Richard, we haven't had sex since the babies were born.'

'Well, I have to say that is totally normal behaviour in a woman. In a mother, that is. I know that Georgia wasn't remotely interested in having sex after Tom was born,' Richard said thoughtfully. 'Although maybe a lot of that had to do with the way I behaved towards her,' he added, a spasm of shame overwhelming him at the memory of his brief fling with Juliet.

'But we didn't have sex before they were born either. Except of course for the very odd occasion. Like the conception – although I don't even remember that. I'm not an unreasonable man, Richard, don't get me wrong,' Nick said earnestly. 'I'm not driven mad by sexual frustration. I'm not having three-in-a-bed fantasies or nudging up to strange women in the park. I just want to be wanted. By Caroline. Does that sound strange?'

Richard muttered something reassuring.

'I just have this feeling that she can no longer see me as a sexual being. It's almost as if she just sees me as the father of her children. And, you know, maybe I have become a bit of a drudge. Maybe I have lost sight of the old Nick. The one that used to like making love in front of the bathroom mirror. I know I've put on weight – I'm two stone heavier since the twins – and sometimes I wake up in the night and I wonder if perhaps she hasn't found someone else. If she hasn't met someone more dynamic and attractive than me at the office,' Nick said, a little mournfully.

It was certainly true that Nick looked a little podgy and worn down, Richard thought. Not that he had ever been that well turned out. But now he had a slightly dishevelled look. His hair was unkempt, he looked as if he hadn't shaved for a couple of days and there was an unmistakable aroma of baby sick about him. Although the twins were immaculate – now wearing matching outfits in pink and blue – there was something neglected and even slightly slovenly about their father. Not surprising really – Richard looked at his friend and noted the stains on his shirt and jeans – when he was single-handedly bringing up two babies and managing to meet his quota of scripts for The Street.

'Life is too short to stuff a mushroom, Nick,' Richard said with great bonhomie. 'What you need is some time alone – away from the twins. You ought to take her away for a weekend, make an effort to be the old Nick. Try and trigger some nostalgic passion in her. Dress up. You know the kind of thing. Agony aunts are always suggesting it, aren't they? Rekindle the old sexual fantasies.'

'But I can't remember what our old sexual fantasies were. Apart from the bathroom mirror. And I certainly couldn't bear to leave the twins for a weekend. I mean, they need me so much right now. Separation, at this stage, is out of the question.'

'Well, why not make your move this weekend and pounce on her here. There's a big mirror in your en-suite bathroom,' said Richard brightly.

'But I'd look so awful in the bathroom mirror now,' Nick said, looking down at his pot belly and his bulging waist. 'God, I'm sorry, Richard, I'm being an absolute bore,' he added quickly, regaining his smiley self. 'What's been going on here? How are you and Georgia – happy as ever?'

'Like all couples we have our ups and our downs.' Richard picked up Jillie and cradled her gently in his arms. 'As a matter of fact, this weekend it is literally our ups and downs. She's in charge of upstairs and I'm in charge of downstairs. She seems to resent my involvement in the running of the house. I suspect that while she claims to adore the fact that I have become so – well – so home-based she doesn't much like my invading her territory. God, this baby thing is more blissful than I can remember,' he said as he received a joyous smile from Jillie.

'Why don't you and Georgia have another child?' asked Nick.

'Maybe, maybe. It would be nice to be as involved as you have been. To really bond with a child. But I'm not sure Georgia would agree.'

Rather reluctantly they made their way down to join their wives, each carefully carrying one baby.

'Caroline,' said Nick sweetly, 'it's time for the twins' tea. Why don't you come and help me feed them?'

'Oh, Nick darling, you know how much better you are with a clear run. I'm so terribly clumsy, and Georgia and I are having such a lovely chat.'

'Yes, Nick,' added Georgia. 'Richard would love to help you. Wouldn't you, Richard? Perhaps the babies would like a little of your starter – that unpretentious little *moussette de saumon fumé*,' she said, raising her eyebrows at Caroline.

'Oh no, I've got all their food with me. I've got them on a rather strict regime of organic vegetables – no salt, no sugar, no additives. Just pure goodness,' said Nick with another beatific smile.

'Well, Nick, I'm sure Richard could help you there, too. He grows his own veg now. In fact, you two must have so much to talk about nowadays – marrows, courgettes, runner beans and the meaning of life,' Georgia said with a mocking laugh. 'Meanwhile Caroline and I are going to open a nice bottle of Bollinger.'

★

When the Minters arrived, some half an hour later, they were received by a hysterical and slightly tipsy Georgia who sent Annie and Steve 'up to find the boys' and took Amanda off back into the parlour.

'Richard and Nick are bathing the babies, Steve,' she said. 'And I'm sure that another pair of strong male hands won't go amiss. Tamsin, Emily and Tom are in their sitting room, Annie darling. They are so looking forward to seeing you.'

Steve was rather shocked by the offhand way in which Georgia had dismissed them but he wandered upstairs and took Annie to the children's den and then, through a process of opening and closing most of the doors on the first floor, finally located his own friends. Richard was giving Jillie her bottle while Nick gave Jack his. The twins smelled of sweet Johnson's baby soap and powder and were wearing matching his'n'hers (blue and pink) babygros. Nick held a finger to his mouth to stop Steve from saying anything and motioned him to sit on the bed while the babies finished their bottles. Presently, when the babies had been winded and settled in their travel cots, the men made their way downstairs.

'Where shall I plug in the baby alarm?' Nick asked Richard anxiously. 'Somewhere where I'll be able to hear them if they wake or need me.'

In the end they decided on the kitchen since Georgia was now so tiddly – the three women were half-way through another bottle of bubbly – that it looked very much as if it would be down to Richard to cook and serve the food that night (not just his precious starter).

In fact, the weekend, as far as Richard was concerned, was in danger of turning into a disaster. Georgia didn't seem to have given a thought to the children and he found himself, before he cooked the adults' dinner, making a quick spaghetti bolognese for Tamsin, Emily,

Tom and Annie. Steve and Nick helped, of course. And they managed to exchange a little news with Steve while they busied themselves with blenders, saucepans and hotplates.

'I'm at a bit of a crossroads,' Steve said sheepishly to his friends. 'Johnny Britten – as you probably read – was acquitted, which represents something of a reversal of fortunes for me.'

'You mean Johnny has sorted things out for you?' asked Richard, a worried frown creasing his usually beaming face.

'Yes, although of course I want no part of any of that business now,' said Steve hastily. 'Amanda and I have given an interview to the *Sunday Times* this week. I've sort of come clean. Given them the details of all the offshore accounts. Turned the money over to the receivers and, hopefully, a little bit back to the investors.'

'Good show.' Richard smiled encouragingly.

'In fact, I do hope it doesn't overshadow this weekend. They're running the thing this Sunday. We decided that it was the only way to go. I trust, I hope, that no further prosecution will follow the disclosures, although I am sure that Johnny Britten will take out a contract on my life.'

'Surely not. Everyone knows the man is a crook. Always has been. Long before he got involved with Minter Investments,' said Richard.

'Yes, but even if the Director of Public Prosecutions decides against taking my case further, she'll definitely go for Johnny. And he isn't going to like that.' Steve sounded nervous.

'But you are doing the right thing. Cleaning the slate will give you and Amanda and Annie the chance to really start again. Let's have a glass of champagne to celebrate, if the girls haven't consumed it all,' Richard said.

It was nearly 10 p.m. before the six of them finally sat down in the family dining room for dinner. Georgia, Amanda and Caroline were in high spirits. Sharing a number of clearly private jokes, sniggering to each other and making silly asides to one another as the men served their supper.

'Darling,' said Caroline, 'I've never seen such an . . . such an . . . ORIGINAL . . . flower arrangement. How daring to mix wild flowers with what look to be organic vegetables.'

'It's Richard's arrangement,' Georgia said, to the evident amusement of her girlfriends.

'My goodness, Richard,' said Amanda pointedly, 'I can remember a time, not so long ago, when you thought a luscious bloom was the happy glow of a sexually serviced woman.'

The three women fell about laughing while Richard attempted to regain a little dignity by serving his carefully constructed *moussette de saumon fumé* (accompanied by warm Melba toast). He glanced anxiously at Nick and Steve as they took their first mouthfuls of his creation. There was a tension in the air, and a tightness on Richard's face while he waited for their reaction.

'Er, let me see,' said Nick thoughtfully, 'a touch of coriander, maybe a tiny bit of basil?'

Richard nodded earnestly.

'Marco Pierre White?' enquired Steve.

'No, Raymond Blanc,' said Richard.

'Marvellous,' said Nick, 'light, tangy, just the right balance of seasoning and a perfect consistency.'

Richard beamed with pleasure, which only served to amuse the women even more.

'Nick's the same,' said Caroline with a giggle. 'When he's not nursing the twins he's fiddling about in the kitchen making roulades and ragouts.'

'And Steve,' said Amanda, 'if he's not working on his petit point or his patchwork, he's creating culinary masterpieces in his perfectly designed kitchen.'

'It's scarcely believable, isn't it,' said Georgia thoughtfully, 'that less than a year ago Richard was praying for a welcome return to the traditional roles of the sexes?'

This time Caroline and Amanda did not bray with laughter. Rather, they were silent for a while, the only noise being the periodic hiccups of the hostess.

'Well,' said Caroline, 'there's been a national change of mood since then. Perhaps the Labour Government are making us rethink how we return to those old family values. Maybe in direct opposition to Richard's old ideas they think that it is men that should be kept in the home – or should I say the kitchen,' she went on as the three men returned to the table each carrying a steaming dish.

Heaven knows Richard had done his best with Georgia's rustic casserole. He had thrown in a few herbs, tarted up the veggies and made a quick salad of home-grown rocket and radicchio with a balsamic vinegar dressing. But it didn't balance well with his *moussette* and he felt oddly let down by the slipshod way in which she had gone about preparing what should have been a memorable meal.

There was a noticeable divide between the men and the women that evening. While the women tittered and twittered and attempted light and witty conversation the men talked earnestly about the very things that, just a few months before, might have dominated their partners' conversations. Richard was worried about Tamsin's progress at school, Steve was full of anecdotes about the PTA and Nick fretted about whether or not he could hear the babies crying on the alarm in the kitchen. Eventually Steve and Richard suggested that the 'boys' adjourn to the kitchen to clear up, talk and listen out for the babies while the women could remain giggling and guzzling their drinks in the dining room.

'Isn't it the ladies that usually withdraw,' slurred Georgia at the retreating male figures, 'and the men who pass round the port and tell filthy jokes?'

'My God,' said Amanda, 'what have we DONE?'

EIGHTEEN

Richard was in a huff. He was disappointed by the way Georgia had behaved the previous night and he had decided that he would not be easily placated. There was far too much to do. For while he had, with the help of Steve and Nick, cleared up the mess from the night before he was well behind with the lunch and dinner preparations for the day.

He got up before seven – leaving Georgia snoring in her sleep – and made a start on breakfast. The children were already up and he cooked them pancakes as a treat. Then he began to organize things for the adults. Making stacks of toast, whipping eggs ready to scramble and grilling crisp slices of bacon which he kept warm in the bottom oven of the Aga. Nick and the babies didn't make an appearance until nearly 8 a.m. Richard helped make up their bottles and cereal and sat chatting while he shovelled the food down their little gaping mouths.

'Good night, Nick?' he asked tentatively.

'In what way?' said Nick gloomily.

'In the way we were talking about. You know, the bathroom mirror . . .'

'Nothing could have been further from either of our minds. Jillie woke at 2 a.m. and Jack at 4 a.m. Even if I had still been on speaking terms with Caroline, I would have been too tired for anything but sleep.'

'They were odd last night, weren't they? Do you suppose they don't like the way in which you, Steve and I have become so friendly? I was wondering if Georgia resented how well we all now get on together. As if we were in some way treading on their territory.'

At this point Georgia made an entrance and began fumbling round the kitchen drawers and cupboards looking for something.

'The Nurofen is in the top cupboard,' Richard said coldly.

'It never used to be. It used to be in the third drawer on the right,' said Georgia irritably.

'Where the children could reach it,' said Richard. 'I reorganized things. You can never be too careful with medicines. Breakfast will be ready in ten minutes.'

'I don't want any. The very thought makes me sick.'

'Well, perhaps you can grace us with your company anyway, even if it is only to drink a large cup of coffee and swallow a couple of Nurofens,' Richard replied stiffly.

Breakfast was rather more dismal than dinner had been the night before. Caroline, Georgia and Amanda were all hung-over and they virtually ignored Richard's breakfast dishes.

'For God's sake, Richard, don't look so tight-lipped,' Georgia said. 'This weekend is about doing what we want, not what you want.'

At this he simply got up and walked out of the dining room.

'That was a bit insensitive after all the work he had put in,' Nick said, getting up himself and following Richard out of the room.

'What time are the others coming?' said Steve in a bid to diffuse the atmosphere that was threatening to engulf them all.

'Very soon,' said Georgia. 'Juliet and Harry were picking Sam up at nine and should be here in about half an hour. Nicola and Carl could be here at any moment. If you'll excuse me, I suppose I'd better go and make up with Richard. Otherwise we'll all suffer for the rest of the weekend.'

She found him, as expected, in his kitchen garden furiously digging the ground.

'Richard I'm sorry,' she said weakly.

He didn't respond.

'I said I was sorry, Richard. I probably didn't behave very well last night. It's been so long since I've seen Amanda and Caroline, and I rather selfishly wanted to enjoy their company.'

'Leaving me to pick up the pieces,' he said with a sigh.

'Well, it's not as if I behave like that all the time,' she said sulkily.

'I don't think you realize how much you left me to do last night. Not only did I help Nick with the babies – you and Caroline seemed completely disinterested in them – I also had to cook supper for the children and then turn your idea of a main course into a meal fit for my friends. Frankly, Georgia, I'm not happy.'

'If I remember correctly, you originally wanted total control of this weekend. Now perhaps you understand how much work is involved. Particularly now we don't have the Hendersons or the nanny.'

'All right, all right, let's not argue,' Richard said, suddenly wanting to make up more than she seemed to. 'I so want this weekend to work. Let's not make a scene in front of our friends. OK?'

'OK then,' she conceded.

'Heavens, I can hear a car in the drive. You go and greet whoever it is while I clean myself up. I must look a total mess.'

It was Nicola and Carl arriving in a rather impressive chauffeur-driven limousine. Georgia waved enthusiastically at them as they drew to a halt and Carl nipped out and opened the other door for Nicola, offering her a helping hand in that gentlemanly way of his.

'Hi Georgia,' he said, beaming from ear to ear as he pecked her on each cheek.

'Darlings,' said Georgia, embracing one and then the other of her friends, 'perhaps your chauffeur could bring your luggage up to the blue room? Then we can have some coffee in the little dining room – the others are still finishing their breakfast.'

'You two go ahead.' Carl exposed his gleaming teeth in a manner that, frankly, made Georgia's heart flutter a little. 'I'll take the luggage up and join you in a moment. I can remember my way.'

Caroline and Amanda were thrilled to see Nicola. If anything, she looked even more polished and sophisticated than she had the last time she had been in England. It must be success, Amanda decided, because whilst she herself had always had her own inimitable glamour she knew that her present progress at work had given her an extra glow.

'You look wonderful, Nicola,' said Caroline.

'I feel wonderful. Everything is going so well. With the launch and, of course, with Carl,' she said as Carl walked into the room and greeted the women.

'Oh Carl,' said Amanda, 'you never met my husband Steve. Carl – Steve – Steve – Carl.'

'Hi Steve,' said Carl.

'Why don't we go and find the other men,' said Steve, smiling broadly and taking Carl off to find Nick and Richard.

They were sitting at the kitchen table, each with a baby in his arms. Richard was a little disconcerted when he saw Carl. The memory of the way in which he had treated him at that dinner flooded his mind and flushed his face. Jumping up and putting Jillie carefully back in her cradle chair, he shook Carl's hand and offered him coffee.

'Would it be rude if I helped myself to some of that breakfast? I can't get enough of that traditional English food,' said Carl, to Richard's apparent delight.

'Of course, old man. I hate waste and I was beginning to think I had made too much,' Richard said, happily ladling out a pile of scrambled eggs, five slices of bacon, some mushrooms and fried bread.

'You mean you cooked the breakfast yourself, Richard?' asked Carl incredulously. 'Last time we were here you were extolling the virtues of keeping women in the kitchen and men in the workplace. Whatever can have happened?' he added with just a touch of irony.

'It's a long story, Carl,' said Richard with a short laugh. 'Let's just say that my life has been completely turned around. We lost the election, I resigned my seat, gave up my interest in politics – Christ, I even gave up my mistress – then I accepted a peerage and discovered what I had been missing all those years. I think you find before you now a much happier man than you encountered when you were last here.' He slapped Carl on the back in a comradely fashion.

'A much happier man, eh?' said Carl as he sat down at the table to eat his food. 'Or a much changed man? A controlled man?'

'Well, I suppose I am more in control of my life,' said Richard cheerily. 'I mean, when I was Secretary of State for Social Services responsible for working out the basic minimum the unemployed could live on I didn't even know how much a loaf of bread cost. But now I do. And I'm in control of my life in so many other ways. I grow my own vegetables, I can cook my own food, I work out each morning, I'm in charge of my body, I am involved in the lives of my children and I am passionately in love with my wife. Well, most of the time.'

'My goodness, that is a total turnaround,' said Carl with another winning smile.

It was at this point that Harry burst into the kitchen to enthusiastically greet his friends. First he kissed Richard on both cheeks, then Nick and finally Steve.

'Why Carl,' he said, smiling down on Nicola's partner, 'how good to see you, too.'

Richard was rather surprised by Harry's appearance. The pony-tail had gone, the ripped jeans had been replaced by cord turn-ups and the leather coat by a tweed jacket. It was, Richard thought, as dramatic a change of style as his own new Lauren-and-loafers look. Carl, too, noted the difference.

'Harry, you are a changed man,' he said.

'You know, Carl, it's odd the way we seem to have come to re-evaluate our lives at much the same time in much the same way. Richard and I seem to have gone through twin mid-life crises and Steve and Nick have been involved in momentous changes in their lives, too.'

'For the better?' asked Carl.

'Absolutely' the four of them answered in unison.

'Isn't that an extraordinary coincidence?' said Carl.

Lunch was not an enormous success. Richard had, again, been rather over-ambitious and the plan to include the children – Tasmin, Emily, Tom, Annie and poor little Sam – backfired. He had served up a 'hearty country soup' followed by wood pigeon with celeriac purée accompanied by a ballottine of cabbage (from his patch) and chicory.

'Yuk,' poor little Sam had proclaimed when he had been served his pigeon. 'What on earth is this, Uncle Richard? It looks like something the cat brought in.'

For the first time a remark from Sam amused his cousins. Probably because for the first time Sam had said something observant. The family cat often brought in headless offerings rather like that which sat on the plates in front of them.

'But it's absolutely delicious,' said Carl to the children in a placatory fashion. 'Taste it.'

Richard found criticism terribly hard to take nowadays, even if it was only from a small boy with an underdeveloped palate. In the old days, when the Tories were in government, he had got used to a daily bashing from the media and had, Georgia always used to say, developed the skin of a rhinoceros. But now he was hurt, flustered and deeply bothered by a slight from a seven-year-old.

'Maybe I should have stuck to burgers,' he said bravely, although he wanted to weep.

'No darling, this is wonderful,' said Georgia gently. 'And it's high time the children learnt that there is more to food than sausages, chips and ketchup. Pigeon, Sam, is really very tasty.'

'PIGEON!' said Sam in horror.

In the end Georgia got very cross with the five children and sent them off to the kitchen to forage for themselves while the adults enjoyed Richard's meal (although the pigeon was, Nick thought, a little too rare).

'So when is the actual date of the European launch of this drug of yours?' Steve asked Nicola.

'This coming Thursday. We did a very successful US launch in a big stadium and we are doing a scaled-down version in your Albert Hall.'

'What do you mean, "your Albert Hall"?' said Amanda. 'Heavens, Nicola, you talk like an American now.'

'I suppose that in some ways I am American now,' Nicola said, looking across at Carl and smiling, 'and when we are married I'll be officially American.'

'When will you marry?' asked Caroline.

'As soon as we have launched Manifold. Maybe here in London,' said Nicola.

'Manifold?' enquired Richard. 'I've heard that name somewhere before – I can't think where. What is it?'

There was a silence before Carl replied, 'It's the name of the drug that Nicola's company has patented. It's a revolutionary product that can perform miracles. Turn violent criminals into tame pussy cats.' He gave a broad grin.

Nicola visibly blushed at this remark and the other women round the table shifted awkwardly in their chairs.

'Shall I clear the plates away now?' said Georgia nervously.

'And how is Stella?' said Nicola. 'I have such wonderful memories of her from childhood. Has her divorce from your father come through yet?'

'Oh no,' said Juliet, 'it's not as if she wants to marry again. That was the point of her leaving Daddy in the first place. After spending all her life bending to the autocratic will of a difficult man, she decided that she had had enough. She wanted to be on her own, the independent woman. And I understand how she feels.'

'Oh darling, that's a little harsh,' said Harry. 'You make it sound as if marriage were nothing more than enforced enslavement for women.'

'That's because, Harry,' said Georgia, 'it can be. It certainly used to be that way for me. Although, thank God, it isn't any more.'

'It's rather interesting to note that it is women, and not men, who are choosing not to marry, or making the decision to divorce. Twenty years ago a woman would not have thought she was fulfilled unless she was married. Nowadays she doesn't think she can be fulfilled if she is,' said Caroline thoughtfully.

'You don't have to tell me that,' said Nick, who had just returned from checking on the sleeping twins. 'It seems to me that many women nowadays do not want to be fulfilled in any traditional sense. All they want is career success.'

'Do you suppose that has something to do with men?' said Richard. 'I mean, when I look back I can quite understand that Georgia might not have enjoyed being married to me. Maybe it is men that have got to change.'

'And maybe, if Nicola gets her way, men will change,' said Carl, smiling across at the woman he now privately despised. 'More men will come to understand what Richard, Nick, Steve and Harry now understand.'

'Oh Carl, let's not talk about Manifold now,' said Nicola, signalling like mad to her partner to change the conversation.

'No darling,' said Carl. 'We'll talk about Manifold tonight at dinner.'

It had been Carl's intention all along to bring things to a climax that night. He needed allies in the fight against the grotesque Malestrom creation, and the men gathered at Gallows Tree House, forcibly changed into Nicola's drug-induced pastiche of 'perfect men', were his natural choice. Once they understood what had been done to them. Of course, it wasn't going to be easy. Carl could remember only too clearly how absolutely wonderful he had felt in the early days of the programme. The smile that he now had to force on his lips had been almost permanently present – as it was on the faces of the four Englishmen today. And he had, he realized, genuinely been taken in by the idea of 'achieving his full potential'. His mistake was in believing that he owed his subsequent progress entirely to the drug. His self-esteem, at the time Nicola had plucked him from his prison cell, had been so low that he literally believed himself to be worthless, brainless, incompetent and incapable of achieving anything.

When he began to absorb knowledge, when he began to move forward, to establish a new identity for himself, he had assumed that it was the drug that had made him into the new Carl Burton. But all the drug had done for him, he now saw, was to control his behaviour in the bad days and make it possible for the real Carl Burton to emerge.

In fact, even now he could still see the sense in the idea of using Manifold within the penal system. He could still understand that, controlled properly, it could be positively implemented. What he could not accept, and would never understand, was how that basic idea had been cleverly expanded so that Manifold was a drug for all men. Even men like Richard and Harry – men who were perhaps not entirely honest, noble and principled, but who never were a danger to society. Of course, Nicola would argue that Richard, with his formerly right-wing views and his inability to be truthful publicly or privately, was a very real danger to society. What she didn't seem to understand was that it was the Richards of this world – that is, the old-style Richards of this world – who made things happen. Meddling with the hormonal and psychological make-up of men like Richard was dangerous. She had turned a powerful political figure into an organic vegetable. And look at Nick. A guy who, as Carl understood it, had one burning ambition in life, to create a work of art, and who had now been transformed into a hideous house-husband whose only concern was nappies, feeding patterns and contributing his bit to the lowest common denominator of popular culture.

It wasn't that Carl particularly liked these men – as

they were now or as they had been. It was just that he couldn't bear to see the changes that had been wrought in them – without their knowledge – by a drug that had been developed and tested on murderers.

The thing that had struck him about Harry, a little under a year ago, was the fact that the man was a free spirit. He wasn't the kind of guy who could be tied to anyone or anything. But now his conversation was full of caring, settling down, having roots and raising a family. How long before he too found his yearning for roots turning him into a vegetable? And the one who was making the petit-point tapestry all afternoon in the sitting room? Steve, the man who had made and lost a fortune. What would happen to him as the Manifold he didn't know he was taking took a further grip on his mind and manners?

The problem Carl faced was in convincing them, in their present state of apparent bliss (although he had noticed a little dissent here and there), that Manifold was not going to help mankind, it was going to stifle it. Of course, he had his evidence. But he would have to argue it against the sharpest and most fanatical adversary he had ever encountered – Nicola. He had only one small advantage over her now. She had no idea that he was off the programme. She had no idea that the smile he turned on her was not real. She had no comprehension of the side-effects that she had induced in the man she wanted as her husband. Her Stepford Husband, he thought as he remembered the copy of Georgia's letter that would form a central part of his argument that night.

But she would know soon. Very soon Nicola would find out who the real Carl Burton was . . .

NINETEEN

The atmosphere at Gallows Tree House had lightened and lifted by Saturday evening. Georgia had agreed to help Richard with dinner and for once they seemed to be working well as a team. There was even time, between feeding all the children and settling them in their den, for the two of them to take half an hour alone in their room. Behind the closed door of Richard's bathroom Georgia made magic of the peace that they had achieved that afternoon. She crept up behind him as he was flossing his teeth (a very un-Richard-like thing to do, she privately thought) and put her arms around his naked back, moving her fingers down to his cock, aware of his excitement.

'Richard,' she said coquettishly, 'a prize courgette!'

'An organic prize courgette,' he said, 'and I grew it all on my own with a little help from you.'

He pushed her in front of the long mirror and entered her quickly watching the motions they made as he moved in and out of her.

'Watch it, watch it,' he urged Georgia, taking the weight of her legs round his waist and moving sideways so she too could see their fucking.

'Oh Richard,' she gasped as he thrashed in and out of her with a force that threatened to overwhelm her.

But Richard was not finished. He laid her on the floor and carried on fucking for an inordinate length of time, so that when he finally came Georgia was crying out for mercy. They lay where they were, on the cold bathroom tiles, for a few minutes before Richard suddenly jumped up and shouted, 'My *bouchée* of mushrooms and shallots – I forgot my *bouchée* – it will be ruined!'

'Richard,' said Georgia, reaching up to her husband and pulling him back on to the floor again, 'look in the mirror. Life is too short to stuff a mushroom.'

'Stuff my mushrooms,' said Richard with a laugh as he embraced his wife.

It was, Nick said later, almost as if Richard had slipped something into the pigeon they had eaten at lunchtime. For at about the same moment, in almost the same position, he and Caroline had achieved sexual union for the first time in over a year. She had been putting on some make-up in the mirror over the basin when he had wandered in to run himself a bath. The twins were downstairs being cared for by Steve, who had offered to take over for an hour or so in order that Caroline and Nick could get some rest, and there was absolutely nothing – apart from his nerve – to stop Nick from propositioning his wife.

'Caroline,' he said with a sigh, 'I love you, Caroline.'

And then he had kissed her just once on the nape of her neck. She had jumped at the contact, she was so tense. But when she saw Nick, and the expression on his face, she relaxed and reached up to him and they kissed each other hungrily, tongue fighting tongue, for the first time in much longer than a year. Nick was breathless with excitement. But not so much so that he was going to risk spoiling the moment by being exposed for what he was (flabby and unfit) in the bathroom mirror. Instead he picked Caroline up, still kissing her passionately, and carried her back to the bedroom, which was softly lit by the glow of the baby night-light.

'Oh Nick, oh Nick, if only you knew how long I have wanted this,' said Caroline feverishly.

'Oh darling, if only I had known how long you had wanted this,' said Nick as he entered her and made love to her with the kind of force and energy he had forgotten he had ever had. It was over in minutes, but none the less momentous for the fact that it was so short-lived.

'Oh, Nick, Nick!' shouted Caroline, 'I thought you didn't want me any more. I thought the only thing you wanted now was the babies.'

'And I thought that you had lost interest in me,' said Nick eagerly. 'I thought I had become such a homebody, such a drudge, that you no longer found me interesting in any way. Sexually or otherwise.'

'Oh but I do, Nick, I do,' she said passionately. 'It's just that there seemed to be so much in the way. The babies, my work, and you made me feel so inadequate at home. As if I had no place. As if I *were* just a boring interference in your life.'

By now Nick was erect again and they made love for the second time with less ferocity, but more emotion. And it lasted longer then either of them had ever dreamt was possible.

'Oh darling!' said Nick, 'we must make sure that we don't lose this. We must do this again.'

'In the next year,' said Caroline.

'Tonight,' said Nick, 'tonight after dinner I'll be brave enough to fuck you in front of the bathroom mirror. As long as you don't scream so much at the sight of my nakedness that you wake the babies.'

When Nick came down to relieve Steve and give the babies their tea there was a new glow to his ever-present smile.

'Nick, you look rested,' said Steve.

'Rested and relieved,' said Nick, embracing Jillie and

Jack as if he had been parted from them for several days rather than just a couple of hours.

'Well then, I'll go up and have a bath myself now,' said Steve. 'We're all due down for champagne at seven.'

When he reached their bedroom Amanda was asleep. Her glorious hair streaming around her on the pillows. Steve reached over for the brush and began, very gently, to run it through her hair. She stretched as she emerged from sleep and pulled him down to her.

'You are the most beautiful woman,' he said.

'Why did you never say that before, in the old days?' she replied, looking up at him.

'Because in the old days I didn't realize the value of anything,' he said as the rhythm of the brushing increased.

'And you think you know the value of everything now?' she said teasingly.

'I know your value, and Annie's. I know that you are both priceless. Worth much, much, much more than the old Steve Minter.'

'And the new Steve Minter. I think he's pretty priceless too,' said Amanda kissing her husband, moving over and unbuttoning his jeans so that she could straddle him. It was the way he liked it best. With her sitting naked on top of him, her hair falling down over her bare breasts in a gleaming curtain.

'Ride me, Amanda, ride me,' he shouted as she pushed herself onto him, her hair flying in the air as she beat down on him.

Then, when they had finished and Amanda had bathed and perfumed herself, they sat together on the bed while he brushed her hair until it shone again and she told him, four or five times, how much she loved him.

*

Harry had nipped into town that afternoon to buy Juliet a special gift. He hadn't planned to present it to her until the following day, but when he returned from Henley and discovered that she was upstairs in their bedroom he couldn't help himself. She was sitting at the dressing table looking at herself in the mirror in a distracted way when he came up and put his hands on her shoulders.

'Darling, have you had a good rest?' he said.

She was wearing a long pale pink cotton dressing gown tied round the waist. It was just possible to see, through the thin material, the tip of her breasts and the dark shadow of her pubic hair. He knelt down beside her and laid his head in her lap, sensuously inhaling the aroma he knew he would find. The sweet smell of tea rose. Juliet had been rather cold towards him that weekend – Harry had decided that she found it difficult being a mother and a mistress at the same time – and for the first time since their arrival she seemed to unbend and unwind.

'Oh Harry,' she said, softly running her hands through his newly cut hair, which was, she felt, rather more attractive than that tatty old pony-tail.

His head went down further and he began to nuzzle through the material, one hand creeping up her thigh inside her gown. She leant back and his head went down and his tongue moved inside her making her groan with pleasure.

'Yes, Harry, yes,' she said as he brought her to climax before laying her back down on the floor and pushing his cock into the wetness within her. 'Oh, Harry, yes, yes, yes,' she gasped as they writhed together, their bodies reflected from odd angles, from time to time, in the three-cornered mirror on the dressing table.

They must have made love for more than half an hour, changing positions, moving their bodies round the room in a frenzy of wild and hectic motion. When finally they sank down on the bed they were both so replete, and so utterly pleased with each other, that Juliet managed the words that, of late, had been sticking in her throat.

'Oh God, Harry, I LOVE YOU,' she shouted as she reached what seemed to be her umpteenth climax.

'Do you? DO you really, darling?' he said, aware that, for the first time in his life, he really wanted a woman to love him.

That evening Juliet had finally managed to eclipse from his memory those old visions of Annabel. The sex between them was, well, phenomenal. And so moved was he by her declaration that he found himself searching through the piles of abandoned clothes that lay scattered round the room for the most extravagant present he had ever bought a woman in his life (privately Harry had always been a little mean). Then he made Juliet lie down on the bed, close her eyes, count to ten and then open them again.

When she did Harry was kneeling by her side, stark naked, with a little maroon leather box in his hand. Inside there was a five-carat diamond engagement ring. He slipped it on to her finger – it looked, she thought, as if it had been made for her long slender hands and perfectly manicured nails – and asked her if she would be his wife.

'I can be divorced within six weeks – Annabel and I have lived apart for so long – and we can be married in a couple of months.'

'Yes, Harry,' she said, looking down at her hand admiringly. 'Yes.'

'We'll really have something to celebrate tonight,' he said. 'Wear that pale pink voile dress, with no knickers.'

*

It might have seemed that even Carl was affected by whatever exotic herbs Richard had slipped into their lunch. Because he, too, was moved to make love to Nicola in the hour or so of privacy they had put aside before dinner. What spurred him this time was not the thought of the red-headed whores or the last effects of the wonderdrug (which, as the four English men were just discovering, had an extraordinarily beneficial effect on their sexual potency), but the thought that by the end of this evening he would be his own master again. She would understand that she had lost control of him. And that, moreover, her plans to control all men with Manifold would be lost, too.

He gave her a lavender aromatherapy massage first to relax her. And when she was ready – he loved to keep her waiting, to drive her wild with desire whilst he calmly continued working the oil into the small of her back – he pushed her on to her back and entered her. He took it slowly, moving with deliberate, long strokes in and out of her until she, with fevered motion, took over and moved down to take him in her mouth, her tongue working on him in a way that – she imagined – he liked.

He didn't do what he wanted to. He would save that for later. For after dinner that night. For now he settled for a lazy fuck, the way she liked it. Bearing down on her with that big smile on his face so that she wouldn't suspect anything.

'Carl, I'm so happy,' she said sweetly as they lay snoozing together after their love-making. 'I can't think of anything that could make me happier. Can you think of anything that could make you feel more fulfilled?'

He could, but he didn't say so. He just smiled benignly at her and reminded her that they had only twenty minutes in which to make themselves decent for dinner.

TWENTY

There was, Richard thought, something wonderful in the air that night. When they all gathered together in the main drawing room to have some champagne before they went in to dinner they seemed to positively radiate happiness.

Nick and Caroline sat on the love-seat whispering to one another and giggling like teenagers. Steve and Amanda stood together by the french windows holding hands. Juliet and Harry were entwined on the sofa, she already quite tipsy from the alcohol and he feeling, for the first time in months, as if what he wanted in life was finally within his grasp (one of his fingers gently played with the big ring on Juliet's left hand).

Georgia looked divine. She was wearing a deep, dark green velvet gown that accentuated her petite shapeliness. Her soft, creamy skin, in the carefully lit room, seemed so irresistible to Richard that he had to stop himself from going over and kissing her fabulous cleavage. Even Nicola, whom Richard had always regarded as a rather asexual woman, seemed to have a sensual glow this evening. She was wearing a shocking-pink short tight dress that should have clashed terribly with that hair but somehow served only to make it look more dazzling.

Carl was the last to arrive. Walking into the room with a smile of apology on his face, he joined Nicola and gently kissed her. When Richard had filled everyone's glass Harry pulled himself up from the sofa and coughed loudly.

'Juliet and I wanted to make a little announcement,'

he said, turning round and pulling her up alongside him. 'We have decided to get married and we wanted to share our news with you all. I put a couple more bottles of Bollinger in the fridge, Richard.'

There was a general burst of enthusiastic chatter as everyone congratulated and embraced the happy couple.

'Well, of course my divorce won't come through for a few weeks, but we are hopeful that we'll be able to marry within a couple of months,' Harry said.

'Juliet, I'm so pleased for you,' said Georgia with a sincerity she didn't often feel when addressing her sister. 'I do hope you will be happy together.'

'Do you really?' said Juliet, looking Georgia in the eye. 'You don't still hate me for what I did, do you? You do understand that it was just a terrible time in my life, a frightful mistake. And that, anyway, Richard was a different man in those days.'

'Of course he was,' said Georgia. 'Well, they all were, weren't they? Harry – my goodness, how he has changed. And Steve and even Nick. Who would have thought we would all get on as well as we do now? Who would have thought that we could all feel so well, so content with our lot?'

'And we owe it all to Nicola,' said Amanda, interrupting Georgia. 'God knows how we would all be, or where we would all be if it weren't for her.'

'Yes,' said Carl, joining the women, 'I know I owe Nicola everything.'

'So do we,' laughed Caroline.

. They were all so relaxed and intent on enjoying themselves that they drank, even before they had sat down to dinner, nine bottles of champagne. By the time they did sit down round Richard's extravagantly dressed table they were all a little light-headed. Apart, that is, from

Carl, who had managed to make one glass last nearly an hour and a half. In fact, Richard was rather relieved that his guests were half-cut because they would be less aware of what they were eating. Lunch had been such a disaster that he had been cautious about this evening's meal to the point of giving in to Georgia (whose culinary advice he nowadays tended to ignore), substituting a starter of plain smoked Scotch salmon for his planned soufflé *Suissesse*. Harry was attempting to engage Carl in a conversation about marriage.

'There comes a time when you think to yourself, what's the point of all this? My life, Carl, had become so utterly, utterly empty. My work was so repetitive that I had lost interest in it, my home was just somewhere I collapsed when there was nowhere else to go and my inner life – and this is the really interesting thing, Carl – my inner life was non-existent. My God, when I think back to the way I was, I realize that I was like one of those hamsters upstairs in the children's den – just pushing my way round and round a wheel that took me nowhere. I didn't have relationships – I just fucked a string of women. I didn't have conversations, I just exchanged clichés. I was lost and I didn't know how to get off that wheel,' he slurred.

'And now?' asked Carl.

'And now I've found the way off. I've found true happiness. I'm going to marry the woman I love, I'm going to put some meaning back in my life. I'm going to move to the country, have some children, put down roots. Now, Carl I'm my OWN man.'

One by one Carl drew the men out that night. And each of them, in his cups, made a similar declaration of happiness and completeness, aided, no doubt, by the fact that each one of them felt sexually sated after their pre-drink activities in their respective rooms. It was,

Carl thought, a little like finding yourself at a meeting of Alcoholics Anonymous, with each of the men wanting to portray his old life in the worst possible light so as to make his new sobriety seem all the more attractive. Only, of course, what Harry, Richard, Nick and Steve should have belonged to was All Men Are Bastards Anonymous, so determined were they to put down what Carl now believed to be true 'male characteristics.'

In fact, he had to fight to suppress a giggle at the idea of the four men at some AMABA meeting standing up and saying, 'My name is Richard James, I am a bastard. For forty years I gave in to the basest male instincts, I was unfaithful to my wife, unpleasant to my fellow man and indifferent to my children . . .' Rather like recovering alcoholics or born-again Christians these artificially created model men, these Stepford Husbands, were almost fanatically committed to their new selves, and absolutely contemptuous of the way they had been before they saw the light (or, if they only knew it, swallowed the Manifold).

The women were rather more interesting. It seemed clear to Carl that although they must know that he was Nicola's own Stepford Husband, apparently carefully controlled by a weekly dose of Manifold, they had no idea that he knew they knew. Carl had guessed that part of Nicola's pep talk to her friends about her drug would have included the revelation that he had been plucked from a prison scrap heap and chemically converted into a civilized, sensitive, caring Manifold model man. But nothing about them, nothing about the way in which they chatted to him or looked across the table at him, betrayed what they knew. When he and Nicola had alluded to Manifold by name during lunch none of them had shown any reaction. They had played dumb when Richard had repeated the name and when Steve had asked about the European launch. Of course, they were part of the conspiracy now. As guilty, in their way, as Nicola. They had become keepers of their men. They were in control. If they had experienced any qualms or doubts about secretly putting their partners on the Manifold programme – and Georgia's letter suggested that she had been initially reluctant – they had long since abandoned them.

Not that they were as happy or as content as their men folk now were. Amanda had the look of a woman who wasn't sure what she wanted any more – success or personal fulfilment. Caroline, prior to this evening, had seemed utterly miserable and detached from her husband and children, while Georgia's role as mother and home-maker had been diminished since her husband had become such a domestic dolt. And Juliet, well Juliet was clearly never going seriously to settle for a man like this new vision of Harry, even with a five-carat diamond ring on her finger. Carl wondered if they were perhaps frightened and trapped. On one level repelled by the prattling paragons that their partners had become and on another terrified of returning to the way things had been.

He decided to start with Juliet. To work away at her, as someone had worked away at the diamond in the ring that she kept glancing down on with pride. Turning towards her, out of earshot of the men, he asked her about her forthcoming wedding.

'Have you found a house yet? Harry says you want to lead the rural life after you are married. Lots of babies, livestock and the simple pleasures of the country.'

'Well, of course that's Harry's fantasy, Carl. The reality, I imagine, will be a little different.'

'And I hear he's going to take Sam out of boarding school and that he plans to give up the kind of work he's doing now. Abandon the glitz and the glamour and devote himself to hearth and home. It all sounds so, so cosy,' said Carl.

'And you, Carl,' said Juliet sharply, 'are you and Nicola planning a similarly cosy future?'

'You mean like you and Harry, Richard and Georgia, Nick and Caroline and Steve and Amanda? No, I don't think I'm the, well, the house-husband type.'

'But the last time we met you seemed exactly the house-husband type, albeit the academic house-husband type. Well, you seemed, at least to us, exactly the kind of caring, sensitive man that we all dreamed of finding.'

'Didn't it ever strike you as strange, Juliet, how very similar Richard, Harry, Nick and Steve have become since we last met? I mean, look at them. They even appear alike. The same grinning countenances, the same sincere eyes, the same thick, glossy hair, the same awful platitudes about family values and roots spewing out of their mouths. And yet nine months ago they couldn't have been more different, could they?'

Nicola, who had been listening with mounting alarm to Carl's odd assault on Juliet, was relieved that at this moment Richard brought in the main course – sautéed guinea fowl with a *bouchée* of mushrooms and shallots (or rather a burnt *bouchée* of mushrooms and shallots), new potatoes and a variety of home-grown veg.

The food might have sobered them up a bit if it had been edible (and had it not seemed so frightfully similar to the wild pigeon he had cooked for lunch). But the fine wines that Richard had been liberally filling their glasses with had rather compounded their intoxication. In fact, Carl wondered if the men might not be too far gone to understand what he would, in a very short time, reveal to them.

Meanwhile he had a go at Amanda. He sensed that she, of the four English women, was the one with the most reservations about the moral implications of what they had done. They chatted about her work, her promotion and how it had transformed her life.

'The thing is, Carl, that I was only ever what you Americans call a trophy wife. I mean, I never did anything before I met Steve and I never did anything during the ridiculous years, and it was only when it had all gone – and Steve had been convicted – that it ever occurred to me that I might be able to earn my living. And now I get a real kick out of it. I mean, I understand the value of money now.'

'And the value of human relationships?'

'Those, too. I mean, I didn't really KNOW my daughter until we lost everything. She had been brought up by nannies. I didn't have a relationship with her. I kissed her goodnight when I was home, which wasn't all that often.'

'And Steve, did you know him?'

She went very quiet.

'Well, of course I knew him.' She paused. 'But he was different, then. Being in prison changed him.'

'Being in prison changed him from the violent man Nicola told me about into the sweet, malleable guy I met today? The man who talked to me for an hour about the art of tapestry and who, when we went out for a walk this afternoon, discussed colour schemes with Georgia for an hour and a half?'

'Well . . .'

'Because, Amanda, as you doubtless know, prison changed me, too. Only not the being behind bars bit. That had no effect at all. No, what changed me was something that was made available to me in prison. And the effects, strangely enough, were very similar to those

269

that I see in your Steve. And Harry, and Richard, and Nick . . . Although I have to say that I never really got into embroidery, wet-nursing or fancy cooking.'

'CARL,' said Nicola sharply, 'that's quite enough. I really don't think Amanda wants to hear about what happened to you all those years ago.'

'Amanda might not want to hear what happened to me all those years ago, but I think that Richard, Nick, Harry and Steve would be very interested.'

'CARL,' Nicola shouted, 'I FORBID you to say any more.'

'You FORBID me to say any more, do you, Nicola?' said Carl. 'Well, I'm afraid that tonight I am just going to have to DISOBEY you.'

An eerie silence had descended on the table. The women were alert to the possibility of what was about to happen but the men, overtaken by alcohol and unaware of the undercurrent in Carl's conversation, obviously thought that what had just occurred was nothing more than a private spat between Nicola and Carl.

'Amanda,' said Carl, 'I think you should go and make some strong coffee. What I have to say tonight is of great importance. It is essential that everyone understands.'

'Look here, old chap,' said Richard, 'I don't want to be rude, but if you want to have a row with Nicola perhaps you should go upstairs and do it. We were all having a rather jolly time.'

'Yes,' chorused Harry, Nick and Steve.

'And has it ever occurred to you four men why you were having such a jolly time? Why, in the last few months, you have become such wonderfully domestic, docile, decent, happy, caring and committed husbands? Has it ever, for one second, crossed your minds that there was something rather odd about the transformation that came over each and every one of you at roughly the same time?'

'ENOUGH, Carl!' screeched Nicola. 'I will not have you behave like this in my friend's house. How dare you be so rude.'

'Now, now, old girl, I don't know that he's being rude,' said Richard. 'He's probably just trying to get his own back for the unpardonable things I said to him when he was last sitting round this table.'

'No, Richard,' said Carl, 'I'm not trying to get my own back. I'm trying to get you back, to reach the real Richard, not this ridiculous pastiche I'm talking to now.'

'How dare you, Carl, how DARE you,' Nicola was screaming. 'After all I've done for you. After the way I dragged you from the gutter and gave you the opportunity to be a decent, civilized human being. How could you betray me in this way?'

'Nicola, if we are going to talk about betrayal, I don't think that you should single me out in this company this evening,' Carl spat back.

Georgia had begun to cry. Tears were streaming down her face as she listened to Carl.

'RICHARD!' shouted Carl. 'You must listen to me very carefully. Do you remember what you said to me that night? What it was that you now think was so unpardonable? In case you have forgotten, you suggested that I was not what you might term a "real" man. I think you described me as Nicola's "fancy new house-pet". Does that description of me in any way now apply to you – or to Harry, or to Steve, or to Nick?'

Nicola was holding her head in her hands and sobbing 'No, No, No,' throughout Carl's speech. But she was incapable of stopping him now. She had lost control – of him, of herself, and, if he was leading where she now thought he might be, maybe of her entire life.

'I don't understand you, Carl. I don't know what you are driving at,' said Richard obtusely.

'What I am trying to say is do you think there might be another reason why the only thing you now dominate is your vegetable patch, why Steve is obsessed with patchwork quilts and tapestries, why Harry wants to marry and have children or why Nick is more interested in nappies and nursery rhymes than he is in creating his great work of art?'

'What possible reason could there be?' said Richard.

'I give you,' said Carl removing a crumpled piece of paper from his pocket, 'Exhibit A. A letter from Georgia James to Nicola Appleton dated October 1996. "Dearest Nicola," it says, "I am so sorry I got so emotional on that last night. I was simply in denial. I couldn't see what Richard had become. And I couldn't see what you were offering me." Is the light beginning to dawn, Richard? Have you made a connection between yourself, myself, the state of your male friends here and the work of Nicola Appleton?'

Amanda came back into the room with a tray of coffee and gave large cups to the men. Georgia was still weeping and Nicola was still mumbling denials under her breath.

'I will give you all a copy of the letter later, but for now I will read out the most salient points. Georgia goes on to say, "But a few days after you left, overcome by anger, I think, I gave him the first capsule. (I told him it was Vitamin B12!)." Ring any bells yet, Richard?'

'Richard, Richard darling, you have to understand that I was desperate,' Georgia shouted between sobs. 'I'd just found out about you and Juliet. I hated you, I wanted revenge. I didn't expect to fall in love with you.'

'Shut up, Georgia,' said Amanda. 'I think that we

might as well let Carl finish, don't you? And then make our excuses.'

'Thank you, Amanda, I suspected you were the only one with any real conscience about what has gone on here,' Carl said before returning to the letter he held in his hand. 'Georgia continues, "Suffice it to say that now, six weeks on, he really is my Stepford Husband. He isn't just the man I used to love, he's more than that. He is my perfect man!" Then she goes on about a birthday gift and their love-making before commenting about how sensitive, caring and SMILEY he is.'

Richard was listening to Carl intently now, an expression of confusion replacing his more usual smile.

'Georgia tells Nicola about Richard's political conversion and his new compassion. "It must sound silly," she says, "but he thinks like a woman but remains a man (perhaps that was the aim of Manifold?). Thank you, thank you, thank you," she continues before asking Nicola to please, please, send her some more Manifold. "I couldn't bear to run out."' He paused for a moment and looked round the table, trying to gauge the reaction to his words. There were tears, denials and sobs from the women but precious little response from the men.

"But perhaps the most chilling line, gentlemen, is this last one: "The funniest thing of all is that all four of the men have become best friends. They even get together for suppers like a bunch of girls! Can you imagine Richard and Steve and Harry and Nick (who's now the most frightful baby bore!) talking for hours together and chatting on the phone every day?" Are things a little clearer now?'

'Am I right in thinking that this Manifold,' said Richard slowly, 'is the drug that Nicola has developed and launched in the States and will launch here next week?'

273

'Yes, Richard,' said Carl. 'A drug tested within the American penal system on murderers like me.'

'Like you?' said Steve.

'Yes. I was serving life when I was picked as one of the volunteers for the human testing of Manifold. Not that I was human. I was, to quote Nicola, an "animal". It did civilize me, it did help me to regain my self-respect, to discover another way of life. But it never occurred to me, when I became involved in the promotional propaganda, that the creators of Manifold had wider plans for its future. That within a year of its launch – that is, within the next few months – it might become as common a prescription drug as penicillin or Prozac. That it would be marketed to appear as the panacea for men. A cure-all for every psychological ailment, every depression, every insecurity, every sexual or behavioural problem known to man – or perhaps I should say known to woman. It never occurred to me that Manifold would turn out to be a hideous feminist plot to suppress and control the most creative and natural characteristics of man.' Carl looked meaningfully across at the snivelling women.

'Those discs you sent me,' said Richard suddenly snapping out of his alcoholic stupor, 'they were full of statistics and plans for Manifold and, what was it now – the Malestrom Foundation?'

'Yes, Richard. We are fellow guinea pigs. Of course, I was a volunteer so I really can't complain. But you – the four of you – you were unaware of the chemical changes that were taking place. And of course after a few weeks, as Georgia's letter says, you were all feeling so happy and smiley that you didn't think to question what was happening to you. And why should you? You all trusted the women you were involved with, didn't you?'

The four men were fighting to come to terms with the

effects of the alcohol and what they had been told. They didn't doubt that Carl was telling them the truth. They could tell from the behaviour of the women round the table that it was all horribly true. But none of them could quite face the implications of what they now knew. None of them could face the women who, just hours ago, they had believed to be perfect.

'Nick, I know it all sounds terrible,' said Caroline, 'but I couldn't see any other way forward. It was either this, what I did, or us splitting up. Don't you remember the pact – the no-children pact – and how you accused me of betraying you by getting pregnant? If you think I betrayed you again by giving you Manifold, then maybe you are right. But I didn't do it for me, but for you. Would you be without the babies now?'

Nick looked at her, shaking his head.

'I wouldn't be without the babies now. But Christ, I don't know who I am NOW . . .'

Amanda got up and walked over to Steve.

'I hated the whole idea from the start. You have no idea how Nicola sold the thing to us. With a dinner and a video presentation and a truth game that involved Juliet telling Georgia that Richard had fucked her when she was in hospital giving birth to Tom. I said at the time that I thought it sounded a bit like the chemical equivalent of crushing the balls of a tom-cat between two bricks. I think I called it feminist fascism. I said it was dangerous to interfere in the balance of nature and that I deeply disapproved of what Nicola was doing. But the thing was that you had started to beat me, Steve. You probably don't remember now, but you came out of prison in such a state of depression and degradation that all you could do was hit out at the people you claimed to love. There's no excuse for what we have done. But remember that for me the last few months with you have been the best of my life. I didn't love you before, but I do now,' she said, bending down and kissing him on his head before walking out of the room.

Juliet was the only one of the four women who appeared unmoved and unabashed.

'Harry, I had never met anyone in my life who could make me do the things I used to do in order to keep you around. I debased myself on such a regular basis, and you degraded and emotionally abused me in return. And all I thought I wanted was you. I wanted you to commit to me. To be with me. Not happily ever after in the country with children and livestock. Just to come and live with me. You were the only person in the whole world I couldn't control and Nicola offered me the means of control and I took it. But hey, I'm not sure that I like what I got. I am beginning to think that the only reason I wanted you was that I couldn't have you. And tonight, and for the last month or so, I've HAD you. And it was quite enough to last me a lifetime.' She paused and removed her ring and put it on Harry's plate. 'Shame about the ring, but we'd never have been happy,' she added before leaving the room.

Caroline turned to Nicola, who was sitting staring down at the floor.

'What happens now, Nicola? What happens to them when they stop taking the drug? Will they revert back to the men they were? We need to know.'

Nicola looked at Caroline and at Georgia, who was still softly crying, and then glanced across the table at Carl.

'I guess you'll have to ask Carl about that. It would seem that Carl is now off the programme. He behaved like a brute tonight. But then maybe it was optimistic of us to ever imagine that Carl could be anything other than an animal.'

She wanted to say that she was sorry. But she wasn't really. She still thought that what she had done, in interfering in her friends' lives, had been for the best.

'I won't let this affect Manifold,' she said, looking across at Carl. 'You are trying to suggest that the drug is some kind of giant plot against men hatched by women. But you are wrong. Manifold is the greatest medical advance that has been made in the second half of the twentieth century. And I am not going to let a piece of scum like you ruin it. Anyway I don't feel in a fit state to defend my work right now, so if you don't mind I'll go to bed and we can talk about it all in the morning.' She got up, kissed Georgia and made her way out of the room.

Georgia got up then and went over to Richard and embraced him. He held her to him and kissed her and told her, very softly, that he still loved her.

'Although I might not when this drug begins to wear off and I turn back into that bastard you were once married to,' he said pulling her up and leading her upstairs, oblivious to their remaining confused guests and the frightful mess on the table.

Then Nick went over to Caroline and held out his hand and took her out of the room and up the stairs to their room. Steve followed shortly afterwards. Which left Harry and Carl. Or rather Carl since Harry had slumped into a deep and apparently contented sleep, his head resting slightly to the side of his untouched plate of sautéed guinea fowl, the sparkling diamond just visible within his *bouchée* of mushrooms and shallots.

Carl realized now that he should have picked his moment more carefully. That having chosen tonight was a mistake. The impact of what he had told them had not properly penetrated their brains, which were, it seemed, overwhelmed by alcohol. But he realized, too, that even when they were sober they would not appreciate the enormity of the Manifold plot. They were too close to the drug. Their actions, their feelings, their very inner selves were so dominated by the effects of those big yellow capsules that they were incapable of comprehending what had happened to them. It would be months before they would be able to see, as he was seeing now, the terrifying potential of the drug.

His plan had failed. True, he had shamed the women and made them cry, but he had done little to alert the men to the evil that had been perpetrated against them. He had believed that once Richard realized what had been happening he would help Carl to crack the Malestrom Foundation. He had been sure that once the free spirit had been woken in Harry he would rear up in defence of the civil liberties of men in the face of the threat of Manifold. He had been certain that Steve Minter and Nick Evans would be so disgusted by their women and so frightened by Nicola's plans that they would join the fight against this monstrous drug. But he now realized that only he could do anything to curb the awesome and inevitable progress of Manifold into the bodies of men throughout the civilized world.

He looked at Harry snoring in his supper and felt a terrible surge of anger overwhelm him. If he couldn't enlist the help of these men, then he would have to use other means to foil Nicola. He would have to fall back on the old Carl Burton in order to rid the world of Manifold. What Carl had done that night, he had done for mankind and not for any personal gratification or need for revenge.

He went upstairs to the room he shared with Nicola. It hadn't occurred to her to lock the door against the man she had loved but now saw as her enemy. She was lying on her side, that hair plastered across her face, breathing heavily in a deep, alcohol-induced sleep. He locked the door behind him and went into the bathroom to find what he needed. Then he returned and carefully gagged her with a black Lycra stocking that still held the imprint of the shape of her leg. She didn't resist. She didn't really stir, although one eye opened briefly. Then he pulled her up and tied her arms behind her back with the cord from his dressing gown.

It had to match his other crimes. It had to be seen as the final act of the Red Avenger. It had to lead them to Manifold. Linking those sordid murders with the drug was, he now thought, the quickest and most effective way of alerting the world to this foul female plot to make mice of men. He pushed her face down on the bed and entered her the way he had entered the others. He was vaguely aware of a resistance, a moaning through the gag, but he was so angry now that it only served to push him on. He fucked Nicola as he had never fucked her before, his hands tightening round her neck as he came. The only difference between this bitch and the others was that this time he had not worn a condom or a pair of surgical gloves. This time he wanted to leave them clues. He got up, went back to the bathroom and retrieved a box of the capsules from the cabinet and laid them next to the body. Manifold had killed Nicola as surely as it had killed those other women and as surely as it would, ultimately, kill Carl.

EPILOGUE

Caroline was the first to arrive in the crowded and cramped restaurant. She confirmed the reservation – made in Georgia's name to ensure a good table – and sat self-consciously staring at the menu as she waited for her friends to join her.

Amanda arrived minutes later, propped up by stilettos and propped out by the newly fashionable wide-shouldered eighties-revival scarlet jacket she wore. Her hair, as luxuriant and darkly glossy as ever, fell in folds around her, and her mouth – the same scarlet as the jacket – was set in the kind of brilliant smile that had been a permanent accessory on the faces of their men in the period before Nicola's death. Despite their extraordinarily different personal styles – Caroline still kept her short helmet of white-blonde hair, her severe suits and her flat classic brogues – they were comfortable together, thrilled, in fact, to see each other.

The regular meetings of the four women – so much a part of their social lives since they had left school – had stopped after the dramatic events at Gallows Tree House. It had been Juliet's idea to revive them again, and tonight's meeting – on neutral ground – had a special poignancy for them all. Although no one, Juliet had commanded, was to wear black.

'God, it's good to see you, Caroline,' Amanda said as she slipped her jacket on to the back of her chair and sat down opposite her friend. 'You look great. How are the twins?'

'Don't ask me or I might tell you. I've even brought

some photographs, although I'll save those until Georgia arrives. More importantly, how is Steve?'

'The DPP has agreed not to prosecute, which is just such brilliant news. Of course, Johnny Britten's going to go down and he will no doubt try and take Steve with him. But I think we are safe. It's good still, Caroline.'

At this point Georgia entered the restaurant and made her way, in stately fashion, to the table.

'Darlings,' she gushed as a waiter pulled her chair out for her and she rested her heavily pregnant frame on the seat. 'I can't tell you how wonderful it is to be together again. To put the past behind us.'

'It looks very much, Georgia,' said Amanda, 'as if you are carrying the past before you.'

Georgia flushed slightly and passed her hand across her swollen tummy.

'Well, you know I really think that this is what I was put on this earth for. Babies. It's the one thing I can do really well. And it's probably the only good thing to come out of that awful business.'

There was a silence then, a moment when all three of them were suddenly lost in their own thoughts.

'And Richard? How does he view the forthcoming happy event?' Amanda asked.

'Well, you know Richard. He certainly wanted it at the time,' Georgia said with a chuckle, 'but now he's got drawn back into politics and he's so busy in the House I think he's hardly aware of what's going on at home. Even his precious vegetable patch has gone to seed, rather like me, really.'

'But are you happy together?' asked Caroline.

'I don't know, Caroline, I just don't know. I do know that he was driving me mad in his digging-for-victory period. And, as he always used to say, there is a great deal to be said for the traditional sexual roles. You know where you are. Before Manifold I didn't have any real identity problems – I was the home-maker and he was an elected member of the House. And then the lines got blurred and I wasn't sure who I was or, more to the point, who the hell he was. But now I've got my own area of expertise back. I suppose you could say that I have lost and gained. No more Marco Pierre White recipes, thank heavens. But then again, rather fewer prize organic courgettes,' Georgia added with a wicked giggle.

'And how's Stella?' Caroline asked fondly.

'Would you believe she's in love?' said Georgia enthusiastically. 'She met some man. In fact, I suspect that she knew him all along. All that stuff about how she didn't need a man, she wanted space, she wanted her independence. What she wanted, despite her protestations, was her fantasy Mr Right. She's frightfully ashamed, it took her months to pluck up the courage to tell us. But she's happy and I'm glad for her.'

There was, as ever, something of a stir in the little restaurant as Juliet entered through the door and made her way to the table.

'Sorry,' she said as she took her seat and kissed each of her friends – and her sister – on both cheeks. 'Have you ordered?'

They poured her some wine and called over an eager waiter to arrange some starters.

'Well, Juliet,' said Amanda, 'how is everything with you?'

'Good. Business is fine – I've been approached about a possible merger that could make me very rich. AND I've met someone new who is absolutely my type.'

'You mean, your prince has finally come?' said Caroline.

'Good God, no. You know what I realized through all

that business? I realized that however much I might have thought that I wanted my prince to come, I would much rather settle for a frog. Or at any rate a swine. I absolutely hated Harry when he turned into my prince. When he wanted to sweep me off my feet and live happily ever after with me.'

'So this new man is not quite so user-friendly?'

'He's exciting, sexy, young and utterly unscrupulous. Perfect for my needs,' Juliet said, her brilliant artificially coloured eyes gleaming.

'And what did happen to poor Harry? Has anyone seen him?' Amanda asked.

'It's funny, you know, but about three weeks ago I saw him walking along Bond Street entwined around this frightfully nubile blonde and just for a moment I re-membered why I had found him attractive. He's totally regressed – same old salt-and-pepper pony-tail, leather jacket, tattered jeans and leering expression. Just for a moment I had a pang of regret for having lost that rough diamond – but not that five-carat diamond ring. Or what would have come with it.' Juliet glanced shiftily at Georgia's bulging body.

'Do you remember that first night when Nicola came back from the States?' said Caroline thoughtfully. 'When we all sat round and created our perfect man, our idea of the Stepford Husband? Did it ever strike any of you as a kind of portent of what was to come?'

'Darling, I don't think any of us, even with the aid of Manifold, achieved a man with Hugh Grant's grin, Mel Gibson's eyes and Linford Christie's lunchbox. And in any case I have discovered that imperfect men are far more attractive,' Juliet said.

'And Caroline,' interrupted Georgia, 'have you settled back down with the imperfect man or has Nick been permanently changed?'

'Well, it was difficult after that night. I mean, he was so shocked by the whole thing, so utterly amazed that the changes in him had been chemically induced – well, you all know how obsessed he had become about a chemical-free diet. And he was angry with me. But he's come to terms with it now. He accepts that Manifold improved his quality of life,' Caroline said cautiously.

'And he's not turned back into the self-obsessed, morose drunk that he once was?' asked Juliet.

'He's still devoted to the children, but rather less interested in the consistency of their stools,' Caroline said with a smile. 'But then he's on a reduced dose now.'

There was a collective gasp from the three other women.

'He's not . . . you didn't . . . you aren't still doctoring his *chilli con carne*?' said Georgia.

'No, it was his choice. Quite simply he decided he was a happier man for it. And, needless to say, I'm a happier woman,' Caroline said sheepishly.

'What was it that Nicola said? "A greater step for womankind than gaining the vote, achieving equality in the workplace or the advent of the pill",' said Juliet slowly. 'But how do you equate what happened to Carl with all that? Christ almighty, we all thought he was a happier man on Manifold and Nicola a happier woman.'

'I knew that none of you would approve. I know that for your own reasons you rejected the concept of the ideal man but if you had to choose between the old Nick and the new man I'm with now I am sure you would do what we have done. Keep taking the pills,' Caroline said defensively.

'But doesn't he remind you of Amanda's castrated tomcat? Aren't there moments when you wonder if Carl might not have been right? Not in murdering Nicola or all those other women, but in his concern for Manifold's hidden agenda?'

'Oh God, that's nonsense, Juliet,' Amanda interrupted. 'What we did in giving it to our men without their knowledge was wrong, we all know that, even if it did make them temporarily happier. But if a man, as Nick has done, chooses to take it, then it is quite different.' She paused for a second. 'And contrary to Carl's deranged expectations Manifold has turned out to be a force for good. Do you remember my friend Debbie – the one who lived next door to my old flat, the one with the children and the awful boyfriend Dean? Well, the GP at the Featherwell Estate Health Centre prescribed him Manifold and he is completely reformed. He's working, helping Debbie, involved with the kids. This drug has the potential to improve society, not destroy it,' she concluded.

'Apparently, according to Richard, there is some kind of governmental directive on Manifold. Some move to create a situation where a persistent offender is given the choice of a custodial sentence or going on what they are now calling the Manifold Rehabilitation Programme,' Georgia said.

'I'm not sure I like it, though,' said Juliet. 'I mean, isn't it a little creepy? I'm with Carl on this. I can believe that the whole thing has sinister implications for the future of mankind. It's fundamentally a feminist plot to suppress the natural instincts of man for the good of women. I hope to God you haven't still got Steve on it, Amanda.'

'No, but Steve acknowledges how it helped him. Helped us. I'm not suggesting that Manifold should be forcibly administered to all males over the age of fourteen, but it can work. Look at what it did for our men.

We might not have liked all the effects but, shit, life was better than it had been. And it's left Steve with a very positive legacy. The talent he discovered while he was on the drug and the natural business acumen that returned when he came off it have combined to enable him to start again. One of his properties was featured in this month's issue of *Architectural Digest*. He's doing a series of loft conversions that are stunning. And he's making money,' Amanda said, playing with a tiny – but clearly expensive – gold heart that she wore round her neck.

Georgia's spirits rose when the attentive waiter delivered the food. Richard's regression back into politics (and Tory politics at that) had been matched by her own return to the emotional and physical comfort of food.

'Georgia darling,' said Juliet as she observed her sister tucking in, 'you're eating for two, not for all four of us.'

'Do you know what worries me most about Manifold?' said Georgia between mouthfuls. 'It makes men effeminate. Not limp-wristed and anally obsessed – although from what I hear that could be said of Carl – but womanish. And in Richard's case *old-womanish* at that. Oh, I know I sort of fell in love with him when he was so transformed – when he talked to me, cooked for me and did the Waitrose shop. But I must say – and I know you are all going to think I am terrible – that in many ways I preferred the old man to the new man. God knows we shouldn't be trying to turn men into women or, for that matter, Juliet, turning women into men. We should be playing to our different strengths. We should recognize, appreciate the difference. We can't – we shouldn't try – to change each other. We should have seen what Carl was trying to tell us.' She was blushing slightly as she finished.

There was a silence, then, as the four women looked more closely round the brightly lit, fashionably cluttered noisy restaurant.

'It's too late to do anything about it now,' said Juliet, glancing across at her sister. 'We are surrounded by them. Look at that blond man at the corner table and that guy with the moustache at the bar . . . not to mention the waiter.'

They all watched attentively as the waiter made his way to their table. It was as if their composite picture of that perfect man had come to life. He was tall, of course, and muscular, with brilliant blue eyes and hair that flopped alluringly across his forehead when he moved. He even, they all silently noted, had a little cleft in his chin. So intently were they watching him that it seemed like minutes, rather than seconds, before he reached them and pulled up the notepad that was attached by a piece of cord round his waist.

'Is there anything else I can do for you, ladies?' he asked with a chillingly familiar smile.

Ⓢ
SIGNET

Published or forthcoming

No Fear

Sherry Ashworth

**Joy Freeman, a Jewish English
teacher in a Catholic college, could win
an Olympic gold medal in worrying.**

When Sister Maureen, the college principal,
tells her that she stands a chance of promotion
– *if she can stop worrying* – Joy knows she must
change her attitude if she is to change her life.

Deciding that the only way forward is to
confront her anxieties, Joy tackles her
problems head on and finds that risk need
not be a four-letter word!

Published or forthcoming

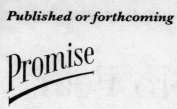

Mark Crompton

In the slick world of the conman, there's only one way to catch a thief . . .

Patrick Old, late of Army Intelligence, is now a private detective and a missing-persons specialist. Fed up with tracing errant spouses, he's intrigued by a new commission – to track down a conman who duped Barry Mee and nine of his friends out of a great deal of money.

Barry Mee ought to have known better: a multi-millionaire porn-king, he's no stranger to the seamier side of life. And nor is Patrick Old. As he delves deep into the world of conmen, he encoúnters a variety of people who make a very healthy living out of being dishonest. And when Old eventually finds his man, he knows that the only way to catch him is to sell him a scam that will prove irresistible . . .

Published or forthcoming

For a Mother's Love

Helen Brooks

The bond between a mother and her child is precious. But when the bond is broken, pain is the price to pay . . .

Growing up in the shadow of her adored sister, Kate Henderson knows what it feels like to be deprived of a mother's love. Now a junior doctor, Kate is engaged to be married to dashing American Hank Ross. But when she discovers she is pregnant – and Hank is not the father – the only choice she has is to keep her baby secret.

As her wedding day nears, Kate's emotions are in turmoil. Hank's family fills her with dread and confusion – does she really know him well enough to marry him? Or should she follow the instincts of her heart? The feelings that are crying out *For a Mother's Love* . . .

SIGNET

Published or forthcoming

Daring to Dream

Holding the Dream

Finding the Dream

Nora Roberts

A glittering sequence of novels following the fortunes and failures, scandals, successes and seductions of three young women.

From dazzling Big Sur, California, to the cat-walks of Milan, Margo, Laura and Kate live, love and work to fulfil their dreams . . .

Published or forthcoming

Marina Oliver

Kind, lovely Nell, fleeing her slum home and brutal father; determined Gwyneth defying her father, a narrow-minded Welsh preacher; wilful Kitty, rich in possessions but not family affection – three girls overcome the social barriers of 1920s Birmingham to become friends and allies in their struggle to succeed on the music-hall stage.

Constant threats from their families – and the pleasanter distractions of men who attract and admire them – make the hard road stonier still. Yet, against the odds, the three battle on through setbacks, squabbles and outright disaster, united by their dream: to dance in Paris at the Folies-Bergère.

SIGNET

Published or forthcoming

Walking in Darkness

Charlotte Lamb

Beautiful heiress Catherine Gowrie had spent her life protected and sheltered by a wealthy family and successful husband. Now her all-powerful father was close to his greatest ambition – nomination as presidential candidate. Nothing must be allowed to stand in Don Gowrie's way.

Sophie Narodni shared only Catherine's beauty. The young journalist had worked her way out of poverty to travel the world. But she carried a secret that could destroy everything Don Gowrie had dreamed of . . . if he didn't silence her first . . .

They came from two different worlds. But the dark eyes that watched over each were the same . . .

BORN IN SHAME

Sarah Hardesty

Shannon Bodine, a tough, ambitious New York designer, thought she'd had the perfect childhood. But when she discovers that she was born of her mother's fleeting love affair in Ireland, her past is suddenly shattered.

Torn between the life she knows and the need to understand her heritage, Shannon travels to County Clare to meet her half-sisters. They are family by blood, but can they learn to become family in their hearts?

Soon the mystical beauty of Ireland, its ways and its people, awakens new feelings in Shannon's soul that she cannot understand. Nor can she define the sensations that surge through her in the presence of Murphy Muldoon, handsome as an angel but with the devil in his eyes . . .

SIGNET

Published or forthcoming

ANGELFACE

Lilie Ferrari

London in the 1950s. The streets of Soho are bustling, cosmopolitan and lively. But inside the Imperial Café the Peretti family is face to face with its Sicilian enemies, who have come to call in a debt of honour incurred back in the old country.

Marionetta Peretti, although bound by the duties of an Italian daughter, despises the cowardice and caution of her family. But it is Marionetta herself who is forced to make the harshest payments: the sacrifice of her love, her freedom, and finally, herself ...

SIGNET

Published or forthcoming

IT TAKES TWO

Maeve Haran

Hotshot lawyer Tess Brien and her ad-man husband Stephen know that a good marriage is hard to keep. They should. Enough of their friends' relationships are crumbling around them. But theirs is a happy home, a secure base for their two lively teenagers.

But when Stephen suddenly gives up his job, leaving a stressed and angry Tess to pick up the bills, and another woman seems determined to have Stephen at any cost, distrust and disruption threaten to destroy their idyllic home ...

'Maeve Haran has a feel for the substantial concerns of her readers ... which is why she has become required reading for modern romantics' – *The Times*

By the same author

HARD PRESSED

Sex-crazed Celebrities. Weeping Widows. Tragic Tots. Kathy Wells, top columnist on the tabloid the *Sketch*, has covered them all. When it comes to distorting the truth, Kathy's a true professional. But what about the lies in her own life?

When Kathy finds herself in war-torn Bosnia, she grabs the chance to catch up on what she's been missing. In her work. In her marriage. In her bed . . .

It's Kathy's biggest deadline: time to set the record straight about what it is she really wants.